Twilight in Djakarta

MOCHTAR LUBIS

translated from Indonesian by
CLAIRE HOLT

edm EDITIONS DIDIER MILLET

© Mochtar Lubis 1968

Translated from the Indonesian *Senja di Djakarta*
First published by Hutchinson & Co. (Publishers) Ltd. 1963

Published in 2011 by Editions Didier Millet Pte Ltd
121 Telok Ayer Street, #03-01
Singapore 068590

www.edmbooks.com

With permission from Yayasan Pustaka Obor Indonesia
Jalan Plaju 10
Jakarta 10230
Indonesia

Cover image © Editions Didier Millet

ISBN: 978-981-4260-65-7

Printed and bound in Singapore

To Hally
to whom I owe a debt of love

PUBLISHER'S NOTE

At the time the novel was written in the early 1960s, the city was spelt as Djakarta (1942–1972). In 1972 the spelling changed to Jakarta as part of Indonesia's spelling reform. Indonesia's capital city has taken different names since it was first founded: Sunda Kelapa (397–1527), Jayakarta (till 1619) and Batavia (till 1942).

CONTENTS

TRANSLATOR'S NOTE

Translation or rather transposition into English of any other idiom naturally presents a great number of problems. Among those peculiarly related to Indonesian is the absence of a pronoun for *it* and the avoidance of pronouns *you*, *he* and *she*, including their possessive form. This often produces a repetitiousness in the naming of a subject or object. On the other hand it was, or may have been, the intention of the author to hammer away at a certain concept (e.g. truck, woman, stepmother, horse, etc.), thus evoking a semi-obsessive or all-pervading presence. This translator was inclined to retain some repetitive structures wherever the boundary between the original idiomatic necessity and the stylistic intention seemed to overlap, and thus to retain the flavour of both language and style. The difficulty of finding some convincing equivalent to the colourful and phonetically idiosyncratic Djakarta dialect spoken by the uneducated city workers and the impossibility of rendering its full local flavour need not be belaboured. As for the transcription of Indonesian names and terms, the reader will come closer to their sound if he gives the vowels approximately the following sound-values: *a* as in father; *e* as in pet in closed, and as in gale in open, syllables; *i* as in see or pit; *o* as in law; and *u* as in boot.

The translator is deeply indebted to a generous friend, who does not wish to be named, for many excellent suggestions, incorporated in the final version, which he made after careful comparison of the Indonesian and English texts,

ACKNOWLEDGEMENTS

The author thanks **Arthur Koestler** for permission to reproduce the following introductory quotation from *Arrow in the Blue: An Autobiography*.

... Now this Wang Lun had one secret ambition in his life, but it took him fifty years of strenuous effort to realize it. His ambition was to be able to behead a person with a stroke so swift that, in accordance with the law of inertia, the victim's head would remain poised on his trunk, in the same manner as a plate remains undisturbed on the table if the tablecloth is pulled out with a sudden jerk.

Wang Lun's great moment came in the seventy-eighth year of his life. On that memorable day he had to dispatch sixteen clients from this world of shadows to their ancestors. He stood as usual at the foot of the scaffold, and eleven shaven heads had already rolled into the dust after his inimitable master-stroke. His triumph came with the twelfth man. When this man began to ascend the steps of the scaffold, Wang Lun's sword flashed with such lightning speed across his neck that the man's head remained where it had been before, and he continued to walk up the steps without knowing what had happened. When he reached the top of the scaffold, the man addressed Wang Lun as follows:

'Oh cruel Wang Lun, why do you prolong my agony of waiting when you dealt with the others with such merciful and amiable speed?'

When he heard these words, Wang Lun knew that the work of his life had been accomplished. A serene smile appeared on his features; then he said with exquisite courtesy to the waiting man:

'Just kindly nod, please.'

ARTHUR KOESTLER
Arrow in the Blue

May

*S*AIMUN TIGHTENED his belt. His stomach was rumbling with hunger again. He'd had nothing to eat since morning. And it was still early. The drizzle which had started at dawn increased his hunger; Saimun blamed the rain. His bare and grimy foot – mud, filth and germs were stuck to that bare foot – kicked a refuse-filled basket off the top of the rubbish heap. The basket rolled down till it was stopped by the dilapidated wall of a hut, so very battered, so very rotten, so sadly dripping in the drizzling rain. A woman stuck her head out and shouted hoarsely,

'Say, take it 'bit easy! Where're your eyes?'

Saimun started a little, looked up and stared at the woman. He laughed roughly, without anger or malice, just because he always laughed that way; momentarily, lust stirred in him at the sight of the breasts of the woman in the hut, visible through the rents of her worn and ragged blouse. For an instant the desire flickered up to go down and get that woman, but then he heard the rumbling of the municipal garbage truck. Turning quickly he sprinted off and jumped on as it was moving away.

Saimun crouched down at the side of Itam, who was lighting a kretek cigarette. He looked at his feet on the truck's dirty, wet floor, felt the hard boards against the bones of his behind shaking loose all the tense muscles of his body, leaned against the wooden wall of the truck and stretched out his hand towards Itam, saying,

'Please, just one, 'Tam.'

Itam looked at him, the reluctance behind his eyes vanished quickly and he handed his kretek to Saimun, watching closely how Saimun inhaled deeply, deeply, retaining the smoke in the hollow of his chest, long, returning the cigarette to Itam, who immediately took a long drag, and then, together, they blew the smoke through their nostrils, slowly, and for the moment they forgot the drizzling rain, the dirt and smell of the truck, forgot themselves; there was only the scent of the kretek, the warmth of the cigarette upon the tongue and the relaxation of the body.

Itam inhaled the smoke once more. He handed the cigarette to Saimun, and while scratching the back of his ear with one hand, reached with his other hand to brush off the flies swarming around the scabs below his knee.

'I'm hungry 'lready, 'Tam,' said Saimun.

'One more, then we'll go get our wages. While waiting for wages we can first stop 'n eat at Mother Jom's.'

'Thinking o' food, my body's limp, no strength left,' said Saimun, his stomach feeling emptier and emptier, as if that emptiness was draining the last bit of strength left in his blood. He leaned back against the truck wall. Suddenly he felt exhausted and very faint.

Itam offered Saimun another draught from his kretek. Saimun inhaled avidly, Itam watching anxiously how rapidly the glow moved towards the end of the cigarette. As soon as Saimun finished, Itam retrieved it hastily, drew on it until it burned his fingers and then threw the tiny stub out of the truck.

Saimun pondered. How come that when something is difficult to get or you don't have it, and you just get a chance to taste it for a moment, a small matter can become so big, doubling, trebling, growing ever larger? This morning one kretek cigarette dominated his whole soul. As if his life depended on one cigarette and if he could get that cigarette his life would be prolonged, as it were, for ever. One cigarette could fulfil his existence. He remembered, when he was still in his village, before it was attacked by the grombolan,[1] and his father and mother died,

---

1 Bandits.

slaughtered by the grombolan, and he fled to the city – when the harvest was over, he didn't think twice before throwing away a half-smoked cigarette; or throwing away a boiled yam after only a few bites. And when there was a wedding feast, or lebaran,[2] or some other celebrations in the village, no one ever cared for just one drag on a cigarette.

Now, to smoke a kretek with Itam was just like a grand ceremonial. Each inhalation was of enormous significance; it was done carefully and with undivided attention. All one's senses were keyed up to tasting this one drag on the cigarette. A kretek never tasted as good as in this dirty and stinking dustcart.

Meanwhile, if one remembered life in the village before it was attacked by the grombolan, it all felt just like a dream. And sometimes he didn't believe that he had ever lived in such a village. As though it had been another person altogether, not himself, who had worked in the rice-field, who had bathed in the river with the carabao Si Putih[3] – got his name because of the white colour behind his left ear – ah, he still remembered it all so well, but did not believe that it was really he who went bathing with Si Putih. It was as though a man's existence was shut away in different boxes, and one part of it shut up in one such box stayed in it, and had no connection any longer with the life in the other box. As though he had become a stranger to himself – with no connection at all any more to the man who had been himself in that other life-box.

He remembered how in the first weeks after his arrival in Djakarta he wept when evening came and he knew not where to wander any more, and looked for a place to sleep under the awning of a shop. Until he met Itam who befriended him, and they got work as garbage-removing coolies. And later they were able to rent lodgings in the hut of Pak[4] Idjo, the driver of a delman pony-

---

2 Celebration at the end of the Mohammedan fasting month.

3 'The White One', or Whitey.

4 Pak; short for *bapak*, father.

cart. Just one room, next to the room where Pak Idjo slept with his old wife and their three children. But the hunger which gnawed at his guts never ceased, and the weariness in his bones never really went away.

'How 'bout driving a betja,[1] isn't it kind of better than this sort of work?' said Saimun suddenly.

'Nuh,' said Itam, 'don't lu[2] remember that Pandi, the betja driver, died just like that, was spitting blood? Ran a betja only one year. Upset his heart!'

Saimun scratched with his toes at the floor of the truck, its thick crust of dregs, and for a moment all life around him seemed to vanish, himself remaining in a dismal void, suspended alone in that void, as if all dimensions of life were lost: there was no past, no present and there was no future. Only himself alone in existence.

He woke with a start as the truck stopped, and Itam called,

'Ayoh,[3] this here is the end.'

Saimun felt stiff all over as he forced himself to get up, jump off the truck and lift a basketful of refuse into it.

By noon the truck was back at the dump, and as he was unloading the rubbish, Saimun remembered the woman in the hut whom he had seen that morning. He stepped down towards the hut. The woman was there, bathing in a small pool, a few yards from the hut, its stagnant water dirty and yellow. Saimun shouted to attract the woman's attention, and his desire revived as he saw her all naked, bathing in the shallow pool. The woman laughed at him, turning her body, challengingly, and Saimun only unwillingly turned away, hearing Itam call his name and the sound of the truck's engine. But he called to the woman, saying he would be back.

Garbage carts and trucks were assembled near the office

---

1 Tricycle-carriage with driver pedalling from elevated saddle behind the open passenger-seat.
2 'Vulgar form of address, second person singular.
3 Exclamation of encouragement

where they were to be paid. There was a row of vendors of cigarettes, of cooked rice and fried bananas. An Arab with a blue notebook and an umbrella and another heavy-bodied man sat eating fried bananas under a tree. The distribution of wages had not yet begun, but Saimun caught a glimpse of the cashier, busy counting the paper money, quarter and half-rupiahs, rupiahs and ringgits[4] stacked behind the small window.

He walked with Itam to the place where Mother Jom was selling rice. And as soon as they were seated Mother Jom served them, she knew what they wanted to eat.

'When you get your pay, don't run away,' she said in way of reminder.

Saimun and Itam were silent; they ate ravenously.

'Aduh,[5] the debt there's 'lready close to five perak.'[6] said Saimun. 'And Tuan[7] Abdullah with his Mandor Besi will have to wait. How much you owe him, 'Tam?'

'About five rupiah! He's the very devil, that Arab, never ends a debt with him!'

'Me, I'm lucky, only a ringgit I owe him,' said Saimun, 'but I must repay him four rupiah this week.'

Saimun calculated his wages. Garbage coolies were paid twice a month, every third and eighteenth day of the month. This was the third, and from the last eighteenth he had worked only eleven days, because there were two Sundays when people do not work and for which there was no pay. Because he was a new coolie, his wage was only four and a half rupiah a day. So he would get only eleven times four and a half, just forty-nine and a half rupiah. Deducting the debt to Pak Imam in the office, who sold him a pair of shorts for thirty rupiah on the instalment plan, each instalment being ten rupiah, he would get only thirty-nine and a half rupiah.

---

4 Two and a half rupiah, formerly the largest silver coin.
5 Exclamation of pain and surprise.
6 Lit. 'silver' = one rupiah.
7 Sir, Master, Mister.

It's lucky that this was the last instalment. But the shorts too were almost worn thin, made as they were of green twill that is not too strong. Then, taking off the debt to Tuan Abdullah, the Arab, there remained thirty-five and a half rupiah, and then the five rupiah debt to Ibu[1] Jom plus one rupiah for the meal now, there remained only twenty-nine and a half rupiah. Bewildered, Saimun counted and recounted: and with these twenty-nine and a half rupiah he would have to live fifteen days longer, until the next eighteenth day of the month. If one eats only one plate of rice with vegetable broth, its price alone is already one rupiah, and one must eat at least twice a day. Coffee and a fried banana or yam – half a rupiah, so he needs for this alone fifteen times a ringgit, which means thirty-seven and a half rupiah.

Already he's short eight and a half rupiah, and no cigarettes have been allowed for. Were one to smoke just 'kawung' cigarettes, one would need one and a half rupiah a day, or 'kretek djinggo', a packet of ten, gone are one and a half rupiah, too. And not yet counted is rent – five and a half rupiah a month.

Finally Saimun stopped counting and resumed his meal, eating avidly. His eyes caught a piece of chicken meat. For an instant he was tempted to ask for a piece of fried chicken. But he remembered the price ... calculations ran through his head, with heavy regret he suppressed his appetite and drank his coffee, to the last drop.

The other coolies had already started to line up before the cashier's window. Itam was urging Saimun to join the line, and Ibu Jom presently called,

'After getting your wages don't forget to pay your debts, yah!'

'Wah, what a nagger,' said Itam, 'as if of course we never paid our debts.'

As soon as they joined the line, Itam said,

'I'll just stop eating at Ibu Jom's and find 'nother place. She's

---

1 Mother.

too cranky. As for me, it's forbidden not to pay a debt. Even if your jacket goes and only your pants are left, a debt's got to be paid. All th'more a debt for food.'

Saimun felt refreshed by the food and coffee. He said,

'Ah, she's just nagging, but her heart, that old woman's, 's good. When we're still in debt she never refuses. But the one I hate is that Tuan Abdullah and Mandor Besi. What's a body worth who doesn't come across with payment of a debt to them?'

Itam spat, hitting the foot of the man who stood before him.

'Where are your eyes, spitting no matter where?'

Itam was quiet.

'There was a man, wanted to run off without paying his debt to Tuan Abdullah. The outcome? He was beaten up by Mandor Besi.'

'Where we going after pay?' asked Saimun.

'Who knows, I don't know yet,' Itam replied. 'You – where to?'

At that moment Saimun remembered the woman in the hut near the garbage dump, but said,

'Don't know.'

After he had received his wages from which the instalment of ten rupiah for the shorts had been deducted, paying four rupiah to Tuan Abdullah, and six rupiah owed for food to Ibu Jom, Saimun stood at the roadside waiting for Itam who was still busy calculating his debt to Ibu Jom. He bought himself one loose kretek cigarette, feeling guilty and rather extravagant, but unable to resist the craving for the aroma of cloves from the cigarette. He crouched on the sidewalk, at the edge of the water ditch, smoking with deep relish. Calm now reigned in his heart and he felt at peace with the world and man. In his pocket were twenty-nine rupiah. He felt very rich. But his thoughts kept returning to the young woman in the hut near the dump. His existence was no longer filled with one kretek cigarette, or a dozen kreteks which he could buy. His mind was filled with the image of the woman. Yet his thoughts did not disturb his feeling of peace, they were even accompanied by most delectable visions, burning and enchanting. And he fingered the little roll of money in his pocket.

On that morning, while Saimun the garbage coolie was busy unloading basketfuls of refuse on to the dump in the drizzling rain, Suryono was stretching his body in his warm bed, too lazy to get up; how pleasant was the feel of lying this way, looking out at the drizzling rain blown by the wind against the window-pane. For a while Suryono lay very still in the dim light, contemplating his room, and then he recalled his room in New York. Three months ago he was still in New York, only three months ago he was still in that giant city. And now, three months later, he was back again in Djakarta. He still felt ill at ease in Djakarta after working three years abroad. Djakarta had so many shortcomings, he felt.

It is decidedly more pleasant to live abroad. One is frustrated here. It's annoying to work in an office which is all confusion. He was still attached to the Ministry of Foreign Affairs, but had not yet been given a definite assignment. He was also dissatisfied by the way he was treated. Going to the office was difficult as he had no car. He was sorry not to have brought his own to Djakarta from America.

He looked round his room filled with things he had brought from overseas. A radio, an electric record-player. In the corner, on the table and on the floor were piles of books in French and English, on economics and on international politics and dozens of other subjects. Everything still looked quite new and very pretty. On his desk and on his night table were stacks of Westerns and sex novels from abroad with covers depicting women in a variety of poses. One was sprawled on the floor with her thighs bared, her eyes closed and a part of one breast in view, while behind her in the shadows loomed the figure of a masked man; and the title of the book was *The Sex Murders*.

In the bookcase were stacked records; from the works of

Mozart, Haydn, Beethoven and Chopin to tangos, sambas, rumbas, foxtrots and American jazz.

Suryono turned over, overtaken by laziness and remembrances of his life in New York, so marvellously luxurious and pleasant compared with his boredom and desolation during these three months at home. It seemed as if there was no place for him in his own country. He was at a loss as to what he should undertake. Nothing really seemed to attract him.

His stepmother suddenly opened the door and entered the room, saying,

'Yon, are you still sleeping?'

Suryono smiled at her, unashamed to be seen in bed with only his short underpants on, and said,

'Ah, what's the use getting up in the morning? You come to the office and there is no work there, anyway.'

His stepmother moved past his bed to open the curtains, but as she passed Suryono caught her by the hand and pulled her on to the bed.

'Fatma, has Father left?' he asked, kissing her neck intensely.

'Yes,' she said, 'but don't be naughty now, the babu[1] is sweeping the middle room.'

She stood up, opened the curtains and Suryono looked at his stepmother, Fatma, who was still young, his age-mate in fact, just twenty-nine years old. His father had married her while he, Suryono, was abroad, a year and a half ago. His father, Raden Kaslan, was fifty-six years of age; his mother had died when he was fifteen. When he heard that his father had remarried, Suryono had only shaken his head in surprise. And now, lying on his bed and looking at his stepmother, Suryono was surprised again, wondering how it was possible for a relationship between himself and his stepmother to have developed as it did. When he returned from New York his father was absent from home, and

---

1 Maid; servant-girl.

19

for two weeks he was alone with her. They lived together, went together to shows and went dancing together, and then Fatma told him not to call her mother, it was enough to call her just Fatma, and then ... and then ... Suryono smiled to himself recalling what happened between him and his stepmother for the first time, and in his father's room at that. They had just returned from a dance, and his stepmother had already gone into his father's room. There was not a soul in the house. He remembered that he had wanted to see an old family album, and went and knocked at the door.

'Come in,' he heard Fatma's voice. He opened the door, and saw that Fatma was changing her clothes within the screen near the wardrobe.

'I want to look for Father's album, Fat,' he said. 'Do you know where it is?'

'Here,' said Fatma, 'come and take it.'

He hesitated at first, but then went up to the screen after all, and saw that Fatma had already taken off her clothes and wore only a very thin nightdress. Suryono could not clearly remember how it began, all he remembered was how later he was getting up from his father's bed, with Fatma still lying on it with no clothes on her at all, and himself rushing out, back to his room. In his perturbation he was surprised nevertheless to find that he did not feel remorse, but was filled by a feeling of satisfaction. True, for a moment his innermost conscience spoke, but he quickly suppressed it with the thought – Ah, it's Father's own fault. Why did he marry a young woman?

And then he fell asleep. And when his father, Raden Kaslan, returned, the situation was further eased when, hearing how Fatma and Suryono addressed each other by nicknames (they did not try to conceal this), he said,

'Ah, I see you two have already become close friends. Fine!'

Raden Kaslan worked as director of the trading company Bumi Aju and was a member of the council of the Indonesian

Party. Formerly he had been a government official, but after the transfer of sovereignty he withdrew from the bureaucracy which did not offer him the desired satisfaction. His enterprise grew rapidly. It was easy for him to secure support because of his party connections.

After the first incident the second one occurred easily, and so it continued. After that first night, during a whole week he slept every night in his father's room with Fatma. They were both as if drunken. And only when the cable arrived from his father asking to be met at the Kemajoran airport did they come to from their intoxication, and Fatma said,

'What if your father finds out?'

But there was no fear in the question of the woman, nor was there any trace of anxiety. The question had a taunting tone, as if she were convinced that she could manage to deceive her old husband.

Also, in bed, Suryono once asked her,

'Whom do you really like, my father or me?'

And Fatma, with a little laugh, bit his cheek and embraced him with ardour.

'You're crazy to ask that. Don't you know?'

And Fatma told him that his father was impotent, and had married her only for the satisfaction of having a young woman at his side, which gave him self-assurance, and could be shown to other people to cover up his own weakness.

'It isn't even once a month that he comes to me,' said Fatma.

At first Suryono felt uncomfortable discussing his father with his stepmother thus, as if his father were a stranger. But this feeling was soon drowned by the passion inflamed by the body of the young woman who was his stepmother.

Nor did they ever raise the question of love. Whether he loved his stepmother or whether she loved him. It seemed that what they were doing was sufficient reason for doing it.

A week after his father's return all tension in him disappeared, as if nothing had happened between them, and his father oftentimes even asked him to accompany his wife to a show, to a feast or some such other occasion, when he himself could not join her.

This is how it came about that Fatma's neck was kissed this morning on his bed. The drizzling rain continued to fall outside, and he felt Fatma's body becoming tense and taut under his hands, and the woman embracing him hard, kissing his mouth and then suddenly extricating herself and running to the door.

'Aduh, you are really naughty,' she called, opened the door and went out.

Suryono laughed to himself, feeling excited and gay, and rejoicing in his male superiority, even defeating his own father.

He put on his bathrobe and went to the bathroom. As he undressed to bathe, he stopped naked before the tall mirror on the bathroom wall and contemplated his own body. Too thin, he thought, gripping his thigh, and the chest is not full enough. I must go in more for sport, he thought further. Then he examined his face. The features were handsome, and his new moustache was just beginning to grow. The eyes were too hollow, the hair was wavy. And he rubbed the cleft in his chin. He was rather pleased with that cleft; he shared it with Cary Grant, the film star. He got out his razor, soaped his lips and chin and started shaving, looking at his face in the mirror and humming away. He was really pleased this morning, there was nothing to trouble his thoughts. There was no work in the office to give him headaches and there was not a thing to worry about.

On this morning he almost felt at peace with himself, and his disappointment at having to stay in his own country was almost forgotten. A fleeting thought passed through his mind. If I have patience enough for another year they're sure to send me abroad again. It was a cheering idea and he whistled repeatedly a tune, very popular at that time in Djakarta – 'High Noon'.

He had breakfast together with Fatma, who awaited him. The two of them sat at the table, and Fatma sliced the bread for him and spread the butter on it.

'What would you like this morning – chocolate or marmalade?'

Suryono, looking at her, said,

'Wah, the goodness of this mother, it's truly marvellous. I want a layer of butter, with a layer of thinly sliced cheese on top of it, and over the cheese, a layer of marmalade, and then ...' Suryono nudged Fatma's foot under the table and Fatma giggled with pleasure.

'You are a bad child, unmannered, and with your own mother at that,' she said.

And they both laughed.

Before going to the office he kissed and caressed Fatma in her bedroom, then combed back his dishevelled hair, and just before leaving the room he held for a moment Fatma's breast, then went out whistling, hailed a betja and was off to his office.

'What's in the newspaper this morning?' he asked Harun, who sat at the desk next to his own.

Harun threw the newspaper which he was reading on to Suryono's desk.

'Read it yourself,' Harun said. 'You're late again. Only the day before yesterday the Secretary General issued a circular warning all officials to be in on time.'

Suryono laughed. 'Let him arrive precisely on time himself. It's easy to make rules. He has a car which brings him to the office. How about us?'

And again he felt resentment. Resenting the Secretary General of the ministry, resenting Harun who faithfully appeared at the office from day to day and then sat at his desk without anything to do, resenting the whole ministry, resenting his country, his people, resenting humanity, resenting life.

He threw the paper back to Harun.

'Read it yourself first,' he said. He was bored no end, knew not what to do with himself. He sat down and picked up the telephone. He waited for a long time, but the switchboard operator did not respond. After a while the operator answered. Suryono gave the number, and soon afterwards heard the ringing tone at the other end.

A woman's voice, caressing his ear, came floating over the wire,

'Hallo!'

'Is it you, Ies?' asked Suryono.

'Yes, so early in the morning, and you're on the phone already, Yon!' The voice was full of smiles and laughter.

'You know that you're in my mind day and night!'

'Ah, where did you learn to say such things?'

'Ies, what are you doing tonight?'

'I don't know yet.'

'I know what you want to do.'

'Yes?'

Then Suryono suddenly changed his playful tone and said seriously,

'Ies, I want to come tonight.'

'I won't be home.'

'Don't play with me.'

'No, I certainly will not be home. I am not home for a man who is bored, annoyed and depressed. Don't think I don't know you, Yono. You're coming to me only when you are bored and lonely. Good morning!'

Ies put down the receiver, and Suryono banged down his. Harun regarded him with lightly smiling eyes.

'No luck?' he asked.

Suryono looked at him, annoyed.

'You're rather eager to overhear other people's conversations, aren't you?'

Suryono sat in his chair, took out a pack of Lucky Strike cigarettes, lit one and after only two puffs threw it on the floor and crushed it with his shoe. Even the cigarette had no taste that morning.

When Sugeng returned home from his office at the Ministry of Economic Affairs he found his three-year-old daughter crying and screaming in the front yard.

They've been fighting again, he thought, approaching the child. 'Come, Yam, why are you crying?'

The little girl, Maryam, raised her head at the sound of her father's voice, stood up and jumped to hide her head at Sugeng's knee, and said between sobs,

'Iwan took away my marbles!'

Sugeng picked her up, held her in his arms and kissed her lovingly,

'Nah, it's all right, don't cry. Father will buy you new marbles!'

Inwardly he sighed and cursed the necessity of living in a house shared by three families: children got into fights every minute, and oftentimes this caused rows between the parents too. It was a year now they had been staying in this crowded house with two other families. In the beginning there was always hope of getting another home, as promised by the ministry. But now it looked as if they would have to live like this for ever.

The house was an old-fashioned one, with a long verandah running along its front, now divided in half by a bamboo screen. He had one front room and one part of the verandah which was screened in front as well as at the side. This was the sitting-room, as well as the kitchen – with an oil stove to cook on – the dining-place and also the place for ironing the laundry. The room behind it was the bedroom. The bath and the lavatory were in the passage at the rear of the house and were used jointly.

When he entered, carrying Maryam inside, he saw that his wife was not in the verandah-room.

'Hasnah!' he called, 'why do you let Maryam stay all alone outside, crying?'

Only a moan, coming from the bedroom, answered his call.

He stopped on the threshold and saw his wife who lay on the bed. She slowly opened her eyes.

'Are you sick?' Sugeng asked anxiously.

'Yes, I am dizzy again and suffer so much nausea. It's already a week late!'

Sugeng quickly put down Maryam, stepped over to the bed and held the head of his wife.

'Maryam will get an adik?'[1] he asked joyfully. 'I hope it is a son.'

His wife looked at him. Something in her face disturbed Sugeng, so that he asked,

'Aren't you happy? We have wanted little Maryam to have an adik for a long time. She's already three years old. And we do want a son, don't we?'

Hasnah nodded, then said,

'Yes, but when Maryam's little baby brother arrives, and we are still here ...' And Hasnah looked around the room meaningfully; its appearance told the whole story of their difficulties in such overcrowded conditions.

Instantaneously conscious of all this, Sugeng was saddened too, but he said,

'Ah, before the baby is born we surely will get another house. My ministry keeps on trying and they say they're beginning to build houses for their employees in Kemajoran. Don't you be afraid!'

Hasnah blinked and said,

---

1 Younger sibling, male or female.

'When we moved into this house you also said it would be for only a few months. Now it's over a year. I cannot live here, with two children. And with a baby at that. Where will we put him? How about his health? If you are not sure that we'll really get a house before then isn't it better that we don't have him? I heard there is a doctor who can help, with just an injection. It's only a week now, there is still time.'

Sugeng suddenly went very pale and then quickly embraced her.

'Aduh, don't speak this way. I swear to you that before the baby is born we are sure to move to our own house.'

There was a ring of conviction in his voice, which caused Hasnah to open her eyes, raise her head; she embraced Sugeng, and she kissed him.

'I, too, want another baby. How happy Maryam will be with a little one.'

And they fondled each other until Maryam came and climbed on the bed, clamouring for food.

During the meal Maryam announced that the family next door was going to move the following week.

'Their mother told them they are going to move to Kalimantan!' said Maryam.

'Wah, at least Maryam will not be bothered any more by that wicked boy Iwan,' said Sugeng laughing. 'I only hope that whoever moves in next will not have such naughty children.'

City Report

The night was like any other night. Evening crowds at the Glodok bazaar. Thousands of electric bulbs gleamed like fire-flies dancing in the night. The lamps of moving motor-cars were like yellow balls of light. The smell of food which exuded from the restaurants hung heavy in the air, almost as if one could touch it, put it into one's mouth, munch it. The two — their mouths watering, saliva gathering in the throat, marble-sized — spewed out together, and the spittle spattered at their feet.

'Come on, let's eat,' said one, nudging the other's side.

They entered a small restaurant and found a place in a corner.

The Chinese 'baba',[1] who ran the restaurant and was also the cook, approached their table. He was wiping his neck, his cheeks, his chest and his armpits with a dirty cloth, taking up the sweat of his body overheated by the large brazier in the other corner of the room. His smooth, oily skin glistened.

'Fried bihun,'[2] said the one. 'You?'

'Okay, beer.'

'Okay, beer.'

The baba nodded and waddled back to his kitchen. The fat under his skin below his armpits wobbled as he moved. The baba wiped his chest once more, then took a plate from a stack on the table, wiped it with the same rag, took a second plate, and wiped it too. And then he started to cook fried bihun.

Both portions of bihun were consumed. Greasy. Three empty beer-bottles stood on the table. Their two glasses were still about a third full.

'Where to now?' asked the man in the Hawaiian-style shirt with green flowers on a yellow background. His hair was smooth, oily, heavily smeared with brilliantine and brushed up high over his forehead like a woman's waved hair-do.

'Ah, we'll just go home. Not much money. He just looked rich, all show. But his wallet was empty. Only thirty-five rupiah. You were wrong again sizing him up,' said the other.

'You were the one to pick him out, Tony,' said the effeminate-looking man.

'Hm, yes. Otherwise I'd have liked to go again to the house of

---

1 Indonesian-born Chinese.
2 A dish based on fine translucent Chinese noodles with vegetables and bits of meat, or shrimps.

that Arab woman. But the money isn't enough. You'll sleep with me!' Saying this, the man with short crude fingers pinched the thigh of his friend, and his heavy-lipped mouth opened a little, showing large, strong teeth.

Three men entered and sat down at the table next to theirs. The baba came up, waddling ponderously – his fat wobbling in his skin, oily and glistening – and wiping his sweat with the dirty cloth.

They stopped talking as the three new arrivals sat down. And they listened to their talk.

'Good luck today, took in over seventy-five,' said one. He was a little man, oldish, his shirt and trousers of cheap cloth.

'It's fine to own a taxi oneself,' said one.

'Yeah, and show off one's profits, too,' said another. 'Yesterday I got thirty, but today only fifteen.'

Tony looked for a moment at the three taxi drivers, then his eyes rested on the man who said in the beginning that he had made more than seventy-five rupiah.

'Another beer, Djok?' he asked.

'Okay, beer!' shouted Tony.

They paid no more attention to the three taxi drivers who were now eating.

The night outside the restaurant was still as any other night. Electric lamps of vendors. People crowding.

'Do you see that man in the blue tropical, Djok?' said Tony slowly. Djok's eyes followed Tony's glance. They fell on a man who stooped over a pedlar's table.

'The usual way,' said Tony slowly.

Djok nodded, and took off. He looked about, to the left and to the right, like someone who is out to buy something and scans the place for the things he wants to buy. Yet like someone who doesn't particularly care whether or not he really finds the things he is looking for.

Behind him Tony walked on. When close to the man in the

blue tropical jacket Djok pretended to slip, and his body fell hard against the man's back. Tony stepped up quickly, his hands moving with lightning speed to the trouser pocket of the man, and as Djok was murmuring 'I beg your pardon, tuan,' Tony was already lost in the crowd, crossed the street and then walked on slowly. Djok stepped back without haste, as he would if he indeed had tripped over that man. After the apology he went on. And that was that.

A few minutes later Djok also crossed the street at a leisurely pace, and found Tony awaiting him in front of the Orion Cinema. Djok saw already from afar that Tony had not been successful.

'He was very cautious, his hand stayed right on his pocket,' said Tony.

'The louse,' swore Djok.

'Where now?'

'Ayoh, home,' said Tony.

They walked on, passed the police station, and under the big trees before the dark Lindeteves office they came upon several women who stood there waiting. Because he was so annoyed, Tony pinched the breast of one too hard, so that the woman shrieked and scolded; they both laughed and went on.

The vituperations of the woman pursued them in the darkness of the night.

They walked on. Crossed a bridge. Entered the shroud of darkness under old tamarind trees. Yellow balls of light, of taxicabs, came and went. Laughter of women was scattering in the air. Grasping hands invited. A hoarse voice swore obscenely. Then burst into roaring laughter. Like the devil's glee at startling human beings. Three betjas raced. The winning driver yelled in triumph.

Tony and Djok continued walking.

Tony took out a pack of Lucky Strike cigarettes, put one into his mouth.

'Smoke?' he asked.

Djok took a cigarette, pinched it with his lips. He got out a match and lighted Tony's cigarette. The light of the match flickered and lit up Tony's face – the thick lips, the hard and cruel lines of the sensual mouth, suggestive of a sadist.

'Taxi, sir?' A taxi moved slowly alongside.

Djok looked at Tony.

'Why not?' said Tony.

At the intersection in front of the Thalia Cinema and the Olimo Store Tony ordered the driver to turn left, towards Prinsenpark. The light of street lamps at the intersection illuminated the driver's face through the windscreen. And instantaneously they both thought of the scene in the Chinese restaurant in Glodok, with the three taxi drivers chatting and eating at the table next to theirs, and the baba-cook with his smooth oily skin, sweating and constantly wiping himself with the dish-towel. And their taxi driver was the one who had said,

'Good luck today, got more than seventy-five rupiah.'

As the driver started to turn into Prinsenpark, Tony ordered him to keep straight on; then to turn right and to follow the railroad tracks. It was dark here. There were no lights. A deserted street. And all houses already shuttered.

'So, I'll go to that Arab woman after all,' said Tony suddenly, and he half rose from his seat, tapped the driver on his shoulder and said, 'Stop!'

Something in his voice, some hidden menace, the tone which was not like the usual tone of passengers who wish a driver to stop, struck the driver's consciousness and, gripped by fear, he didn't stop the car immediately.

Resentment and anger rose in Tony.

'Stop!' he said again.

But now the threat and danger carried by the voice were stronger and more startling, and the driver, in growing terror, lost his head. He stepped on the accelerator as Robbers! flashed through his mind, and the whole menace, frightfulness, pain, loss and terror contained in that word flooded his soul and mind.

Djok noticed an iron rod on the floor and picked it up.

'What a blockhead,' he swore, and raising the rod he swung it in the direction of the driver's head. Tony tried to stop him, but before the driver could utter 'Don't hit ...', there was the thud of the iron on the skull, the stifled blood-curdling scream of the driver, blood from the head .... And then the cab, continuing to move as if drunken, careered left and right, eventually landing in a ditch at the roadside near the railway line.

Tony and Djok jumped out, looked around, there was no one in sight; they ran a short distance to a side street, walked on rapidly and Tony struck Djok, swearing angrily,

'Why did you hit him, you pig?'

And Djok said, 'I didn't intend to hit him hard. Just to make him afraid.'

'You never wait for orders,' Tony raved on.

'It's true, I was going to knock his head just a little, to frighten him,' repeated Djok.

They walked slowly, as was usual, when they turned into another street which was still somewhat enlivened by people and betjas. A few servant-girls were joking with betja drivers.

Tony's anger began to subside. Djok continued blubbering, 'It's true, I didn't intend to hit him hard!' until suddenly Tony burst into loud laughter.

'"It's true, I didn't intend to hit him hard. Only to frighten him",' he jeered. 'But you struck so hard that his head was broken, and how could he be afraid – dead? Ha-ha-ha!' he laughed, pleased with the wit of his own joke.

Djok tried to laugh too, but deep in his heart something stirred, not yet fully emerging, but beginning to rise, a chill which made him shrink.

And Tony, who had laughed his fill, was now saying in a cold, sharp voice,

'It is you who hit him, Djok, not I!' Djok knew that it was he. He would be alone with this feeling of terror which had begun to grip his body, The terror of a murderer. He glanced at Tony out of the corner of his eye. Hatred rose in his heart. Hatred of Tony who laughed at his terror.

Tomorrow, in a few hours now, the police will start looking for the taxi driver's killer. Is the driver dead? He's dead! No! He is dead! You've killed him! I have killed him! He is dead! He is dead!

Fear and horror enveloped and choked him, and as Tony pinched his buttock and said, 'I'll sleep with you anyway, Djok!' he swung his arm and hit Tony in the face. Tony fell with no chance to parry, and Djok, whirling round, ran, ran swiftly, Tony shouting after him,

'Haai Djok, here, where are you going? I'm not angry! Djo-ok!'

Djok kept running, turned and Tony's calling voice was lost behind him.

He turned into a narrow alley, ran on – running where, running where, running where, drummed in his head, and deep in his heart he knew that he wasn't running anywhere, and knew that the hunt was on, that he was the hunted one and that he was running away, and that he couldn't run away.

Djok was still running, panting, his rasping breath like the sound of rusty hinges opening, running, running. And in the night only the trotting of his shoes was heard as he ran, turning this way and that, endlessly. Running and unable to run away. For ever.

June

THE CROWING of a cock behind the hut, loud and clear, pierced the dawn. The sun's rays, still feeble, tried to creep through the cracks of the decrepit, darkened bamboo wall whose paint was peeled off by rain and the hot sun in turn. The wobbly and crooked window, blown by the strong night wind, was half open, and through the opening a flowering djambu tree was visible outside.

Saimun stretched himself on his balai-balai,[1] under his covering of two mats, slowly opened his eyes and then looked at the young woman who slept beside him. The woman's small mouth was half open. Her camisole was undone except for the lowest button, and her kain[2] enwrapped her limbs loosely, untied around the waist. Saimun was very still as he regarded the woman; he was at peace and happy, and when he laid his hand on the woman's belly she moved a little and her hand held Saimun's hand.

'Neng,' whispered Saimun, and his hand moved upwards, his blood rising. The previous week he had gone back to the dump and brought the woman to his hut. Just like that. He was surprised at his own daring. But also that the woman had so readily decided to follow him.

All he'd said was,

'Come with me!'

And she got up, tied her clothes into a small bundle and the two of them walked over to his hut. Neneng, the woman, was his. Slept on his balai-balai. Itam slept on his own bench, not two yards away from theirs, separated from them only by an old batik cloth which

---

1 Bamboo sleeping-bench.
2 Rectangular batik cloth worn as a straight wrap-around skirt, from waist to ankle.

was hung up at night near the edge of the bench. Neneng slept with Itam too, but she always returned to Saimun's sleeping-bench.

They never discussed it, but everything seemed to arrange itself on its own. That week it was Neneng who cleaned their little room. And they gave a part of their coolie wages to her for cooking.

Suddenly Saimun embraced the woman with ardour, his body burning. Neneng, awakened, smiled at Saimun, aware of his intent, and happily gave him what he desired. The hunger, which never loosened its grip upon him, so easily fanned his passion for the woman. That which consumed his body in the embrace with her seemed to dispel the hunger which nagged at his guts, gave him a feeling of power and confidence in himself: he too was a man, he was human, and in such a moment he was a male all alive, and the breath of life stormed through him, and the moans and little cries of the woman under him proved the force of his male assault.

The more the woman moaned, the stronger he felt his maleness and power, and he was great and strong, and not a little garbage man of no significance.

Then he lay back, Neneng tied up her kain, got off the bed.

'We're late,' she said, pushed back the batik hanging and looked over to the balai-balai where Itam was still lying, but with open eyes.

As Neneng passed by his balai-balai he caught her hand to pull her down, to sit on his bed, but Neneng laughed, extricated her hand and ran to open the door.

Saimun got up, put on his pants and said to Itam,

'You're not quick enough! Tonight, you!'

Behind the thin bamboo partition they could hear Pak Idjo's family beginning to stir, and Pak Idjo complaining that he was sick, saying to his wife, 'Aduh, I am feverish. Look at the boils on my back! But if I don't go out to earn, how then?' And the voice of his wife said, 'Just be careful!' Then Pak Idjo's little child started to scream and cry.

They went down to bathe in the stream where many people had already gathered, and then, after coffee had been brewed by Neneng in an empty tin that once held butter, Saimun and Itam hastened to the meeting place of garbage carts. The truck was there with Bang Miun, the driver, inspecting its engine. He was swearing to himself when they arrived. The engine wouldn't start. Again the battery's dead, Bang Miun muttered, how many times has it been to the repair shop, but it doesn't want to go. Itam and Saimun stood behind Bang Miun watching how he scraped the cables of the battery. Saimun was always amazed when he looked at the engine of a car. He could not understand how a dead thing like that could move such a big and heavy truck, but neither was the driver able to explain it to him clearly. Saimun had once asked Bang Miun to teach him to drive. This was the highest aspiration of his life. To become a driver like Bang Miun, to get higher wages, to sit comfortably behind the steering wheel, and to control the engine and the truck. Bang Miun had said jocularly that he would teach him if Saimun were diligent and would wash the truck every evening. Saimun had been washing it every evening for a whole week now, but Driver Miun still had not started to teach him. Saimun was full of dreams of how he would drive that cart. He was afraid to press Driver Miun to start the lessons lest he become angry and refuse to teach him altogether. Suddenly Miun turned to him and said, 'Saimun, get in, switch on the ignition and step on the starter. Put your foot on the accelerator a little.'

Saimun's heartbeat quickened, so unexpected was such an order from Driver Miun. This was the beginning of his driving lessons, he thought. By now he knew where the ignition key was, where the starter and where the accelerator were.

Saimun climbed into the truck, sat down at the steering wheel, turned the ignition key and pressed on the starter-pedal with his foot. How proud he felt, and smilingly he looked around at Itam who regarded him with envy.

But the motor still wouldn't start. The first garbage carts had already arrived, and coolies started to toss the refuse into the truck.

Driver Miun shouted for the coolies to stop filling the truck.

'Ayoh, come on, push, the engine is dead.'

The whole crowd of them pushed the heavy truck, and at last the engine started but only after they had pushed it repeatedly and were all out of breath, panting; and Saimun and Itam felt a smarting pain in their insides because their stomachs were still empty. But the moment the engine started they all jumped on the truck, shouting and cheering, and under the hubbub the truck returned to the place for the reloading of rubbish from the carts.

Saimun was overjoyed because Driver Miun had said that at about noon he would begin his lessons.

'I'll ask that lu be moved, become knek,'[1] said Driver Miun. 'Knek Ali, three weeks not come. Sick. He 'lready back country, maybe not coming back!'

Sitting on the truck, now piled full of refuse, Saimun told Itam of his dream of becoming a driver.

'And when I 'lready got my permit I look for work, become an oplet[2] driver and lu I teach to steer,' said Saimun. 'Driver Miun, he drives a taxi after hours too. An oplet, he says, brings in a lot of money, y' can take home up to twenty, or fifty, a day. Just think!'

Itam joined in day-dreaming of how Saimun would be an autolette driver — a vivid, resplendent vision, which filled him with gladness. Thus they dreamed on together, sitting on the garbage truck, its stench gone, all the rubbish gone, only the dream filling them with joy.

Hasnah was busy sewing a dress for the baby she carried when Dahlia knocked at the door and immediately entered, without

---

1 From the Dutch *knecht* = manservant. Here = an assistant to the driver.
2 Oplet = autolette ('opellette'), a small urban bus.

awaiting a response.

'Idris is off on an inspection tour again, this time to Kalimantan, for ten days.'

Hasnah smiled and invited her to sit down.

'You're only one year in Djakarta, and fed up already?' Hasnah asked her.

'What do you think—staying in a house like this, who can stand it? It's almost the same as before, when we stayed in the hotel. And my husband constantly going off, too. How can you stand it? The more so with a child. I don't have a child but I'm almost losing my mind staying here.'

Hasnah smiled and said,

'Soon we'll move to another house. Sugeng promised that before our baby is born we'll move to a house of our own.'

'Ah, lucky you. I don't know when we will get a house to ourselves. My husband is too obedient a government official. He doesn't want to keep on begging for a house. If there's no chance yet, that's that, he always says. What's the use of having a husband like that!'

Dahlia stood up to look at her face in the mirror near the window, stroked it in several places and said,

'It's time to go to the beauty shop again. Make-up and a permanent wave.'

She turned around and said to Hasnah,

'Don't you ever get a permanent for your hair? Why? Your husband doesn't like it?'

'Not at all,' said Hasnah. 'It's too expensive, no money.'

'Nonsense. You're just lazy. Don't be like that, Has. Just try and see how it'll change you. Your face will be prettier when your hair is all done up.'

Dahlia took hold of Hasnah's hair, got out a comb and went to work with zest. At first Hasnah protested, but she did not interfere. When Hasnah's hair was done, Dahlia got out a lipstick from her handbag and painted Hasnah's lips. Then she got the mirror off the wall, held it up to Hasnah and said,

'Nah, look, isn't it pretty?'

Hasnah looked into the mirror, looked at her face. Very embarrassed, but inwardly pleased, she asked,

'Is it really proper for me to be made up like this?'

'Of course. Don't let yourself go ungroomed. All men, including your husband, like to see you pretty like this.'

'Ah, but my belly, it's quite some weeks already, what's the use of prettying up?'

'It's needed all the more, so that your husband forgets your big belly and keeps looking only at your face.'

They both laughed.

'I am so pleased that you live next to us,' said Hasnah. 'The family before you had too many children, there was constant uproar and Maryam got into fights with their children. How long have you been married?'

'Three years!'

'You don't want to have children?'

'In the beginning I did too. But it seems it's not our fate. And now, with housing conditions as they are, I'm not eager to have a child.'

'Don't think that way! Every child brings its own luck. Our second baby here will bring us a house.'

'How come you're so sure that you'll get a house?'

'Sugeng has promised it.'

'And if he said so does it mean that you're sure to get it?'

'Yes.'

'You have no doubts whatsoever?'

'No. Why should I doubt if Sugeng has promised it?' asked Hasnah, astonished.

Dahlia shrugged her shoulders, and said,

'Who knows, maybe your Sugeng is an exceptional person. But

I never believe people's promises. The more so, promises made by men. Even more so, promises made by my husband. Idris is an idiot. He's an inspector of the Ministry of Education. His friends are all rich by now, but he isn't worth even a half a cent.'

'But you, you don't seem to be at a loss. Look at your badju,[1] they're always beautiful. The material is always new. No lack of perfume, either,' said Hasnah.

'Yes, but I didn't get it from him.'

Hasnah was about to ask her where she did get it from, but something kept her back.

'Women today must be smart, look out for themselves,' added Dahlia. 'You must always be pretty. It's the only thing men want from a woman.'

'Ah, not Sugeng. He also loves his child.'

'That's what you say. How do you know he's not playing around with another woman?'

'I know Sugeng is not like that,' said Hasnah.

'How do you know?'

'Somehow, I'm just convinced. Besides we were married by our own choice.'

'You're lucky,' said Dahlia. 'Do you like to go to shows?'

'We do. But it's been a long time since we've seen a show, because of this.' And Hasnah pointed to her growing belly.

'If you go out to a show, invite me sometimes?'

'All right.'

'Which film star do you like?'

'Male or female?'

'Ah, I like to see Gregory Peck, but he's not quite forceful enough.'

'Do you know who I like? Gary Cooper! There's a real he-man for you!'

'But he's already old …!'

---

1 A jacket made of very light material.

Sugeng was busy reading incoming mail when he got a call to appear before the chief of his bureau. His heart beating fast, he went to the office of his chief, hoping that the problem of his house was at last solved. The nearer Hasnah's confinement came, the more nervous he had felt. He had fought who knows how many times with the people in charge of housing for the ministry's employees. But he was constantly told just to have patience: he, at least, had a place to live, while there were many other employees who were separated from their families for lack of housing.

The bureau chief ordered him to sit down, and then said,

'I have good news for you. According to the minister's decision' – and here he handed Sugeng a letter – 'beginning with the end of the month, i.e. on the first of July, you will be promoted to the head of the import section.'

Sugeng shook the hand of the bureau chief and quickly went out. He was very happy – his salary would be higher and the chance of getting a house, as head of a section, would be greater. How pleased and happy Hasnah will be, a real professional advance.

They had been debating in the room for over two hours already; the problem they were discussing was turned over time and again, returning to its starting point, but it still looked as if the end was nowhere in sight. Suryono looked around him, and was amazed: were all these friends really convinced of what they were saying, and were they serious in believing that what they were doing here was of benefit to the nation? He felt somewhat trapped, because Ies Iskaq had once challenged him by saying that if he was so completely dissatisfied why didn't he join them, to think about the nation's problems, and she brought him several times to these meetings.

There were only six of them in the room. Ies, himself, Pranoto, the well-known essayist, who often wrote on Indonesia's cultural problems and was considered to be the driving force behind this small club. His face was that of a thinker and he always spoke with sincerity. Achmad, a labour leader, and Yasrin, a poet, who as time went on felt that there was no chance for him to grow and develop in his own country, and Murhalim, a young provincial comptroller who was constantly enraged by the conditions in his office.

'Is there a crisis, or isn't there?' said Pranoto. 'Actually, the fact that this question is being raised at all, shows that a feeling of responsibility already exists in society. And …'

Suryono stopped listening to Pranoto's exposition and thought of how time and again he had heard such discussions – about the function of culture in building up the country, of the individual's loneliness in Indonesian society and where was Indonesian music going, and he recalled a particularly heated debate about Europeans having reached a dead end, and how the debate finished with a question from one of the people in the gathering – who was it?… he forgot – why were we worrying whether the peoples of Western Europe were stalemated or not, were we West Europeans?

He was aware of Ies sitting at his side, her fine face, the full curves of her breasts, and in his imagination he saw her without a badju on, lying beside him in bed, and was comparing her with Fatma. The young woman, feeling his stare, turned her head to glance at Suryono. What she saw in his face caused her to blush and she quickly turned away. Suryono woke with a start, and heard Yasrin saying,

'I received an invitation to visit Peking at the expense of the Ministry of Education. In my conversation with the minister I explained my desire to go to R.R.T.[1] to study how they develop art among the masses over there. In my opinion, the problem of social integration in our nation is very closely connected with the development of a national culture, I even think that the problem of our society is a cultural problem.'

---

1 *Republik Rakjat Tionghwa* = People's Republic of China.

'Just what do you mean by national culture?' asked Murhalim. 'I know — people are already sick and tired of hearing this problem discussed, but why get excited about the problem of a national culture? Why do people want to synthesize regional cultures in order to produce one national culture? Why do people want to synthesize Western dancing with the S'rimpi[2] dance, or nationalize the S'rimpi? Why must gamelan[3] music be "national-orchestrated" with the addition of a viola, piano and cello? Why don't we view the problem from an angle in which the gamelan is national music, as the Sundanese angklung and ketjapi[4] are equally national music, and the S'rimpi dance of Central Java, the dances of Bali, the plate and handkerchief dances of Sumatra, the tjakalele[5] of the Moluccas, the pakarene[6] of Sulawesi, etc., all are national dances, because aren't they all the property of the Indonesian people, but only of different regional origin? I believe the problem does not involve national culture, but the Indonesians who are not as yet mature enough to feel themselves as one nation, and who still differentiate between the regions.'

'I protest, I protest,' said Achmad. 'What Murhalim just said is surely nice to hear. But this means being blind to history, and to reality as it actually is. The problem of national culture *does* arise, because the Indonesian people indeed do not have a national consciousness. This is why a national culture must be created, to achieve our national integration.'

'Is it possible to organise a national culture when the people don't have a national consciousness, as you've just said? Which comes first, a national culture, or a national consciousness?' retorted Murhalim.

'Ah, your thinking is rather naive, brother,' said Achmad. 'It's

---

2 Originally a court dance, S'rimpi is the classical dance for women in Central Java.
3 Javanese orchestra composed mainly of percussion instruments.
4 *Angklung* — percussion instrument made of bamboo tubes; *ketjapi* — a type of lute.
5 *Tjakalele* — a war dance in the islands of East Indonesia.
6 Pakarene — ritual dances in South Celebes (Sulawesi), esp. in the regions of Makasar.

decadent bourgeois thinking. It is necessary to establish a concept of national culture at the top and then to spread it downwards. This is why I agree with brother Yasrin's plan to study the development of the people's culture in R.R.T. He will probably learn a lot and be inspired by their example.'

'But maybe what is possible in R.R.T. cannot be applied in Indonesia,' interposed Ies.

'What do you mean?' asked Achmad.

'In R.R.T. power is in the hands of the communists and everything is run by a dictatorship. We in Indonesia have high respect for democracy.'

'What does democracy mean today to the Indonesian people?' asked Achmad. 'It is the voice of the bourgeois class wanting to retain its power over the ignorant and confused masses. How do we stand with our democracy? Is the provisional parliament democratic? Are our people already capable of realising a democracy? Can you answer that honestly?'

'Eh ... certainly not ripe yet, nevertheless ...' said Murhalim.

'Nah, there you have that lack of certainty, the lack of courage of Indonesians to face the true reality. That's why our country is confused. That's why a moral crisis, a cultural crisis and all sorts of crises arise. Permit me to speak, and I hope Murhalim and Ies will refrain from interrupting me before I have really finished.'

Achmad drew breath, looked around with the air of a man confident of his coming victory.

'According to Marx and Engels, it is the system of production which determines the process of social, political and intellectual life of man. This is the very root of our crisis. Because the system of production in our country is not only imperialistic, but at the height of capitalism. All sorts of crises are certain to occur, so long as their roots are not eradicated. And is any effort made to eradicate them, or to attempt to eradicate them? No! You, brothers, are worrying about a cultural crisis, but the discussion is all up in the clouds, because you don't want to face reality. The bourgeois spirit causes all this, brothers.'

'I protest,' shouted Ies.

Pranoto pounded on the table.

'Let Achmad finish speaking first,' he said.

Achmad looked around again, and this time his expression conveyed that it's done, he must win. The little wheels in his mind strained, and all the arguments that had to be advanced became clear and precise.

'It is not man's consciousness that determines the condition of the self; or the personal condition, but it's the social self or the social situation which determines the consciousness of the individual. And because the system of production determines also the social life of man, it is clear therefore that a certain type of production system, such as capitalism, is a chain which constricts the social self of man, which further means pushing self-consciousness towards a conception of individuality. So it's clear that capitalism directly enslaves the human soul, and that from such a system of production inevitably arise all sorts of crises, especially because of the conflicts among peoples who wish to free themselves from enslavement to this capitalism. So, if we discuss cultural crisis, we really should be discussing the basis of our economy.'

'But you seem to propose that Indonesia should become a communist state?' said Ies. 'Our state is based on Pantjasila.'[1]

'Ha, Pantjasila,' said Achmad. 'I can muster arguments which will convince people with equal success that the Pantjasila aims in fact at an Islamic state, or a Christian state, or a socialist-welfare state, or at a communist state. I'm not going to discuss the Pantjasila, because its philosophy is not fully thought out; but how can we debate here? Ah, brothers, I beg you not to interrupt me.

---

1 The Five Principles: Belief in God, Nationalism, Humanism, Sovereignty of the People and Social Justice, proclaimed in 1945 by President Sukarno as the basis of the Indonesian state.

Permit me to speak until I have finished. As I said before, you, brothers, are not realistic in viewing the problem. We cannot discuss the cultural crisis which confronts us without touching on the economic system which still prevails in our country. The political development, law, philosophy, religion, literature, art and so forth, are all based on economic development, so said Engels.'

'Brother Achmad, have you finished?' asked Murhalim.

'Yes.'

'May I ask a question?'

'Please,' replied Achmad.

'I want to ask only one thing,' said Murhalim. 'Are you, brother Achmad, a communist, or a member of the communist party?'

'What connection is there between my being a communist or a member of the communist party and the problem we're discussing?' asked Achmad resentfully.

'If brother Achmad is a member of the communist party then it would be futile to continue this debate,' said Murhalim, 'because, to the end of days there would be no meeting of minds between us. I believe in democracy. Marxism, as practiced by communists, doesn't bring freedom and happiness to man, but actually ends up bringing enslavement and loss of humanity. What brother Achmad wishes is that a dictatorship of the proletariat be established in Indonesia. But brother Achmad has forgotten that human beings are not machines who can be ordered to become parts of a production system. Next to materialism, there are also spiritual values of no less importance for ensuring the good way of life. If a man's stomach may not be empty, neither may his soul be starved, and it must be able to live and flourish in freedom. Brother Achmad wants an economic system wholly controlled by the state, one hundred per cent. Such a totalitarian system must, of necessity, control the lives and thoughts of people, because without such absolute control and authority it would be impossible to attain what brother Achmad wishes for. I can agree that some parts of an economic system can influence the cultural development of a people. But one cannot completely disregard the human factors. The peoples of Persia, India, Egypt, Rome, Greece, all attained the peaks of their cultural glory under a system of absolute monarchy, which, according to communist theory, could not possibly produce highly prized values. The painter Picasso, who glorifies the communists, is himself the product of a bourgeois society and of capitalistic Western Europe. And I want to ask further, where are those cultural products that are supposedly coming out of Russia today? But – to return to my question – are you a communist?'

'Your question implies a confession that you're unable to carry on the debate. I am not a communist, but if conditions in our country should continue as they are today, with a leadership which continues to deceive the people, with corruption on the rampage, disintegration and confusion, then I shall become a communist.'

Murhalim shrugged his shoulders.

'It's a bit difficult to continue a debate when one is accused of inability to continue it.'

'I am not an expert on Islam,' intervened Ies, 'but I want to introduce a thought for all of us to consider: could not Islam be made the mainstay of our people's spiritual uplift? A modernised Islam, with a new dynamism?'

'Ha, Islam, what naivety. Very naive,' interposed Achmad quickly. 'I once talked to a man who came from a Middle Eastern country and had visited its Islamic university, one of the highest, most widely acclaimed centres for the study of modern Islam in the world today. Do you know, sister, what he said? He was very disappointed. Disappointed no end. What he found was incredible dirt, people sleeping on dirty floors and nothing organised. And what did this Islam bring to these Arab countries? All we see is that one class of society exploits the masses who for hundreds of years have lived on the brink of starvation and in darkest ignorance.'

'But this is not yet reason enough to reject the idea of seeking a new dynamism in Islam,' Ies replied. 'Probably, with sufficient conscious stimulation, some Islamic thinkers capable of finding it could emerge in Indonesia, too! The conditions we see today in Islamic countries are not the fault of Islam, but of some Moslems who disregard the teachings of their religion. They make the study of Islam a completely dead thing – no different than if one made a mynah bird recite the verses of the Holy Qur'an, or from putting the verses of the Qur'an on gramophone records and then letting them play day and night. Since the majority of our people adhere to the religious teachings of Islam, and if some Islamic leaders would come forth bringing a new dynamism into Islam, couldn't Islam then become a tremendous force in the development of our people?'

'Theory! Vain hope! Impossible!' exclaimed Achmad heatedly. 'There isn't a single proof in history that religion can bring about a good human society. Christianity at the time of its greatest glory, Islam at the time of its greatest glory, Buddhism at the time of its greatest glory, which of these really succeeded in eliminating the contrasts between the classes and bringing justice to humanity? The time of Islam's glory was, as we saw, an era of royal power; enslavement is still the order of the day, so where is your just society? As Christianity flourished with its crusades, so also the Spanish Catholic Church going to South America has spread death and hatred.'

'Brother Achmad appears to be completely anti-religion,' interposed Murhalim. 'And, to criticise religion, he uses communist clichés. What Ies meant was to seek out and develop the valuable principles contained in Islamic religion, just as there are valuable principles in any religion. Values which now are buried and dead should be revived, given a new life. That was the problem suggested by Ies's question. Could Islam with a new dynamism be used to become the mainstay for the development of our people? This question was posed, I believe, because with the exception of you, brother Achmad, all of us here reject communism with its totalitarian system as a means to build up our nation.'

'I don't reject communism,' said Suryono, speaking up for the first time. 'Why should communism be rejected? Look at Russia where it succeeded in freeing the people from feudal oppression and provided them with livelihood. Look also at R.R.T., how tremendous the progress which has been initiated by Mao Tse-tung in all fields – the liberation of the people from the oppression and corruption of Chiang Kaishek's clique. If it can be done there, why not here?'

'Suryono, don't play!' Ies exclaimed. 'I know you. You don't believe your own words!'

'You're right, Ies,' replied Suryono. 'Of course I don't believe what I've just said. Has it never occurred to anyone that we do not live today in an atomic age, but in an age of unbelief? An age of unbelief caused by the deep frustration felt by mankind since the end of the last world war, when they saw that this war would not end all wars either? Isn't it evident that the Americans are afraid of their own atomic and hydrogen bombs, do not believe in themselves, and the Russians, too, don't dare trust each other, that the Asians do not trust the West, that the West fears and doesn't trust Asia? Malan's racialism in South Africa, the white-skin policy in Australia, suspicion against foreigners in Indonesia and in other Asian countries, discrimination against Negroes in America – all this underlies this absence of faith. Because people don't trust each other they do not believe that human beings are equal and that they can and must be able to live together. The communist is like this, the imperialist is like this, the democrat is like this, the merdeka[1] man is like this. They're all the same.

---

1 *Merdeka*, lit. freedom, is a much used Indonesian slogan and greeting, hence 'merdeka man' implies an Indonesian.

There's little use spending oneself on exchanges of ideas, as we do here. Isn't it best to take care of oneself, seek one's own happiness in any way one chooses and to the devil with the world?'

'You're joking!' said Ies accusingly.

'No, he's not joking,' spoke Achmad with a light smile. 'It's quite true what he said about that non-belief. But he forgot to clarify the cause of this lack of faith in the world today. It is the evil outcome of capitalism and imperialism which still—'

'And therefore we should all become communists,' broke in Murhalim.

Achmad glanced at Murhalim with great resentment.

'It's hard to exchange ideas in an intelligent manner with people who are as prejudiced as brother Murhalim here.' He pretended to be plaintive.

'I want to intervene before the discussion strays off elsewhere,' said Suryono, a smile playing on his lips. 'If this discussion should be continued without a change of direction we are sure to get absolutely nowhere, because, friends, you're all taking the wrong view of the problem. Achmad, who adheres to historic materialism, is wrong, our friend who wanted to put forward Islam is also wrong. The root of the matter is man himself. That which is called crisis of leadership, cultural crisis, economic crisis, moral crisis, crisis in literature, is nothing but man's crisis. That's why an Indonesian must first of all realise that he exists, and that his fate is in his own hands. That his life is not determined by society or his family, or by the economic system, but that he has enough inner strength to determine himself.'

'Ah, existentialist! Pessimistic bourgeois ideas!' sneered Achmad promptly.

Suryono laughed and looked at him.

'I admit frankly that what I've just said is lifted straight out of Sartre,' he said. 'But, of course, only people who are half informed on existentialism always assert that it is a pessimistic philosophy.

Yet, it is quite the contrary. Existentialism is the most optimistic of philosophies because it says that man, and not outside influences, can determine his own self. Sartre said it in *L'existentialisme est un humanisme* − have you read it, brother Achmad?' he asked, taunting, which made Achmad look at him furiously, and Suryono, smiling, continued,

'In fact, Sartre himself opposed Marxism, because Marxism conceals the truth that man is fully responsible for his attitudes and choices. Sartre's argument is that the individual is fully responsible for what he is and what he does. That's why there is no other philosophy that is more optimistic than this existentialism, optimistic in the recognition of the individual's capacity to determine himself, and to act as an individual, which is the only hope for humanity, as only by acting can man survive.'

Pranoto coughed lightly, looked round, saw that Achmad was tearing to jump into the debate again and quickly said,

'Ah, we hadn't realised, it's almost seven o'clock already. I'm really sorry to have to adjourn our meeting at a time when the discussion was becoming so very interesting, especially since Suryono, who kept quiet at the beginning, has now jumped into the arena with both feet. Although we have not arrived at any conclusion, I believe that many valuable ideas have been expressed, whether one agrees with every one of them or not. That such ideas are present, as well as the readiness of us all to discuss them and to listen, shows that we have high enough expectations from this exchange of ideas that it will enable each of us to clarify for himself the essence of the ideas touched upon here. I think that the most fortunate man among us is brother Achmad because to him everything is already clear. For him, the road to our people's development and human happiness is communism, while the others are still questioning and still searching for the way which seems best according to their views and convictions.'

'I cannot discern the good fortune in Achmad's situation. His thoughts are no longer free,' interjected Murhalim. They laughed, and Achmad joined in laughing with them. Pranoto stood up and said,

'Before we adjourn – remember that the meeting next week is on Wednesday.'

Outside Suryono said to Ies,

'I will see you home, Ies.'

'It's not necessary,' said Ies. 'I have a bicycle.'

'Leave it here, I have Father's Dodge. Father just bought himself a new Cadillac! Tomorrow's time enough to pick up the bicycle, or get your younger brother to fetch it.'

Ies looked very hesitant.

'You're angry with me,' Suryono said. 'You suspect that I was being sarcastic and was making fun of them with this existentialism?'

Ies regarded him for a moment and then said,

'All right, you see me home.'

They rode in the car of Suryono's father, a new Dodge. 'Aduh, it's embarrassing to be seen in such a luxurious car,' sighed Ies. 'They will suspect me of riding with a black marketeer or a corrupter.'

'Ah, why these allusions?' Suryono asked. 'If Father is wallowing in money made in business, why throw it in my face?'

'Forgive me, I'm wrong,' said Ies, and, sincerely regretful, she patted Suryono's neck lightly and playfully wiggled the edge of his ear, gently.

No little startled, Suryono glanced at Ies, a thrill passing through him, but he quickly suppressed it. He was afraid to disturb the mood in the car. Never before had he felt so close to Ies.

'I swear I wasn't mocking with this existentialism, Ies,' he said. 'I really, really believe that man has the strength to determine what and who he is.'

'Ah, I'm already tired of pondering these involved problems,' said Ies. 'I just want to rest.' And she leaned her head on his shoulder. 'Let's not go home directly,' said Ies. 'Let's first take a little ride.'

Suryono smiled happily and pressed Ies's hand with warmth.

In front of the restaurant rows of new motor-cars were parked at the kerb. That evening the restaurant was crowded. A dark-red Cadillac arrived, seeking a place to park, but the places at the kerb were filled, and finally it stopped with its two left wheels raised on the pavement.

Raden Kaslan was at the wheel, and at his side sat his wife, Fatma. From the dark-red Cadillac, up to Fatma's finery, her elaborate gilt slippers, her coiffure fresh from the hairdresser's salon, emanated an air of luxury and wealth. Also from the smile which Fatma directed at Raden Kaslan.

Thus, on that clear evening, Raden Kaslan and Fatma, exuding wealth and luxury, left their beautiful car which glistened in the light of the setting sun, half-raised on the pavement, the other half tilting a little over the roadway.

They seated themselves in the garden in front of the restaurant, at a table somewhat isolated from the others, and having settled they exchanged views on matters that were rather expensive and rather luxurious.

From the loud-speaker behind the restaurant's bar came gay music; at the tables people ate, drank, chatted and laughed.

Raden Kaslan ordered the meal without first consulting the prices listed on the menu opposite the names of the dishes and drinks, and then they returned to the rather expensive and luxurious ideas, to which Fatma responded with a luxuriant smile.

It was extremely pleasant, that atmosphere of the clear evening, the deep blue sky overhead and the fresh breeze.

An old delman carriage, empty, drawn by an old emaciated horse, and its driver, Pak Idjo, dozing in his seat, came by, passing in front of the restaurant. For years the horse had been accustomed to pulling the delman through the big city, and even if the driver fell asleep, which often happened on hot days – and Pak Idjo hadn't had any passengers since morning, until he dozed off hungry – the horse continued drawing the delman by himself, stopped by himself when hailed by a passenger, awakening the driver by the shock of the sudden stop. Or when a traffic policeman barred the traffic's progress, the old horse stopped too, its muzzle pressed against the side of a car or a truck.

In this way the horse which pulled the delman cart trotted on along the street also on that gay evening. Near the restaurant, from behind the fence of the house across the street, a big dog chasing a cat suddenly jumped out, barking loudly. The horse, badly startled, tried to dodge the dog and the cat at its feet, slipped and fell; the left pole of the delman with its blackened copper capping hit the side of the red Cadillac at the roadside, damaging its chromium and paint, and the protruding iron brace of the cart roof struck the car's side window, shattering the glass.

Pak Idjo, jolted from his nap, staggered out, helped the old horse to its feet and just stood there, dazed, stroking the horse's knees and head.

The noise of the collision also alarmed the guests who sat eating, drinking and laughing in the restaurant. Raden Kaslan jumped up and hurried to the street; the moment he saw the damaged chromium and paint on his car, and the shattered glass of the door, he flew into a rage.

'Hai, you idiot, where're your eyes? Look, you've mangled my car, do you admit it or not? You'll pay for all this damage!' Raden Kaslan shouted, beside himself.

Pak Idjo, white in the face, his whole body shaking and his voice quivering, was like a man seized by an attack of malaria. He was sick already, anyway. His ragged and dirty clothes hung on a thin body, and his inflamed, watering eyes were sunk in the hollows of his cheeks.

He tried to say something, but his voice, quavering with agitation and despair, was lost on his trembling lips, and his hand kept stroking the head of his horse.

Raden Kaslan eyed him furiously, exchanged glances with Fatma, so expensive and luxurious, then he looked again at his damaged car, and his wrath flared even higher.

'I'll call the police, I'll sue you, you'll make good all this damage. Look at this!' – and he jumped to point to the chromium on the car door – 'and this' – and he pointed at the scars along the side where the paint was scraped off – 'and this' – and he kicked a piece of the broken glass. 'You shall reimburse me for all this, at least one thousand, two thousand rupiah,' he roared, castigating Pak Idjo, who almost fainted at the mention of one or two thousand rupiah, but suddenly found his voice and said, weeping,

'I admit my guilt, tuan, you may kill me, but I cannot repay, I am a poor man, it's best just to put me to death!' And his hand kept on stroking the head of his old horse.

The horse licked Pak Idjo's hand as if begging forgiveness for his misdeed.

At Pak Idjo's words, Raden Kaslan, even angrier than before, turned away without another word and walked back to the restaurant where he telephoned the traffic police.

On the street many people stood watching; Pak Idjo still stroked the head of his horse and when Raden Kaslan returned, saying,

'Don't you run away, I've called the police!' he, together with his horse, died a thousand deaths and faced all the fires of hell, until the police arrived on their exploding and roaring motor cycles, like the detonations of guns which kill.

And at that instant in the old man's mind flashed back his village and the sounds of shooting guns, of invading bandits who forced them to flee and seek shelter in the big city.

Meanwhile, the other guests had returned to their tables, eating, drinking and laughing again. A collision was an ordinary matter, and once the police had been called the police would take care of it.

Raden Kaslan met the policemen, identified himself and, pointing to the trembling old delman driver, said,

'It's entirely his fault. My car was parked at the kerb, even half-way on the pavement, and still he ran into it.'

The traffic police inspector was a young man who had dealt with collisions hundreds of times, a routine matter for him, quite an easy case, in fact. Quite clear who was at fault.

'I demand damages,' repeated Raden Kaslan.

At these words Pak Idjo suddenly cried out weeping,

'Just kill me, tuan,' he said, bowing with folded hands to the police inspector. 'I'm a poor man, I have no money at all.'

'You admit your guilt, bapak?'[1] asked the inspector.

'I admit, tuan, just kill me, tuan. I cannot pay for the damage. I am a poor man.'

'Why did you run into my car which was parked at the side of the street?' fumed Raden Kaslan.

'I dozed off, tuan,' replied the old driver, trembling.

'Ha, dozed off! What sort of a driver are you! Dozed off!'

Pak Idjo's reply was truly infuriating.

'If you want to sleep, sleep at home, not in the delman, endangering other people. Why did you fall asleep?' Raden Kaslan snarled.

'Because I am sick, tuan,' replied Pak Idjo, his voice quavering even more.

'Ha,' Raden Kaslan sneered, 'fell asleep, sick; if you're sick you should not work! Stay home! Take medicine! Otherwise you'll cause accidents! What if you run into a little child and kill him, how'd that be?'

Pak Idjo, trembling more violently, said,

'But I am hungry, tuan, and my wife and my children are

---

1 Familiar form for father, papa.

hungry, tuan. And yesterday we had nothing to eat, tuan.'

For a moment Raden Kaslan was still, but then he shouted,

'You lie, what is your sickness?'

Then Pak Idjo, still weeping and shaking, unbuttoned his jacket and bared his back. 'Here, tuan, look!' and with his hand he motioned towards two boils the size of a fist, red and swollen, and then he lifted one side of his sarong and showed a big boil on his thigh. The whole thigh was red and swollen – it made one shudder.

It seemed as if the old man had come to the end of his strength after he had done this, every part of his body shook, his teeth chattered and tears streamed from his eyes.

The inspector looked at him, then looked at Raden Kaslan and then at Fatma, the luxurious one.

Raden Kaslan turned to the police inspector, raised a hand and spoke like someone at the end of his wits.

'How do we stand in this case, Inspector? Who will reimburse me for the damage? Who is responsible?'

'Who is responsible?' he asked again.

Pak Idjo continued to shiver and shake, continued to stroke the head of his old, emaciated horse and as they waited for the answer to come forth to the question, 'Who is responsible?' it seemed as if the shadows of the driver and of the horse were growing longer and longer on the pavement under the setting sun, and they, the old driver and the horse, died and lived hundreds of times.

Raden Kaslan swore again at Pak Idjo, but finally realised how impossible it was for this old, poor driver to pay for the damage to his car.

'That's that,' he said to the police inspector. 'Let's go.'

He drew Fatma back to the restaurant. His joy was completely spoiled.

'The devil,' Raden Kaslan muttered. 'A brand-new car, just purchased!'

City Report

The eyes of Wang Ching-kai, alias Tony, were red because he had cried all night in the detention-room of the police station, calling for his father and mother who still had not come. His cheeks were hollow, his hair dishevelled. During the night he was kicked several times by other prisoners who were annoyed with his incessant crying.

That morning he didn't touch the coffee or other fare distributed to the arrested persons. He waited for his father and mother to come to his rescue.

At ten o'clock his name was called by a police agent, the door was opened for him and he was ushered into an office. When he entered his face lit up as he saw his father seated near the police inspector's desk. But a moment later he became apprehensive, because his father behaved like a stranger and looked at him with such anger and loathing that he was frightened. Tony dropped his face, sat down on a chair in front of the desk as soon as he was ordered to do so.

The police inspector read the report prepared the previous night: '... confesses that he stabbed with a knife a woman named Siti Danijah at Kaligot, number ... in a brawl about payment of money ....'

His father lowered his head, looked at the police inspector with despair and then the police inspector asked his father,

'This is your son, tuan – is that true?'

The old man bit his lip, the words he wanted to utter, a denial that this was his son, had almost escaped; he restrained himself and said in a shaky voice,

'That's true, sir. But now I do not wish to acknowledge him any more as my son. I gave up trying to teach him. He was a scoundrel already at seventeen. We're not able to teach him any more. And ... did that woman die?' asked the father fearfully.

'No, but somewhat seriously wounded. Has been taken to a hospital. Lucky she did not die,' replied the police inspector.

His father tried hard to show the relief he felt at the inspector's reply. Nevertheless, gathering his courage, he then said,

'I beg you in all earnestness, sir, to sentence this boy. We are afraid that if he goes free he will kill someone. He even once stabbed me, six months ago. At that time he stole a gold ring from his mother. He sold it in order to gamble. When I got angry at him he fought, fetched the cleaver from the kitchen and attacked me. But his elder brother arrived and so he ran away.'

His father rolled up the sleeve of his jacket and showed a scar.

'This is the scar!' said the old man.

'He doesn't want to study. If you send him to school he always runs away. His mother is afraid of him. Sir, punish him. He's not our son any more.'

The old man stood up, walked quickly out of the room, the police inspector called after him to return, but was not heard. The old man walked on rapidly, large tears wetting his cheeks, flowing full and swift, dimming his sight.

July

RADEN KASLAN, director of the Bumi Aju Corporation, member of the Indonesian Party, closed the door of his office in his home and turned to his visitor, Husin Limbara, chairman of the Indonesian Party.

'Nah,' he said. 'Now no one can listen to our conversation. Please sit down.'

Husin Limbara sat down in a dark-brown leather armchair, leaned back comfortably and said,

'Aduh, my shoulder still hurts. None of the doctors are able to cure it.'

Raden Kaslan picked up the cigar-box from his table, said something in sympathy with Husin Limbara's shoulder trouble and, as his visitor helped himself to a '555', Raden Kaslan held up to his cigar a silver lighter made by the Jogja silverworks.

Husin Limbara inhaled deeply, puffed the smoke slowly, his eyes steadily fixed on the face of his host. For a moment Raden Kaslan felt uncomfortable, but he dispelled this feeling, after thinking: The party needs money again, and deciding for himself that this time he wasn't going to give them more than one or two thousand rupiah. Having decided so, he felt at ease again, and said to Husin Limbara,

'Nah, what's on your mind? On the telephone it sounded like a very important and pressing matter.'

With a little groan Husin sat up in his chair and said, lowering his voice,

'The executive council has taken an important decision. As you know, the general elections are very near. Our party needs a lot of money. We must establish a trade organisation to raise as much money as possible. Of all our members we have selected you to prepare a plan, because of your long experience in the business world. We want you, brother, to prepare a plan on a really large scale, to cover all economic activities. You needn't worry about your own money. It's not our intention to trade, really. But if some of the arrangements could remain permanent, all the better. Our members who are in positions of authority have already received instructions to support the party's efforts. What do you think?'

Raden Kaslan looked at Husin Limbara. He had heard already of the party's intentions to raise this money, for quite some time he had been hoping that he would be invited to participate. Even though his name was being mentioned among the council's members, he had not failed to solicit on his own the help of friends among the council members. And he had already spent several thousand rupiah in connection with these efforts.

'If the members of our party in positions of authority give their support it will not be too great a problem,' said Raden Kaslan. 'Of all the economic sectors, the easiest to get money from is certainly the import sector, whereas the other sectors will ask for time, ask for organisation, ask for personnel – as for instance transportation, or export, or industry – the import sector will need nothing at all.

'All it will need is a name of a corporation, and that's all. We're just going to sell the import licences which we obtain. I suggest that we make two plans. One for quick results, that is via the import sector of business. And the other, a permanent plan, for establishing banks, industries and so forth.'

'Ah, not in vain do people say that Raden Kaslan is an expert in economics,' laughed Husin Limbara.

'No, it's really not so difficult,' said Raden Kaslan. 'Importers are willing to buy their licences, particularly for ordinary goods which are public necessities, for as much as 200 per cent more. So if, for instance, the price of all licences is one hundred thousand rupiah they could be sold for up to three hundred thousand rupiah. And we get three hundred thousand rupiah clean without investing a single cent!'

'Good!' said Husin Limbara and clapped his hand on the table with delight. 'According to our calculations, our party, in order to win in the coming general elections, will need at least thirty million. Do you think we can raise this amount in six months?'

Raden Kaslan was silent a while, calculating.

'Ah, no trouble,' he said.

'Good,' said Husin Limbara again. 'I leave it to you to prepare the plans.'

'However, there is one more principle which ought to be settled,' said Raden Kaslan. 'What percentage does the party get, and how much for the people who implement the plan? This work involves risks, of course ....'

'Ah, as for risks, don't be afraid. Our ministers will protect them.'

'Oh, that's not what I meant,' said Raden Kaslan suavely. 'But even though these corporations we establish will be fake, there nevertheless will arise financial consequences such as taxes, certification fees and many other things.'

'Ah, now what would be proper in your opinion, brother Raden Kaslan?'

'I think fifty-fifty is fair. Fifty for the party and fifty for the names of the people we will use.'

'Isn't that too much?' asked Husin Limbara distrustfully.

'How come too much? The party will be sure to have the money in six months,' Raden Kaslan answered.

'Brother Raden Kaslan, you realise, of course, the importance of maintaining complete secrecy in this matter?' asked Husin Limbara.

'Ah, certainly! I will exercise the greatest caution. Isn't my own reputation involved too?'

Husin Limbara rose from his chair, and, stooping slightly to favour his hurting shoulder, stepped to the door, then turned to Raden Kaslan and said,

'When do you think you can bring the plans?'

'Give me a week,' said Raden Kaslan.

'All right, a week. Let me know.'

On the front verandah they saw Fatma who sat in a chair reading, and at the piano in the corner Suryono, lackadaisically playing some tunes.

'Are you going directly home, mas?'[1] said Fatma. 'Won't you have something to drink?'

'Ah forgive me, mbakju,[2] another time. Too much work.'

'Suryono, come here for a moment. Meet Pak Husin Limbara, chairman of the Indonesian Party. This is my son, Suryono, just returned from abroad, works in the Ministry of Foreign Affairs.'

'Ah, fine, fine! Have you joined the party too?' asked Husin Limbara, while shaking hands with Suryono.

'It's quite enough with just Father in it,' answered Suryono.

They laughed heartily, and Raden Kaslan accompanied Husin Limbara to his car waiting in the yard.

When he had re-entered and closed the door he rubbed his hands, looked in turn at Suryono and Fatma. And he laughed broadly.

'We're in!' he then exclaimed in Dutch. 'We're made now,' he said. Raden Kaslan sat down near Fatma, called Suryono over and spoke in confiding tones.

'This is very secret; don't tell anybody. A great catch for us!'

And very quickly he described to his wife and son the plans for raising money for the party.

'Nah, it's my intention,' said Raden Kaslan when he had finished his tale, 'to establish a number of corporations of different

---

1 Polite, yet somewhat familiar, Javanese form of address for men, when used without the name.
2 The equivalent polite form for women, from *mbak ayu* = elder sister.

kinds, with Fatma becoming the director of one, you, Suryono, the director of another one and so on with the other corporations, and in every one of them we must have a part interest, so that we get the largest possible share at the division of profits.'

'Ah, I cannot participate,' said Suryono. 'I am a government official.'

'Don't worry, just quit, or ask for a prolonged leave of absence. I'll talk about it with the party. It can be arranged.'

The three of them talked for a long time, making all kinds of plans. Something he had never suspected in himself gripped Suryono, a joy at the thought that he would dispose of so much money.

'Ah,' he said, 'why not? I have decided for myself that I want it. If I get tired of it I'll make another decision, that I want something else.'

By the time they had finished talking Suryono had already convinced himself that what he was doing was in no way reprehensible.

The other parties are doing the same thing, he thought. Why shouldn't I?

Pak Idjo lay sprawled in the semi-darkness of the room in his hut. Since the accident when his delman collided with the car his illness felled him, his whole body consumed by fever. The boils on his body caused incessant pain, and every minute Pak Idjo kept muttering, 'La illa haillallah — la illa haillallah,'[1] moaning with pain; he didn't eat, and only from time to time asked to drink.

When high fever attacked him, he often had nightmares and cried, 'Aduh, the motor-car is attacking me. Have pity on the old horse! Help! Help!'

His wife, Ibu Idjo, was already half-ill herself for lack of sleep, caring for Pak Idjo.

---

1 'There is no God save Allah!'

That morning his fever had subsided considerably, and Pak Idjo called Ibu Idjo,

'How's our horse?' he asked in a heavy voice.

'Amat is looking after him. He's looking for grass.'

'Amat is already ten years old. Tell him to look for work,' said Pak Idjo.

'What a pity he's still so little, otherwise he could run the delman,' said his wife.

'Yes, maybe he can get some light work. Just tell him to look wherever he can. How's the money?'

'Saimun and Itam have paid the rent for their room. There's still a little left.'

'Aduh, be sparing. Who knows when I'll be well again?'

Ibu Idjo stepped outside and called Amat.

''Mat, Father says you must look for work to help bapa who is still sick.'

Sugeng, slumped in his chair, was deep in thought. His face was very tense and pale. Hasnah, his wife, had shut herself up in their bedroom.

They had just had another quarrel. The usual thing. The question of moving to another house. Hasnah's screams still rang in his ears. 'All the promises were false. From month to month you just make promises. Look how my belly is growing. It won't be long before the child is born. Why do you make children if you cannot provide a decent place to live? Just throw it out, this child!'

Their joy at Sugeng's promotion did not last long. The promotion had brought new hope for a house, which had again proved futile.

'Do you want me to become corrupt like other people?' Sugeng had shouted, and these shouted words kept reverberating in his mind over and over.

By God, he swore inwardly, I know that until now I have fought off every temptation with all my strength. But if Hasnah must have a house, and if the only way to get a house is corruption, then I will engage in corruption. For Hasnah, for the baby who will be born, my baby!

He rested his chin on his hands.

How unjust is this world. People who want to be honest are not given a chance to remain honest. A matter of a simple house, that's all, and a man wouldn't need to do violence to his honour. No, not I, I will not succumb. Let Hasnah be angry, let Hasnah hate me! Yet, fused with this stream of thought, there was also the recognition that in the end he too would have to succumb. It was beyond his strength to fight with Hasnah every minute about the house.

He got up, went to the bedroom, straight to the bed where Hasnah still lay sobbing. Sugeng embraced his wife and whispered,

'Forgive me, Has, of course I'm wrong. But this time I promise truly that I'll get a house for us.'

He spoke with such sincerity that Hasnah, discerning this new tone in his voice, turned and embraced him. And they held each other caressingly.

Dahlia was walking along the row of shops on Pasar Baru.[1] Who knows how many shops she had gone into already, she couldn't remember herself. In each shop she had looked at all kinds of materials, but hadn't bought a thing. She was rather discouraged by now. In one shop her chance had seemed almost within grasp. When she had been examining some cloth, a man, with the appearance of someone with money, had stood next to her. Dahlia had flashed him an alluring glance. And she had caught the response in his eyes. But, who knows why, the man had not

---

1   Lit. New Market, the shopping district of Djakarta.

followed up this opening, and while Dahlia was still pretending to bargain he just walked out.

Probably he had no money, said Dahlia to herself.

Soon afterwards Dahlia had left the shop. Practically all men who passed by turned to look at her, but there wasn't a single one who was attractive enough to her. Dahlia walked slowly, stopping before shop-windows to tidy herself up and to look at the displayed goods, alone with her fancies. Her husband would be away another two weeks, and for two weeks she would be alone, quite free.

Suddenly she was startled, uttering a little cry at the shock of someone bumping into her, and a male voice said,

'Aduh, I beg your pardon, nyonya,[2] I didn't see you.'

Dahlia turned round and saw the man who had said it. She saw a young man, smartly dressed, carrying a package. Their glances locked, and they both smiled.

'May I escort you, nyonya?' said the young fellow without hesitation.

'Thank you, if it isn't too much trouble.'

'Ah, not at all. My car is across the street.'

The young fellow held her elbow, helping her across the street, and brought her to a Dodge sedan.

He opened the front door for her, and then climbed in behind the wheel.

When he had started the motor he turned to Dahlia and asked her, laughing,

'Excuse me, we're not acquainted yet. My name is Suryono.'

'My name is Dahlia,' replied Dahlia, smiling.

'A lovely name, and its bearer is as lovely as the flower,' answered Suryono flirtatiously.

'Ah, you've a glib tongue, tuan!' retorted Dahlia.

'You're not working?' she asked. 'How come you can go shopping in the middle of the day?'

---

2 Madame, Mrs., lady.

'I actually work at the Ministry of Foreign Affairs, but am now on a long leave. I work temporarily in business. Playing at imports. My office is N. V. Timur Besar, in the city.'

After leaving Pasar Baru Street, Suryono turned towards Gunung Sahari Avenue.

'Are you in a hurry to go home, Dahlia?'

'Why do you ask?' she answered archly.

'Ah, if you're in no hurry we could first take a ride to Tandjong Priok,'[1] replied Suryono.

'My husband is out of town. He won't be back for two weeks. Hurry or no hurry, it's all the same to me,' said Dahlia.

'Ha, fine, in that case we'll go for a spin first. Is your husband a business man too?'

'Wah, if only he were a business man I'd be delighted,' said Dahlia. 'He's a civil servant, inspector at the P.P. & K.[2] It's really so hard to be a government official these days, as you well know yourself, tuan. The salary gets you through just one week.'

'Of course! How true!' said Suryono. 'It's silly for anyone to want to be a government official nowadays. But if he wanted, he could get along nicely by accepting bribes.'

'That's what I've been telling my husband, and how many times. But he says, if all government officials were corrupt, where would our country be? It would go to pieces!'

'Your husband is an exceptional person,' Suryono replied. 'He's too good. He refuses to see our world here as it really is — whoever is honest goes under. Other people just go ahead.'

'My husband doesn't want to understand this.'

As they were passing the electric power-station at Antjol, Suryono took Dahlia's hand.

'Your hand is exquisite. And you're exquisite, quite in keeping with your name. How lovely you are!'

---

1 Djakarta's port, ca. sixteen miles away.
2 Ministry of Education.

'You're just fooling,' Dahlia answered, and as she smiled her eyes flashed coquettishly.

'Why should we really be heading for Priok, isn't it better we go to your house if indeed your husband is not home?'

'To our house, it's impossible,' replied Dahlia. 'We've only two rooms, too crowded. People can see.'

'To a hotel in the city?' asked Suryono.

'I'm afraid to go to a hotel,' Dahlia answered. 'I have never gone to a hotel.'

'Ah, come, come,' interrupted Suryono.

'It's true. Let's go to the house of Tante[3] Bep on Petodjo.'

Suryono swung the car round and headed back towards Djakarta.

'Does this Tante Bep really have a good place?' he asked as they were approaching Petodjo. 'Where is it?'

Dahlia showed him the way and they finally stopped before a good-sized house.

'This is her own house,' Dahlia explained. 'Tante Bep is already quite old and stays here all alone. She has a son, but in Bandung. And occasionally she's willing to put up people whom she knows well. It's lonely here,' she added.

Dahlia knocked at the door. Waited a moment. There were heavy, shuffling steps inside. The high voice of an old woman asked from behind the door, in Dutch,

'Who is it?'

'It's me, Dahlia, Tante Bep,' answered Dahlia.

'Oh!' said the voice from the inside. There was a sound of a key turning, and an old woman opened the door and said to Dahlia,

'Good morning. Come in!'

Suryono didn't seem to exist for her, she had glanced at him fleetingly, and when he had said good morning to her, her response was very, very short. When they were seated, Tante Bep

---

3 Aunt, in Dutch.

immediately went inside.

'Wait a moment, yes?' said Dahlia to Suryono, and she got up and followed Tante Bep inside. Suryono, left alone, looked around the sitting-room. Though the furniture was old it was well taken care of. On the wall facing him hung a family portrait. In the centre sat a man, still young, in a K.N.I.L.[1] uniform, wearing a bamboo hat turned up at one side, and with a sergeant major's insignia. At his side sat a young woman and two small children, a boy and a girl. Suryono, attracted by the picture, stood up to examine it closer.

Then Dahlia was back in the room, and seeing Suryono standing near the picture came up to him and said,

'That is Tante Bep's husband and Tante Bep herself, with their children, before the war. Her husband is dead. The daughter disappeared during the revolution. The son works in Bandung.'

Her body came close to Suryono's, into his nostrils rose the scent of her perfume and the warmth of Dahlia's body flowed into his own.

Dahlia drew him by his hand into an inside room. She locked the door of the room. The bedroom was very neat. The sheets on the bed were clean and white and freshly laid. In the corner stood a dressing-table. Dahlia closed the window and quickly started to undress.

'You are really beautiful!' said Suryono a few moments later. Sometime later Suryono loosened his embrace on Dahlia, rolled over to the edge of the bed and reached for a cigarette on the bedside table.

'Cigarette?' he asked Dahlia.

She nodded.

He lit a cigarette, gave it to her and then lit one for himself. Dahlia, rolling over, nestled her head between Suryono's shoulder and neck, and whispered,

---

1 Royal Netherlands-Indies Army.

'You're so strong!'

Suryono was quiet. He felt very pleased. He'd had many such experiences since he had become an importer. But this time it was really exceptionally good. Usually there was preliminary haggling. Always these money negotiations. For him, the mention of money beforehand always spoiled the later pleasure. He much preferred to pay more afterwards, provided the woman did not start by discussing prices as if she were nothing but a trader.

This time, from the beginning, not a word had been said about money. He decided for himself that he would give Dahlia a round five hundred rupiah. But not yet, a little later. He had no desire to go home now. Let it get dark first.

'How long may we stay here?' he whispered to Dahlia.

'As long as we like,' answered Dahlia.

'Till dark,' Suryono decided.

But they didn't stay on until dark. An hour afterwards Suryono felt that he'd had enough, and invited Dahlia to go home.

When they had dressed Suryono asked Dahlia how much he owed Tante Bep.

'Fifty rupiah,' said Dahlia.

Suryono took out a fifty-rupiah bill, handed it to Dahlia. As she moved to leave the room he held her back, took out five one-hundred-rupiah notes.

'And this is for you!' he said.

Dahlia looked at him and said, 'I'm not asking for money.'

'Yes, I know. But do accept this!' pressed Suryono.

Dahlia smiled at him, embraced his body and kissed his mouth.

'You really are a sweet boy,' she whispered.

Suryono brought Dahlia to her house, and in answer to his question when they would meet again, Dahlia said,

'Now you know where my house is. Come and ask!'

Dahlia stood at the fence until Suryono's car disappeared

behind the street corner, and then hastened to her room.

'Aduh, what a chic escort you had, his car is quite new,' called Hasnah, shaking her head as soon as Dahlia appeared on the verandah.

Dahlia, turning towards her, said, smiling,

'A new friend, Has!'

City Report

In a room of the Asrama[1] of the organisation for delinquent children Sung Tjay-Yong, sixteen years of age, with an intent expression on his face, was signing a confession, witnessed by the administrator of that welfare organisation and a few other persons of the Asrama:

'... I, Sung Tjay-Yong, aged sixteen, residing at Halimun Street, declare herewith in the presence of the Asrama Administrator as follows: I had not attended school for five months; thereafter I attended a mechanic's school at Gang Spoor, in Kemajoran, paying sixty rupiah a month. Then I left that school also. I have companions, one, Ali, thirty years old, bicycle guard in front of the Roxy Cinema, who claims to be a member of the veteran's organisation, on night duty. And I have known him one week. My other friend is named Idruss, aged thirty-five, residing in Djembatan Merah, and he told me he was a member of K.M.K.B.;[2] also O Bung, a locally born Chinese who lives in Djatinegara and works in Pasar Baru, dealing in foreign exchange; and Sapii, who lives in Gang Mandur, a member of the night watchmen. The four of them usually kept asking me for money. Sapii once ordered me to steal money and things from my parents, and it was Sapii who sold them. I have stolen from my parents seven thousand

---

1 Home, barracks.
2 Military Command of the city.

rupiah in cash in the course of two months. I have sold my father's Philips bicycle, costing nine hundred rupiah, for four hundred. The money I divided with my friends, and we used it for gambling and for having fun. I have also stolen from my father a Parker fountain-pen costing one hundred and sixty rupiah and sold it for ninety-five. I have stolen from his wardrobe seven pairs of woollen trousers and sold them at thirty-five rupiah. One wristwatch which I stole from home was sold for only fifty rupiah. One pair of my father's sharkskin trousers which I took I gave to Sapii.

'I further confess that I began to sleep with street girls on the Gambir Plaza at the age of ten, paying ten rupiah, it was a friend of mine who had invited me. I repeated this often with money stolen from my parents. The latest was when I slept with a woman to whom I was introduced by O Bung in Gang Sadar, formerly Gang Hauber, and I paid twenty-five rupiah for a quarter of an hour. As a result I have contracted a venereal disease, bubonic syphilis. I also confess that I have spent three months in the Training Centre for Boys of the Pra Juwana at Tangerang, because I stole a house-key and gave that key to two betja drivers to rob the gudang[3] of the coffee-shop Njan Tjan.'

'Your father is now applying to the government and the immigration authorities in order to obtain as soon as possible the permits for sending you to R.R.T.,' said one of the members of the administration to Sung Tjay-Yong. 'And in the meantime you will stay here, and we hope you will not make trouble, but will behave properly.'

Sung Tjay-Yong looked at him and burst into loud laughter.

---

3 Storeroom, godown.

August

HUSIN LIMBARA banged his fist on the table, his face purple, his voice choked with rage, 'How did this happen? Here, read all this!' And he pushed towards Raden Kaslan a pile of newspapers on the table. Raden Kaslan remained calm. He glanced meaningfully at Halim, chief editor of the daily, *Suluh Merdeka*.[1]

'You can laugh, brother, but how about our party's reputation?' continued Husin Limbara. He picked up one of the newspapers, obviously reluctant to read it again, but forcing himself to do so.

'"This is How the Leaders of the Indonesian Party Enrich Themselves,"' he read the headline. '"According to a statement made by the Ministry of Economic Affairs, it has been acknowledged that the director of the import corporation Tjinta Hati is Mr. Kusuma, a member of the Indonesian Party; the director of the Barat Laut Corporation is Raden Sudibyo, and its vice-director Tjong Eng Kouw. Raden Sudibyo is also a member of the Indonesian Party. The director of the Timur Besar Corporation is Suryono Kaslan. Suryono is the son of Raden Kaslan. The Bahagia Corporation is headed by Madame Fatma. This Madame Fatma is the wife of Raden Kaslan. And Raden Kaslan is a member of the Indonesian Party. The director of the Sumber Kita Corporation is Husin Limbara, and Husin Limbara is the General Chairman of the Indonesian Party. As is known already, some time ago some members of the Indonesian Party established a bank with a board composed of members of the party's executive council. This is how they enrich themselves."'

---

1 *Torch of Freedom.*

'This ruins our party's reputation. Your plan was all wrong,' cried Husin Limbara. 'Patience, patience,' answered Raden Kaslan. 'It isn't the plan that's wrong. How many million rupiah have already flown into the party treasury during this time? Come on, just count them up, brother. Of course, this matter could not be kept a secret too long. However, we will counter this attack with one of our own. That's why I have invited brother Halim of our newspaper to talk it over. He has an excellent suggestion.'

Husin Limbara looked at Halim.

'Hm,' said Halim, 'I have a great deal of experience in newspaper work and in how to influence public opinion. If we just let the opposition newspapers get away with the disclosure of secrets in this manner, our reputation will certainly suffer greatly. But fire must be extinguished with fire. That's why we must counter-attack. You, brother Husin, must release information, at a general meeting and in an interview, that there are certain groups in our country who are stooges of foreign powers, and that these foreign powers have stored secret funds, just name a sum – ten million dollars, fifty million dollars – anything will do. To mention "certain groups" is safest. People will be certain to suspect the opposition groups. But we're not going to make any direct accusations naming the opposition groups we mean. Thus we'll be quite safe, and we'll be able to counter the accusations made against us.'

Husin Limbara scrutinised Halim in silence at first, then, slowly, his face lit up as if the sun had broken through a cover of dark, driving clouds. He stood up, swaying a little, grasped Halim's hand, pumped Halim's hand, while clapping him on the shoulder.

'Right, you're a genius, brilliant idea. That's high strategy,' exclaimed Husin Limbara.

He released Halim's hand, rubbed his own hands, looked at Raden Kaslan.

'Ah, forgive me, Raden Kaslan. It's understandable that I, as general chairman of the party, think of the interests of the party first. From now on I shall trust you entirely, brother Kaslan and Halim.'

And he sat down again.

'Ahem,' coughed Raden Kaslan lightly. Husin Limbara glanced at him. From previous conferences with Raden Kaslan he knew only too well what that little cough portended. The cough usually preceded a demand for a higher percentage of profit from a special licence because allegedly the risk was greater or under some other pretext.

'Yes, brother Kaslan?' asked Husin Limbara, knowing full well what was coming.

'Ahem, it's really a minor matter for the party, but of considerable importance to brother Halim. And I'm speaking not on my own behalf, but for brother Halim. As you know, brother Halim is for all practical purposes almost like a member of our party, except for not holding a party card.'

'Ah, that's easy, tomorrow we can issue a membership card for brother Halim,' interposed Husin Limbara. He was pleased, just a matter of a membership card, not a demand for a greater share in profits.

'Ahem,' coughed Raden Kaslan again. 'You didn't permit me to finish, so you got the wrong impression. Brother Halim proposes that in the best interests of our party's struggle it may be advisable for him to stay out, to appear neutral. Isn't that right?'

'Ah, what genius, brilliant, right!' responded Husin Limbara.

'Nah, well then, brother, as you know, the parliamentary seat of Mr. Hadiwibrata is vacant, because, being a non-party member, he withdrew. Nah, we thought, how would it be if we proposed brother Halim to fill this seat?'

'Genius, brilliant.' Husin Limbara clapped his hand on the table. 'We can arrange this with the other government parties.

Will you please excuse me now? I have an appointment with the minister.' Husin Limbara rose, but sat down again as he heard,

'Ahem.' Raden Kaslan was coughing. 'One more thing. Quite an easy matter. As you know, brother Halim's daily owns a printing works, and this printing works has obtained a two-million-rupiah loan from the Nusa Bank, but you understand, of course, what newspaper can operate with a profit? And this is no small loan. The bank now wants to foreclose. But, if the bank seizes the plant, aren't we going to lose an important newspaper that can support us? Therefore it is most desirable that the bank be persuaded to desist from pressing so hard.'

'Ah, that can be arranged, too. Don't worry, brother Halim.'

Husin Limbara stood up, shook hands with the overjoyed Halim and went out, accompanied by Raden Kaslan.

When they had left the room, the newspaper man Halim chuckled to himself.

They think they can make me serve as their tool, he was saying to himself. But I will use them for my own ends.

As soon as he heard Raden Kaslan's steps approaching the door, Halim picked up a magazine from the table and pretended to be engrossed in it.

'Ah, the party owes you no little thanks, brother,' said Raden Kaslan as soon as he had closed the door.

Halim looked up at Raden Kaslan and said,

'Ah, there is only one more small matter. The newspaper needs a little money. Only one hundred thousand rupiah. Could you help me out with a loan, for two or three weeks?'

'Hah,' said Raden Kaslan, 'haven't we helped you out already with the bank loan?'

'The money from the bank is already used up for the purchase of machines, paying off old debts and to buy newsprint. I need the hundred thousand rupiah to buy paper and to pay the workers. Besides, it's only a loan. Of course, if it cannot be done, well, it doesn't matter ... but ...' And for a moment Halim looked fixedly and with significance at Raden Kaslan. As though to say, if you don't give me that loan you know what will happen, I will not help either you or your party! And all your secrets are in my hands.

Raden Kaslan wanted to say something, wanted to refuse outright, but he stopped short, and after a moment's thought made an attempt to bargain,

'It's very difficult to find one hundred thousand rupiah now. If it were fifty thousand I might be able to find it.'

'Ah,' said Halim, 'why should we haggle about it? Just last week—' Halim stopped, and looked at Raden Kaslan.

Raden Kaslan understood at once what Halim meant. Because the preceding week Halim had acted as go-between in the sale of a special licence to a foreign company, and this transaction had netted not less than seven hundred and fifty thousand rupiah.

Raden Kaslan went to his desk, took out a cheque-book from the drawer and wrote out a cheque for one hundred thousand rupiah.

As he handed it to Halim he made a strong effort to laugh, and to make it appear a hearty, open laugh, not a forced one.

'Here you are,' he said. 'With someone like you, it's hard to bargain.'

'Thank you, and remember it's only a loan,' answered Halim.

He stood up and stepped to the door, after shaking hands with Raden Kaslan. As he was opening the door he turned round once more, and, looking hard at Raden Kaslan, said,

'Remember, brother, with me there is no bargaining.'

And Halim closed the door very slowly. All sorts of feelings crept into Raden Kaslan's consciousness. There was a great deal he didn't like about this Halim.

Halim smiled to himself as he re-read the editorial he had just written for his newspaper.

'… it appears that the tactics of the opposition is never to give the government a chance to resolve any of the problems which face the people. The opposition's only aim is to bring about the downfall of the cabinet, because they are so eager to fill the ministerial posts themselves. Why are they so very eager to undermine this cabinet which has proven so progressive, so patriotic and so concerned with the people's fate? In this connection, we would like to remind the readers of the speech made by Bung[1] Husin Limbara of the Indonesian Party, which indicated that certain leaders of the opposition are being bought by funds from a foreign country. We leave it to our readers to draw their own conclusions.'

He called in one of the editors and said to him,

'Here is the editorial for tomorrow. It must appear together with the text of Bung Limbara's speech. The speech should appear on the front page. Give it a three-column headline: "Certain Leaders Receive Bribes from a Foreign Country!"'

Halim wrote down the headline on a slip of paper and handed it to the editor.

The telephone on the table rang. Halim picked up the receiver.

'Hallo, this is *Suluh Merdeka*! Yes, it's myself, speaking! Good news? Ah, it's Bung Limbara? What's the news? No, incredible …? Is it true? Ah, I don't believe it! Really? I am appointed to be a member of parliament? Ah, you're joking, bung! True? Well, many thanks! Yes, yes, we've begun the attack. I've just written an editorial linking them with probable subversion from a foreign country. Ah, it doesn't matter. We don't mention any names, but the public will know whom we mean. Yes, quite an easy matter. Thanks again!'

Halim replaced the receiver. He rubbed his hands. Now I'm a member of parliament, he said to himself. Satisfaction and pleasure were written all over his face.

---

1 Very familiar form for comrade, brother.

Dahlia was fast asleep at his side; he gazed at her for a moment, and then Suryono lit a cigarette and slowly inhaled the smoke. He was very pleased. They slept in the room of Tante Bep's house. Since Dahlia had brought him there for the first time, they had come back repeatedly. During the day and occasionally at night. In the daytime, as at this moment, it was particularly pleasant, Suryono thought. Outside it rained in streams, and Suryono let his thoughts drift. All kinds of memories came to his mind. Fleetingly, the time when he was still working in the Republic's office in New York. Decidedly, Indonesian women win out, he thought, remembering his experiences with different American women. Then his thoughts drifted to his stepmother. Ah, there was no comparison between her and Dahlia.

For some unknown reason he then remembered his schooldays during the Japanese occupation. How furious they were when the Japanese ordered their heads shaved. Then the moment he joined the P.E.T.A.[1] Took part in the Sjodantjo exercises. The Proclamation of August 17th, 1945. His division then joined the T.N.I.[2] And mostly he just stayed in Jogja. He had never really fought. When the Dutch occupied Jogja he discarded his military dress. Remained in the city. Then he was obliged to help friends who were constantly sneaking into the city. He didn't do very much. Always haunted by fear of arrest by the Dutch. And later Jogja was surrendered, given back by the Dutch to the Republic. President Sukarno, Vice President Hatta, returned to Jogja. And in the confusion of the first week he managed to secure work with the Ministry of Foreign Affairs. Managed to create the impression that he was a much-deserving ex-guerilla. Later, in Djakarta, he was given the chance to attend the foreign service academy, and at the first opportunity he was sent out to work abroad.

Suryono pressed the stub of his cigarette hard against the

---

1 A para-military youth organisation, youth militia.
2 The Indonesian National Army.

small plate on the adjoining table, extinguishing it. He got out his wallet from the pocket of his trousers which hung on a chair near the bed.

He felt with pleasure the weight of the wallet in his hand. Ah, this is a good life, went through his head. Plenty of money, plenty of women, no worries. What else could one wish?

He suddenly remembered Iesye.[3] Should I ever want to marry I'll marry Iesye, he said to himself. Then an uneasy feeling crept in – but Iesye will never agree to let me play around with Dahlia and other women. Ah, how stupid! Nevertheless— Suryono stopped short in his musings. There was something in Iesye which challenged him. Was it because Iesye was not easy to get, or was it because she put him on the defensive? Yet something seemed to compel him to want to overcome Iesye. But soon the disturbing thoughts about Iesye were pushed away. From his wallet he took out two five-hundred-rupiah notes, placed them under the little plate which had served as an ashtray and returned the wallet to the hip-pocket of his trousers.

Outside the rain poured harder, and Suryono turned over towards Dahlia, who was still asleep. He awakened her.

'Ayuh, we're going home, it's evening already!' he said to Dahlia as she stretched her young body and opened her eyes.

Dahlia threw her arms around Suryono's neck, pulled him down, while Suryono was saying,

'Really— really, ah, after this we go home. I have an appointment. There's a meeting!'

'Aduh, 'm I faint now, hungry!' complained Saimun to Itam, as they got off the garbage truck.

'Money 'lready 'll gone. Wages only day 'fter tomorrow!' muttered Itam in reply.

'Finish, juss go home, 't's raining, see,' shouted Bang Miun,

---

3 Dutch diminutive form, adopted in Indonesian.

the driver, to Saimun.

'Try one more debt with 'Bu Jom,' Itam suggested to Saimun.

'She, no, will not give 's time. Debt of past week, not yet paid,' answered Saimun.

'Aiih, can try, see,' said Itam.

'Get plenty 'buse,' answered Saimun.

'What harm from 'buse, see?' asked Itam.

Because of the rain, Ibu Jom had moved her portable stall across the railway line, to wait out the weather under a coffee-shop's roof. The coffee-shop was empty. And on the small benches owned by Ibu Jom not a person sat. Her eyes were sharp and cold as she saw Itam and Saimun approaching.

'Want to pay your debts?' she asked sharply.

Itam and Saimun looked around, and then Saimun said,

'Wah, 'Bu, when no wages yet?'

'So, borrow more you want?'

'Help out, 'Bu, 'lready hungry, see!'

The old woman food-vendor, with a cold look, told them both to sit down, efficiently filled two plates with rice and then added in each a spoonful of vegetable broth.

'Nah,' said Ibu Jom, 'all I know is debts!'

Neither of the two said anything, but they both ate voraciously. After having eaten some spoonfuls, Itam started praising Ibu Jom. The goodness of her heart, her attractive appearance, her excellent cooking. Gradually the old woman's resentment mellowed, and from a tin she poured them each a cup of coffee.

'What other place 'd do it,' she grumbled. 'Not even for a cent's debt will they give.'

'But not if her name Ibu Jom. Where's 'nother Ibu Jom in Djakarta?'

''Nly one!' praised Itam.

'You two boys, why not look find other work?' asked Ibu Jom later.

'Ah, me, I 'lready learn steering now,' Saimun declared. 'When 'lready can, soon become taxi or oplet driver.'

'Me, I'll work together with Saimun,' added Itam.

'Why you not look find inside work?' asked Ibu Jom.

'In an office? Not possible. How can office people want know garbage man, 'Bu!' Itam replied.

'Yah,' added Saimun, 'ev'n just be watchman, but people 'n office, see, no want noth'n to do with us. Same wages, same per day. But nobody'll want to know us.'

'Ah, rain will not stop, let's go home, 'Mun, 'yo!' Itam prodded Saimun.

They both got up and hurried out into the rain.

'Aduh,' said Saimun. 'My body, see, getting weaker. Hunger, see, makes stomach burn. Too little rice, was 'fraid to ask for more.'

'Me too,' said Itam. 'Neneng, still 'round.'

'Yes. But 'lready gone. She's in the hut of Uwak Salim, in Kaligot now. Wah, one time I see her, 'lready new outfit, powder, lips red. Wants not to see me.'

Saimun kept quiet. Ever since Neneng had left their hut to go to Kaligot and become professional he felt as if he were lost. It wasn't clear to him just what it was that he missed, but it was as if Neneng had left in him a great emptiness. There was nothing to go home to. As if he could now sleep just anywhere. He was really grieved to have been abandoned just like that, without even a farewell. Yet, had Neneng taken leave from him, he wouldn't have known what he'd have done either. He only felt joyless. But could not name that which he felt.

Vaguely, vaguely, somewhere floated visions of life continuing with Neneng, and somewhere far, far away, there was the crying of a little baby, causing confusion in his mind. A small house, a small plot of ground, he and Neneng. But all this was finished now.

Suddenly Saimun was rattled into wakefulness by the frantic blowing of a car horn behind him, brakes screeched on the wet asphalt, he felt Itam's strong push which threw him aside to the edge of the street, felt the impact of his ribs hitting the pavement, knocking out his last breath until tears spurted from his eyes and then a loud voice was scolding him,

'Hey, you fool, want to be killed? Where're you walking? Idiot!'

Then there was the sound of an accelerating motor, and a beautiful car swiftly receded into the rain. Only his body was still wet from the water spattered by the wheels. Itam quickly helped him to his feet.

'You're dreaming about what, 'Mun?' he asked him. 'Lucky I push you quick.'

Saimun stood, followed with his eyes the diminishing form of the car in the distance, not knowing what he ought to think.

In the car Suryono drew Dahlia's body closer to himself and murmured,

'A real inlander.[1] Was almost crushed to death. Doesn't even know how to walk. How can Indonesia make progress?'

Dahlia giggled and laced her arm around Suryono's waist.

'All right, twenty-five thousand rupiah,' said Sugeng to Said Abdul Gafur, the old Arab. He had just inspected a small house on the Probolinggo Street.

'And the housing permit, cleared,' he reminded the old Arab again.

'Ah, the housing permit will be in order, don't worry.'

'I'll pay when the housing permit is issued,' Sugeng reiterated.

'Yes, you needn't pay anything now, tuan. When the permit is assured, and the key is in your hands, then you'll make payment. Why shouldn't I trust a ministry official?' answered the old Arab.

'When can I move in?' Sugeng asked a Dutchman who was

---

1 Dutch term for native.

coming out of the house towards them.

'I am leaving on the M.S. *Oranje* on the tenth of August,' said the Dutchman.

'Ah, I will arrange all that myself. I'll come and bring you the key, I'll have some people occupy the place, so nobody can seize it.'

Sugeng thanked the Dutchman and climbed into a waiting car.

In the car the Arab said to Sugeng,

'Nah, here I'm helping you, tuan, and you, tuan, help me. You will get forty thousand rupiah for the licence which we are getting. I will retain twenty-five for the key money.[2] You know that this house is owned by a friend of mine. We must pay off that Dutchman, we must pay the U.P.D.[3] official to clear the permit. You understand.'

'Yes, it doesn't matter,' said Sugeng. 'What I need is to get the house now. The licence is already issued. Don't be afraid. You may come to the office tomorrow and get it.'

The old Arab took Sugeng's hand and shook it repeatedly.

When the car stopped in front of Sugeng's house he said,

'Ah, please excuse me, tuan, I'll not get out. It's raining. And it's near magrib[4] time.'

'All right,' Sugeng replied. 'Many thanks. And see to it that nothing goes wrong.'

'*Masja Allah*,[5] tuan, don't worry about anything. Be assured it's all clear. I guarantee.'

Sugeng ran lightly across his front garden, and when near the verandah noticed Dahlia standing before the door to her room.

'Ah, caught by the rain?' Dahlia asked him.

'You're wet, too, caught by the rain?' Sugeng answered.

'I just came in,' replied Dahlia.

Sugeng stepped to his part of the verandah and hastened inside.

---

2 Key money = black-market payment for the privilege of renting a house.
3 Housing Bureau of Djakarta.
4 Islamic prayer-time at sundown.
5 'As God wishes.'

Hasnah sat in a chair sewing her baby's clothes. Sugeng went to her quickly, embraced her and whispered,

'The tenth we're moving, Has! I found a house for you.'

Hasnah exclaimed with joy,

'True?'

'Yes.'

'How did you get it?'

'From Housing. The permit is cleared. Got it from the office.'

'Aduh, I know. If only one persists, and does everything necessary the right way, one cannot fail to get it.'

Hasnah drew Sugeng close to herself, and whispered into his ear, 'I love you.'

Sugeng felt as though he were choking. Also as though his body were suddenly drained. It was the first time he had lied to Hasnah. Until now there had been no secret between them. Hasnah, sensing something, asked,

'What is it, kak?'[1]

Sugeng forced a smile, laid his arm around Hasnah's shoulders and said,

'Nothing. I'm just happy that we've got a house at last.'

And inwardly he swore to himself that this would be the one and only time that he would engage in corruption. Never again. Sugeng embraced and kissed Hasnah with such passion that Hasnah was startled and cried out,

'Aduh, my belly. Naughty, that's what you are.'

'Ah, forgive me, friends, I am late,' said Suryono, entering. 'Good evening, Ies.'

He sat down near Iesye. It was the usual evening meeting at Pranoto's house.

Murhalim, who was talking, waved a hand to Suryono and then said,

---

1 Short for elder brother.

'After this brief interruption caused by the arrival of our highly esteemed brother Suryono, may I now continue my talk?'

'It might be good to recapitulate what you've said so far, brother Murhalim, so that brother Suryono can follow this discussion fully,' suggested Pranoto.

'Ah, no need,' quickly responded Suryono. 'Just continue.'

'The problem confronting us with regard to our relationships with Europe is which of Europe's basic values should we accept, and which to reject. This question is obviously not new, and one which our people have been facing a long time. Also, it is not exclusively an Indonesian problem, but a problem that confronts all Asian peoples. We may take as an example the case of the Japanese. As we know, the Japanese have learned all the secrets of Western technological progress, and have used them to build up their own nation. Brother Pranoto once wrote that before they'd be able to utilise Western technology our people must first undergo a psychological change. Just as an example, take our Indonesian fishing community – you can't give them modern equipment, such as motorised boats, etc., before all their old beliefs are changed – only then will they be able to make full use of it. So, for instance, there is one fishing village where, I understand, there are strict taboos connected with their fishing gear which is still very primitive. But the advent of engines and all sorts of modern appliances which will overcome the problems of tropical nature and climate will change all this. Their whole way of life must be changed to conform to the acceptance and utilisation of this European technology. Similarly, the expansion of industry, with the use of machines in factories, in mines, in transportation equipment, on land, at sea and in the air, in the offices of the government and in private enterprise, all this brings new values into the life of Indonesian society. The question of the spiritual values which underlie this technology is rather complicated, and – should Indonesian life be made to conform with this new technological sphere, or must the technology from Europe be made to harmonise with the Indonesian spirit? These are the questions which arise, and it is my hope that we can discuss them tonight.'

'May I be permitted to say a few words first?' asked Pranoto. 'Since brother Murhalim has just mentioned my writings, I'd like to explain that when I wrote that the spiritual life of the people must change in order to receive European technology I didn't mean it as an absolute condition. More precisely, I meant to indicate that if we wish to preserve harmony in our society the acceptance of technology makes a change in the people's mentality inevitable.'

'Ah,' said Suryono, 'I am baffled. Why do we worry about whether or not to accept European values? Considering the developments in the world today, it makes little sense to toss around the problem of ourselves and Europe. It would be more to the point, in my opinion, to discuss the problem of ourselves and America, or our problems vis-à-vis communism as represented by the Soviet Union and the People's Republic of China. As a matter of fact, the perpetuation of Europe's civilisation depends on American help. Therefore this discussion is just meandering and is quite useless. I suggest that we undertake a study of ourselves in relation to America and ourselves in relation to communism.'

'Seeing that the divergence of opinion between me and brother Suryono is so great,' said Murhalim, 'there would be little use of my attempting to convince him of the reason why we're discussing our inter-relationship with Europe.'

'Ah, I can really agree with brother Suryono,' interposed Achmad. 'The present world situation makes it quite impossible for us to consider problems of our relationships with only one part of the world. Moreover, what do we really mean by Europe? Today Europe is no longer the Europe of before the Second World War, the Europe which left such a strong influence in Asia. If we want to look at our problems, the problems of ourselves in relation to the world – and I think that only in this context are they worth considering: our country, and ourselves, and the world – then all this confusion, all the complications will be cleared up if only we apply the principles of Marxism. If we're willing to adhere to historical materialism our problems can be quickly solved. Marx has demonstrated the historical initiative of the masses. Read Lenin's book about Marx, Engels and Marxism ....'

'Ah, this is where we go wrong,' spoke Pranoto. 'If brother Achmad continues to expound ideas based on communist practices in Russia, our debate will never end. As I see it, all of us here have assembled as supporters of the concept of democracy, and we reject a totalitarian system, whether it be fascism or communism, as a method for building up our nation and assuring its progress.'

His face distorted with anger, Achmad stood up, looked at each of them in turn and, when he spoke at last, his voice trembled. 'I greatly regret brother Pranoto's words. Because to me they mean the same as closing the door to my further participation in this study club. If every time I want to express my opinions you all immediately brand communism as evil and unacceptable, then what's the use of my attending these discussions? I've seen it for some time, these meetings of yours make no sense. You keep talking here night after night, but what are you doing? This is the difference, brothers, between you and us. I am indeed a follower of Marx and Lenin. But, in addition to theorising, we also work. We go to the worker and the tani,[1] whom you say you want to protect, but whom you do not even know. We are convinced that we must win. We are convinced that we are right. Even now, brothers, you don't know where you stand and what it is that you should be doing. I bid you all farewell ....'

Pranoto quickly rose and grasped Achmad's hand.

'Forgive me,' said Pranoto, 'if my words have wounded your feelings, brother. Believe me, it was not my intention to offend you. If we must part, let's part in friendship. You, brother, have

---

1 Peasant.

your convictions; we have our convictions too. In our view every advance of man should be attained only by means of and on the principles of democracy. This is, of course, a difficult and probably a slow way, yet we are convinced that it's the one and only way to ensure freedom and human happiness.'

Achmad looked at Pranoto, and in the end their longstanding friendship triumphed, and Achmad, too, shook Pranoto's hand.

Thereafter he shook hands with his other friends, and at the door he said,

'Good night, all my friends!'

After Achmad had left they all sat staring, until Pranoto broke the silence by asking,

'Was he really angry?'

'No, I don't think that he was really very angry,' answered Murhalim. 'He is now active in a workers' organisation, and actually was only waiting for an excuse to get out of our discussion club. It's not likely that he would be angered merely by Pranoto's statement. It was nothing exceptional. We've had much bitterer and more acrimonious debates before, and nothing happened. I think he's received orders to leave our club.'

City Report

He was startled by the words of Mandur Kasir who was busy lighting an oil wall lamp and was saying to him,

'Please, brother, just sit down. My wife is busy with the child in the bath.'

And he felt even more disconcerted when he was left sitting alone in the room with the windows open and the doors ajar. Outside twilight was descending, but the blue of the sky was still visible. His eyes roved wildly around the room. A room with plaited bamboo walls pasted over with old newspapers which were already torn in several places, an old mat on the brick floor, a bamboo sleeping-bench with a thin mattress on it, the worn rattan chair in which he sat, a table to eat on with four dilapidated chairs. A cupboard with one of its doors open, and inside only a few tin plates and the other shelves empty.

From the back of the house he heard Mandur Kasir's voice talking to his wife, and the voice of a woman answering, and then the gay outcries of a child splashing in the water. And he felt increasingly uneasy in this room with its windows and doors wide open, not locked.

He stepped over to the window and looked outside, feeling very odd. And that moment he heard the steps and the voice of Mandur Kasir saying to him again,

'Sit down, brother Abu. We'll have some tea. My wife will come in a few minutes.' He jumped a little, startled, and felt as if he had been guilty standing there at the open window.

He sat down at the table with Mandur Kasir who poured hot tea into cups, carefully spooning out some sugar from an old butter-tin. And then they both sipped their tea in silence. It was difficult for him to start a conversation and he just sat, saying nothing, holding his cup of hot tea with both hands. Finally Mandur Kasir spoke.

'Tonight, brother Abu, you sleep in our house. Tomorrow morning I will see you to the station. Don't be afraid of anything any more. What's past is done with.'

When Mandur Kasir's wife appeared carrying a baby about a year old Mandur Kasir introduced her to the man. He rose to his feet awkwardly, facing the woman who stretched out her hand to him. He was at a loss as to what to say when she excused their poor home. What could he say? The place where he had stayed for the last twenty years could not be compared at all with this room of Mandur Kasir's. That's why he remained silent, and Mandur Kasir's wife went to the kitchen to prepare food.

A few moments later he was again left alone in the room when Mandur Kasir went out to join his wife in the kitchen. And so he was alone in that room, holding his warm and now almost empty cup of tea.

'Without meaning to, you've humiliated the man,' Mandur Kasir said to his wife in the kitchen. 'It's too bad you were apologising for our room, that it's so broken-down and dingy. Didn't you know that he has spent the last twenty years in jail?'

Mandur Kasir's wife exclaimed softly, while Mandur Kasir continued,

'He was released from prison only this morning after having served his twenty years' sentence. He must return to his village in Kediri. But there was some delay with his papers, so he cannot leave until tomorrow. I felt sorry for him and have invited him to stay overnight with us. Tomorrow morning I'll see him to the station.'

Mandur Kasir's wife looked up, full of fear.

'Ah, don't be afraid of anything,' said Mandur Kasir. 'I've known him for the last eight years. He never made any trouble in prison. Just worked quietly. He was sentenced for having killed a man twenty years ago. Why he killed him I don't know either. But, so that you don't feel afraid, I'll sleep in the outside room with him, and you may lock the door of the sleeping-room from inside.'

When Mandur Kasir re-entered the front room he saw Abu tilting one of the dining-chairs which was almost falling to pieces.

'Ah,' said Mandur Kasir, 'this chair really needs to be repaired. I'll bring a hammer and some nails.'

Mandur Kasir went to the open cupboard, crouched down and took out a heavy iron hammer and a box with nails.

'Come, I will fix it,' said Abu shyly.

Mandur Kasir looked at him for a moment, then handed over the hammer and the box of nails to him. Abu quickly went to work repairing the wobbly chair. But when it was done he tackled in turn the other three chairs, so that by the time he had finished nailing together the fourth one Mandur Kasir's wife had finished heating the vegetable broth in the kitchen and had come in to set the food on the table. Abu put away the hammer and the nail-box, setting them against the wall near the cupboard.

After the meal he sat on the balai-balai, watching how Mandur Kasir performed the prescribed magrib prayers, and thereafter the Isa[1] prayers, and after that Mandur Kasir went into the sleeping-room, and he could hear only their voices whispering. Mandur Kasir came out again carrying a rolled-up mat and a kain, and said to him,

'If, brother Abu, you're tired already, just go to sleep. Here's a mat and a kain.'

He took the mat and the cloth, and spread the mat on the floor near the cupboard. Mandur Kasir stretched out on the balai-balai. Abu rolled himself a nipah-palm-leaf cigarette, and Mandur Kasir lit his pipe. They both smoked in silence, while in the adjoining room Mandur Kasir's baby cried from time to time, was soothed by his mother and relapsed into sleep. Gradually the noises around them in the other houses subsided. Only from afar sounds of a radio, turned up to top volume, penetrated the bamboo walls of Mandur Kasir's house, with nostalgic tunes of Sundanese ketjapi music.

'What will you do when you are back in your village, brother?' asked Mandur Kasir suddenly.

Mandur Kasir's question startled Abu. How could he answer it? It was impossible for him to think up an answer to such a question. He didn't know what he would do when back in his village. For twenty years he never had to think about what to do next, now, yesterday or tomorrow, so he'd long lost the ability to think for himself. Since his release that morning he had been at a complete loss. He had killed a man when he was thirty. He didn't really remember clearly that he was thirty years old when he killed the man. Also, the reason why he had killed him was by now dimmed in his memory. The only thing he knew was that he had spent a

---

1   Isa = the fifth daily prayers in Islam, said in the evening.

very long time in prison, until his hair had greyed, his body had become lean, the body of an old man who was always doing hard work, and the leanness of body which hides strength.

Because he could not find an answer, and because he felt upset by Mandur Kasir's question, his voice was abrupt and indifferent-sounding when he said,

'Who knows, I don't!'

Something in that abrupt voice made Mandur Kasir turn and look at him. But Abu's face was already turned to the floor, his eyes fixed on the hammer and the nail-box near the wall. After a few minutes Mandur Kasir said,

'Whatever you do, brother, remember, never kill anyone again. You will be locked up in prison again!'

Thereafter Mandur Kasir turned down the flame of the lamp and lay back to sleep, pulling the sarong over his head to protect himself from mosquitoes.

The old man just out of prison stared at the wall, his open, unblinking eyes followed the images that floated past them. Mandur Kasir's question had increased his anxiety in his out-of-prison situation, and the darkness around him seemed threatening, full of danger. In prison he had felt calm and secure. Behind the iron bars everything was decided for him. But a window one could open oneself; a door that was not locked for him, the freedom given to him after twenty years of regulated life – he, now tossed out into the world outside the prison walls, felt as if he had lost firm ground, as if he were naked … his hand moved towards the hammer; grasping it, he turned around to look at Mandur Kasir who was already asleep, snoring. If I kill him, I'll be back in prison. It buzzed in his brain, and he got up cautiously, approached Mandur Kasir, raised the hammer, but before sending the blow at Mandur Kasir's head something seemed to explode in his brain, he lowered his hand, he felt dizzy and knew not what to do.

He stepped back towards his mat, when the door of the

sleeping-room opened, and Mandur Kasir's wife carrying her baby came in, saying,

'People are asleep already, and here he soils himself again ....' But she stopped dead as she saw in the dimness of the half-dark room that she was not addressing her husband. And as she caught sight of the hammer in Abu's hand she opened her mouth to cry out in fright, which struck the convict with terror. He leaped to shut the mouth of the woman who was going to scream, she pushed him away, they struggled, the baby cried and the ex-convict swung the hammer down on the head of Mandur Kasir's wife. Stunned, she fell to the floor. The baby, lost from her grip, cried on the floor; the convict jumped on the baby. Again he swung the hammer. The baby was still, its head crushed. Mandur Kasir, shocked out of sleep, yelled, and in one leap the ex-convict was near him swinging the hammer .... Mandur Kasir screamed,

'You're mad!'

The hammer crushed his skull and Mandur Kasir collapsed near the wall, slid down on the balai-balai, blood streaming from his broken head.

All was still again in the house, the only audible sound was the heavy breathing of the ex-convict in the dimness of the room.

He looked around the dim room — Mandur Kasir whose head was crushed, the baby whose head was crushed, the woman whose head was crushed and the blood-smeared hammer in his hand, and suddenly he hurled the hammer against the wall and ran to the door.

But the door, when he pushed it, opened wide. Startled, he retreated a step, howled in terror and then burst into laughter, like a madman.

September

HALIM WHISTLED softly in the bathroom. He was in high spirits. Standing before the mirror, he shaved his moustache, glancing from time to time at some neatly typed sheets laid out on the little table near the mirror. Then, turning back to the mirror, he rehearsed passages of the speech that he was going to deliver that night in parliament.

At certain passages of his address, he laughed aloud into the mirror, ' ... there are a number of people nowadays who make special efforts to show that they are genuine nationalists,' he declaimed, assuming the posture of one speaking in parliament. 'Thus, quite recently, brother de Vries arrived in Parliament wearing a sarong, and he told us that he had donned this sarong as proof of his true nationalism. Could anything be funnier? Isn't it like saying that when a lutung[1] puts on a sarong and claims to be human we must believe him?'

Halim paused and looked into the mirror. Here they'll certainly burst into laughter and applaud, he thought. And again he chuckled. His high spirits were occasioned not only by the prospect of addressing parliament that night. Just before he went into the bathroom, a telephone call from the bank had informed him that his application for a two-million-rupiah loan to expand the printing plant of his newspaper had been approved.

'Ah, you Halim,' he said to his image in the mirror, 'they imagine that they will use you. But you're going to use them for your own ends.'

His radiant mood was clouded over for a moment as he recalled

---

1 A long-tailed monkey.

an argument he had had last night with his wife on the same subject. His wife had told him that a lot of people were beginning to talk, saying that the newspaper man Halim had sold himself. And he had denied it heatedly, and he'd asserted that it was he who was making use of the politicians for his own ends. Those people who talk are just envious, don't pay any attention to them, he had told his wife.

Thinking of his wife, Halim smiled. He remembered how a few weeks ago, before he was appointed to parliament, his wife had told him about the djelangkung[2] oracle. His wife, together with four of her friends, all eager to question the djelangkung, had gone to the house of a Chinese family in Djatinegara.

According to his wife's story, the ancestral spirit of the little girls who held the djelangkung had manifested itself. His wife had asked whether Halim would become a member of parliament. And immediately the djelangkung had nodded. And now he was indeed a member of parliament. Halim wasn't usually superstitious. But in this case he too wavered somewhat. For hadn't it come true for himself?

His wife believed strongly in the djelangkung and in dukuns.[3] According to his wife, Mrs. Suroto had gone to the djelangkung in Djatinegara six months ago to ask whether her husband would get the post of ambassador to London. And the venerable djelangkung had nodded. And true enough, three months later, Mr. Suroto was appointed as ambassador and sent by the government to London.

Halim cautiously guided the razor, especially near the scar on his left cheek; he had got it when he was only eighteen months old. He had fallen off a ladder and his cheek had been cut open by a sharp stone on the ground. But after the revolution, however, this scar had come to stand for a wound he had sustained while

---

2 Said to be derived from *tsai lan kung*, a contraption made of crossing boards dressed in a shirt, topped by Chinese inscribed tablets, set in a basket and manipulated by children for oracular purposes.

3 Dukun = magician-healer, male or female.

fighting for the revolution. The story that the wound was sustained then had started when a foreign correspondent who had come to see him had asked,

'Did you get this wound during the revolution?'

'Ah, not at all,' Halim had answered.

Nevertheless, this correspondent later published an article in which he described meeting an important Indonesian newspaper man who had an influential position, and who had been wounded during the revolution. Halim read the article, and when later one of his friends, who had read the article too, asked about the wound, he had replied, 'Ah, it's nothing!' But now there were many people who really believed that he had received the wound while fighting in the revolution, even though no one knew precisely in which of the battles Halim had been wounded.

Halim laughed again at his face in the mirror while his fingers stroked the scar. A little lie like this has its uses. Makes people respectful and a bit different towards you, he said to himself.

He washed his face and took a quick bath. While rubbing his body with the towel he read his speech, and then rehearsed it again, looking at his own face in the mirror.

Udin, Hermanto and Bambang had been waiting for fifteen minutes in the office of the All-Indonesian Dockworkers Union at Tandjong Priok. Three days earlier they had sent in a complaint to the central committee to the effect that all their members insisted that the union take action to alleviate the workers' conditions. For many months now their pay had not been nearly enough to meet the ever-rising costs of living. In the beginning the leadership of the union told them to be patient, the government was busy launching programmes to improve the people's welfare, and that demands for pay increases at this time would in no way improve the workers' living conditions. Even worse, if the wages were raised, the prices for goods would go up also and the workers themselves would be the first to suffer. Therefore the correct thing to do would be to urge the government to force the prices down.

Six months had gone by since the leadership had issued this communication to the workers. Yet during this period the prices, far from going down, had actually shot up higher than ever. And now in the last week the workers again had started to press for action.

'How can they continue ordering us to keep pacifying our people?' said Bambang. 'And especially when the other unions do not stop pressing for better wages. Many of our members have already joined other unions. If we continue our present policies we're sure to lose!'

'Let's hear first what the leadership has to say. They're going to send brother Achmad down to talk things over with us,' said Udin.

'As for myself, I'm with the majority,' added Hermanto. 'If they feel dissatisfied with the present leaders who support the cabinet, while the government pays no attention to the people's welfare, then I'll go along – we should get out of this union and take our members to some other union that really fights for the workers' interests.'

'Hush, don't speak like that, friend,' Udin responded quickly. 'The leadership would be very angry to hear you talk this way. Aren't we always supposed to trust and obey the leaders?'

'Obey, obey,' Hermanto retorted. 'But how can we tell a hungry and suffering worker to keep on obeying?'

Sounds of approaching steps were heard outside, and then the door opened and Achmad came in. The three of them rose to greet him, and Achmad, while greeting them each in turn, was saying,

'Forgive me, I am late. Through no fault of mine. The train was shunted about for ages in front of the station near the harbour entrance. I was delayed by half an hour.'

The four of them settled round the table and Bambang, who acted as secretary of the Tandjong Priok Branch of the All-

Indonesian Dockworkers Union, opened his briefcase and took out some papers. He handed Achmad a typed report, saying,

'This is a copy of the report which we have sent to the central committee.'

Achmad spoke.

'Yes, we've already received and examined it,' he replied. 'The important question now is how we are to retain the trust and loyalty of the workers. It looks as if among yourselves, brothers, there are some who have already lost faith in the party.' And Achmad looked sharply at Hermanto. 'This spirit of defeatism is not permissible. We are in the middle of a struggle to crush capitalism and colonialism, and the reactionaries still have many stooges among our own people, plotting with the foreign capitalists.'

'The question is not one of disloyalty to the party,' Hermanto put in at once. He was a quick-tempered man. He could work tirelessly if he believed in the job to be done, but his anger and hate could be aroused with equal intensity if he felt he was being cheated.

'How can we tell the workers to keep on being patient, and tell them that to go on strike at this time would harm the government now in power, and that this government is really progressive and genuinely concerned about the people's welfare? How can the workers believe us, when they must cope every day with wages that aren't nearly enough to cover their daily needs? And the price of food, clothing and other necessities keeps going up?'

'We understand the difficulties of the leaders on your level, who are in direct contact with the workers,' answered Achmad. 'Nevertheless, the question is one of conviction. Whether you can convince the workers to remain loyal and to support our struggle. It has been stressed by the party, time and again, that the present government is more progressive than any other government Indonesia has ever had. Despite this we are not blind, of course, to some aspects of the government's policies that do not benefit the people. But, for the sake of our party's growth, we must continue to support this cabinet. We do not agree with their economic and financial policies, and we intend to try to correct this in short order.'

'In other words, for the sake of expanding the party's power, you order us to sacrifice the workers' welfare?' asked Hermanto pointedly.

Achmad gave Hermanto a long, sharp look. Through his mind flashed: Hermanto is already spoiled for us! We'll have to be careful with him! He may betray us! Must report to the party!

'You take the wrong view of the problem, brother,' answered Achmad. He immediately decided to change his tactics in talking with Hermanto. Pushing him won't work, he thought.

'It's not our intention at all to sacrifice the welfare of the working people. Far from it. It's actually quite the other way about; the party is working day and night trying to improve the workers' lot. We do not want to strike now, or join in supporting those strikes that are promoted by unions dominated by the reactionaries, because we know that there are other ways for improving the workers' conditions.'

'What ways?' pressed Hermanto.

Hermanto's blood was beginning to boil with anger and resentment. This party man has it easy, just talking, he thought. They never meet the workers face to face. All they can do is dish up theories. Can you feed a worker, or clothe him, with theories?

Achmad looked at Hermanto, then at Bambang, then at Udin and said to himself: This Hermanto is a really stubborn fellow.

'We must have complete and absolute faith in the leadership of the party. It's only the party that understands and can lead the struggle of the proletariat correctly.'

His voice conveyed disapproval of Hermanto's question.

Hermanto felt it, but could no longer contain his pent-up resentment.

'Brothers,' said Hermanto, 'from the time I entered the party I gave all my strength, working day and night, to fight for the workers' interests. I was arrested time and again, accused of agitating when we engaged in large-scale strikes under previous cabinets. And it was always the party that gave us orders to do so, because it was for defending the workers' cause. At present the plight of the workers is even worse than it was during previous cabinets. And the workers urge us to give them leadership in taking action, to demand improvement of their plight. And the party says this is not permitted, that the workers must continue to be patient and must not make demands though strikes. This I do not understand. Are the workers here for the party, or is the party here for the workers?'

Hermanto glanced round him, and then looked intently at Bambang and Udin.

'Brothers Bambang and Udin,' he then said, 'you both, brothers, have heard the workers' bitter complaints yourselves, and the three of us have often discussed them and said that we should urge the party to take the lead by swift action to improve these conditions. Come on, brothers, let's hear your opinions, too.'

For a moment Udin and Bambang just gazed in silence, looked at Achmad, then turned their faces away from Hermanto and didn't say a word. Hermanto regarded them in deep astonishment. He had never seen his two friends act so strangely before.

'Why are you both silent?' he asked them with surprise.

Achmad just kept quiet looking at Hermanto. Something mysterious and uncanny seemed to have crept into the room where the four of them sat, as though the room were permeated by a darkness whose chill gripped the heart. For an instant Hermanto felt as though he were in a remote and eerie world, that he was sitting there with strange creatures, human beings he did not know at all. He was still for a moment, trying to disentangle and understand his own bewilderment. Then, in a rush, he was swept by anger.

'Why don't you speak up? So you're afraid to talk? Isn't it true what I said?' he half shouted.

Udin and Bambang still said nothing, and then Achmad cleared his throat and said,

'Brother Hermanto! Actually brothers Bambang and Udin feel that the policy of our party is perfectly correct, and they don't want to say anything so as not to embarrass you any further. And I advise you, brother, to re-examine your ideas and your attitude; if you persist in thinking as you do now you are certain to become the victim of the reactionaries.'

Hermanto looked at Achmad in perplexity and amazement, and then at Udin and Bambang. All sorts of thoughts darted through his mind. Why have they become like this? Why are they afraid? Are they right, perhaps, and I am wrong? But his anger got the better of him, he rose to his feet, pounded the table and his eyes glowed.

'Now I see what the party's game has been all this time. In order to advance the party, the workers' well-being is sacrificed. This means that the working class exists for the party, and not the party for the working class!'

'Ah, you've got it all wrong again, brother,' spoke Achmad. To himself he had decided to recommend that Hermanto be ousted from the union leadership as soon as possible. Too dangerous, has ideas of his own, undisciplined and doesn't trust the party ....

'The party exists for the workers, the peasants, the whole people. But the party can only do something for the people if the party is in power. In order to attain power, the party must be big and strong. That's why this phase is one of building up the party. And shouldn't we expect everyone to join forces to build up the party, the working class included?'

'Ah, nice words, but is it true? When the party gets into power, won't the workers just become its tools?'

'Brother Hermanto!' Achmad banged the table. 'These are treasonable words! How can you talk this way? I propose that we stop this argument. Come on, let's discuss the report on the workers' demands sent to the party!'

Hermanto, still standing, said,

'I'm not participating. I don't want to go on misleading the workers!'

He walked out of the room. Udin half rose, intending to detain him, but Achmad gave him a sign to let Hermanto go. Hermanto slammed the door and through the window they could see him walking hurriedly towards the highway.

Achmad took a handkerchief out of his trouser pocket, wiped his face and then said,

'He's gone astray! Has no dedication!'

'Better be careful with him,' said Bambang. 'His influence among the dockworkers is strong.'

'Both of you, brothers, watch his activities carefully,' said Achmad. 'If necessary we will take special steps to break Hermanto. Nah, let's now return to the workers' complaints. Once more the party orders you to stress firmly that a strike at this time is something much desired by the reactionaries, as well as by the capitalists and the imperialists. We must not be misled and trapped by them. The workers must be persuaded that whoever goes on strike or is in favour of striking before the party has given its assent, will be lending support to the enemies of the Indonesian people, that is the cliques of the reactionaries, of the capitalists and of the imperialists. Get this done, brothers.'

Achmad stood up, took from his pocket two envelopes and gave one each to Udin and Bambang.

'As deserving activists of the party, you both are again entitled to the party's support. You will find inside two hundred rupiah for each of you, brothers.'

Udin and Bambang expressed their thanks and promised to

execute the party's orders to the best of their ability.

'And watch that Hermanto!' said Achmad, when he was at the door ready to leave the room.

Raden Kaslan, Husin Limbara and Suryono sat at a table in the corner of the Capitol Restaurant.

A waiter came to their table with beer. Raden Kaslan glanced at his wristwatch and then turned to Suryono.

'Does Halim know we're all meeting here at twelve noon?'

'He knows, Father!' replied Suryono. 'I telephoned him myself. He is certain to come.'

Husin Limbara raised his head and said, smiling,

'Ah, here comes one of them.'

Sugeng appeared, approached their table and Husin Limbara, remaining seated, introduced him to Raden Kaslan and Suryono.

'This is brother Sugeng of the Ministry of Economic Affairs,' said Husin Limbara. 'He has joined our party and is actively participating in our programme.'

When Sugeng was seated, Raden Kaslan asked him,

'What would you like to drink, brother? Beer, whisky-soda?'

'A whisky-soda will be fine, thank you!' answered Sugeng. For some time he had been growing accustomed to strong drink, and had even come to like it. At home he now had a refrigerator, a present from one of the importers, and he always had a supply of whisky, cognac, ready-mixed martinis, etc. At first Hasnah objected — why take up the habit of drinking strong drinks, she said — but Sugeng had only laughed and said it was necessary for entertaining visitors. By now he was used to it, and he enjoyed a whisky-and-soda.

A few minutes later Halim arrived, greeted them and immediately sat down.

'This is brother Sugeng of the Ministry of Economic Affairs,' Raden Kaslan said, introducing Sugeng to Halim.

Sugeng shook hands with Halim, and as he looked at him contempt rose in his heart. So he was the man who daily denounced in his newspaper corruption and actions detrimental to the people and the state. And here he was playing the same game! As for himself, he didn't feel too guilty of having harmed his country. What he had done was only to fulfil Hasnah's wishes, and in his view her wishes were just. Especially for his baby. For a baby every man has the full right to do whatever is necessary, he thought. But here was Halim. A newspaper man. He couldn't grasp it. Husin Limbara was another matter, he was a politician. Didn't people always say that politics was a dirty game? What they were doing here was only a part of that dirty politics. The party needed ample funds for the general elections. But Halim, the newspaper man, who day in, day out exhorted people to uphold honesty in their work …!

He could also understand Raden Kaslan. Also his son, Suryono. All they were out for was the money. One cannot blame people whose only aim is wealth so they can do what they like. And he himself? Ah, he was not after money, nor did he seek power. All he wanted was to safeguard the well-being of his family.

Husin Limbara cleared his throat, coughed a little and said,

'Brothers. We have gathered here to discuss the implementation of our programme. As you know, we have been busy for some time collecting funds for the general elections. Thanks to the assistance of brother Raden Kaslan and also of his son Suryono, and of brother Halim as well, much has been achieved already. But now the party has decided to work even more efficiently. Brother Sugeng, who works in the Ministry of Economic Affairs, has been promoted by our minister to head the division that issues import licences. Brother Sugeng has also joined our party ….'

Ah, I joined only for protection, Sugeng said to himself at Husin Limbara's words.

'Our main problem at the moment is that we must work fast.

The opposition groups have already launched attacks against the issuance of special licences. Several of the government parties are beginning to feel that they're not getting their fair share. That's why whatever needs to be achieved must be done before it is too late, Brother Halim's job is to counter all attacks directed against us. We need closer co-ordination. Some time ago one of our applications was delayed for over a month because they didn't realise that this application had come from us. Such occurrences must be prevented. The minister himself will protect Sugeng should anything come up. Yet, everything we do must follow the legal procedures and remain strictly within the law.'

'We have no difficulties at our end,' said Raden Kaslan. 'Our organisations are all established and running smoothly. I'd only like to know whether perhaps there aren't some people in brother Sugeng's division who could obstruct our programme. Also I would like us to be notified immediately if there are any government orders, so we're not late in submitting our bids.'

'As for the government orders, I can arrange that easily,' responded Husin Limbara. 'But on the first question, may I ask brother Sugeng to answer?'

Sugeng smiled inwardly. His regard for political leaders such as Husin Limbara had now collapsed completely. So they're thieves, too, he thought. In what way are they my betters, then? I am really not wrong in doing what I am doing. He looked at Husin Limbara and smiled.

'No one will make any trouble. Provided we "grease",' he said.

'Ah, fine, fine,' said Husin Limbara. 'That's a small matter. We'll leave the greasing to you. Money will soon be easy!'

'Nah, now back to our programme,' said Husin Limbara after his remark. 'There is a large-scale order which we must get ....'

Idris, Dahlia's husband, had been awaiting Dahlia for over two hours now. He had just returned from his inspection tour in

Sumatra and upon arrival didn't find her at home. There was only the babu guarding the house. The place felt rather desolate. The children of the family next door, which had taken Sugeng's place, and who usually filled the place with commotion in the afternoon, were away. The babu told him that her mistress had gone to Pasar Baru. Idris looked at his watch. It was already two o'clock. She takes a long time to shop, he thought, and where does she get the money from? For a moment the thought of this money produced a gnawing feeling in his heart. For a long time he had wanted to ask Dahlia how she got the money to buy such good kains and lovely new jackets. He could no longer believe that Dahlia was so clever at saving money from his salary that she could buy all this. But he quailed before asking her. He was afraid that Dahlia would get angry and accuse him of distrusting her. During their six years of marriage he had never been angry with Dahlia. And when she was angry he just kept quiet.

Idris rubbed his forehead. For some time he had been feeling weak, and he tired easily. Just sitting up in the plane on the less than two-hour flight from Palembang to Djakarta had already strained his back. He got up to get cigarettes from Dahlia's dressing-table. A portrait of Dahlia stood on the table. Idris contemplated the portrait and it made him feel proud to see how very beautiful his wife was. Then, as if something were pulling his face, he looked up into the mirror. Idris saw the face of a middle-aged man, with rather hollow cheeks, eyes bleary with weariness. He kneaded his cheeks and thought, I am old already. Much older than Dahlia.

Their wedding six years ago then came to his mind. It was just after the Dutch had recognised the R.I.S.[1] He had come to Djakarta from Jogja as a partisan of the Republic. Met Dahlia in her office. She worked with N.I.C.A.[2] So did her father. He was

---

1 *Republik Indonesia Serikat* = United States of Indonesia.
2 Netherlands Indies Civil Administration.

immediately attracted to Dahlia. And when he proposed to her Dahlia accepted at once. Her parents, too, were pleased to have him as son-in-law.

During the first years he was happy with Dahlia. It was only in these last months that a distance and a sort of emptiness seemed to have come between them. He had known for a long time that his salary could not cover their living expenses. At first he thought that Dahlia was often cool because of her dissatisfaction with their lack of money. On top of all that came his frequent absence, connected with his work. He hadn't really stopped to think about all this clearly. But now he felt depressed. He had sent Dahlia a telegram from Palembang informing her of his arrival. Usually, if Dahlia did not meet him at the airport, she waited for him at home. But now, for the first time, Dahlia had not been there to greet him. His anxiety grew. He was much disturbed. Then, being a kind man, he began to blame himself. It's hard on Dahlia, he thought, not to have any children. And it's my fault. Three years ago they had gone to be examined by a doctor, and according to the doctor it was he who was infertile. Their initial disappointment was later dispelled as Dahlia seemed to have accepted this state of affairs. For a time Dahlia was even more tender and closer to him, until he too was reconciled to the idea of never having children. But now he felt perturbed and depressed and an intense desire came over him to share in the happiness of having a child.

Idris kept kneading his cheek, gazing into the mirror and saying to himself, I'm older than my real age. I'm only forty-two, but my face is that of an old man of fifty. While Dahlia is only thirty-two, but looks like a young woman of twenty-five. He drew in a deep, long breath and sighed as though accepting a situation that can neither be rejected nor changed. He kept asking himself, what more could he offer Dahlia? And at the same time the answer persistently recurred – he had nothing to offer which could give delight to a young woman like Dahlia.

Ah, let it be, if only she stays with me and we're together always — that's enough. And then he was utterly overcome with a longing for Dahlia to be home. He longed to see her body, her face, hear her voice.

Tired of looking at himself in the mirror Idris rose, taking with him Dahlia's photograph, and lay down on the bed. From the pillow emanated a perfume, a perfume unknown to him, intensifying his desire for Dahlia to return. Without knowing, Idris then dozed off, his right hand still clutching Dahlia's photograph.

When Dahlia returned after a while she found Idris in this position, asleep. She smiled to herself, tiptoed to the bed and kissed him on the temple.

Idris woke up, opened his eyes, smiled to see Dahlia, embraced his wife and she kissed him, whispering,

'Aduh, forgive me. I had a prior appointment with a friend, and that's why I could not wait for you at home. Don't be angry, yes?'

Idris could say nothing since his mouth was covered by Dahlia's mouth; the great happiness that now filled his heart spread through his whole body, and he embraced her fervently. Dahlia's handbag slipped from her hand, fell open as it hit the floor, with a five-hundred-rupiah note half protruding from it. Dahlia, abandoning Idris' mouth, glanced at her handbag on the floor, sat up quickly and said to Idris,

'Hush, wait a minute, I'll change my clothes!'

As she got up she stooped, picked up her handbag, pushed the note back into the bag and hurriedly started to take off her kain and kebaya,[1] Idris watching her with growing desire.

'Nah, you're beginning to get it,' said Driver Miun to Saimun. 'But now there'll be trouble getting the permit. Y'have to know how to read. Better Saimun now learn to read. There're "courses for

---

1 A long jacket of light material for women.

combatting illiteracy" in the kampung.'[2]

Saimun had been learning to drive the truck for several months now. He was overjoyed at Driver Miun's words. He turned to Itam who was busy washing a wheel of the truck.

'Hear this, 'Tam,' he said, 'and when I get my permit, I teach you to steer.'

'We go together to learn read and write. I also want to learn,' answered Itam.

'But number one, truck must be washed!' said Driver Miun.

Saimun and Itam laughed, and readily followed Driver Miun's order. They felt very happy, the future was full of promise.

While wiping a tyre Saimun told Itam,

'When I get permit 'lready, I sure become oplet driver. They say one can get thirty, up to fifty, rupiah one day. Just think!'

And Saimun scratched his head, unable to imagine just how much money he would get every day as an autolette driver.

They gazed into the distance, full of wonderment at the possibilities the days to come held for them, when they could get their licence and work as autolette drivers.

City Report

A whirling wind chased and scattered the flying bits of dry rubbish along the tracks of the electric train between the stop at Nusantara Street and Pintu Air II. The day was blazing hot. This whirling wind lifted the flies, too lazy to move from the tops of rubbish heaps along the road. Car horns blared, punctuated from time to time by the screeching of suddenly clamped brakes, followed by ejaculations from a swearing and scolding driver.

Suddenly the air was rent by the piercing scream of a woman, the sound of someone being beaten, the repeated scream of the

---

2 City quarters, peripheral or enclaved, where the poor working population lives in bamboo dwellings or huts.

woman and then a stream of abuse.

Along the wall near the railway in the ruins of a former half-torn-down train-stop shelter, the city vagrants had their shanties. Old charcoal baskets had been piled up to serve as walls; worn-out, shredded pandanus mats were laid on the earth for floors. The roofs of these shanties were made of blackened and rusty pieces of old cans, patched together with bits of old cardboard. Larger cans which once held butter were set on cooking-stoves made of a few piled-up stones, and these served as kitchens.

A tiny, slender woman was trying to extricate her hair from the grip of a man's fists. The woman screamed. The man was small and thin too, no older perhaps than sixteen or seventeen; he should have been on a school bench at this time of day, not pulling the little woman's hair by the railway line.

The woman was beating the chest and the face of the man who was pulling her hair with both hands. His hands were clenched into small tight fists, and he too screamed. Suddenly he released his grip, and she fell hard to the ground. He stepped towards her, kicked her in the head with his emaciated, dirty, bare foot. Infuriated by the kick, the young woman leaped to her feet, picked up a stick and, like someone who had gone berserk, she swung it against the head of the man. The man, not having anticipated this sudden attack, could not escape the blow and one could hear the sound of the wood hitting his skull.

The man yelled with pain and rage.

'The devil, you stubborn woman!' he cursed in fury and with all his might he pushed with both hands against her chest and she was hurled to the ground once more. He advanced, to kick her again, but the woman jumped up and retreated until her back was against the wall. She was not afraid. Abuse spouted uninterruptedly from her mouth. Three or four vagrants sat and lay inside and outside their shanties, but paid no attention to the raging fight.

'Brave with a woman, lu!' the little woman's ringing voice

reproached. 'If lu dare, just kill me right now! Kill me!' And she bared her chest half covered by her torn kebaya. Her breasts, still round and firm, were bathed by the light of the hot sun-rays.

The man stepped closer, as if wanting to hit her again.

'What good is a man like this!' screamed the young woman again. 'Talks a lot. Brags! Lu promised to marry me. I'm in the third month already. Why lu didn't marry me yet? Lu say, no money! But for gambling there's money! Where's the house? Lu said you had money! Said you had a house! Said you have work! Me – I've become a whore, lu not ashamed! You're eating whoring money, lu!'

She wept and threw herself on the ground, sobbing and hiding her head. The man stood, perplexed. And he scratched his big toe against the dirt on the ground.

'I've looked for work, there is none,' he said vaguely.

'If only I'd stayed in my kampung, I wouldn't have been ruined like this. Why did I follow you?' the little woman wailed again. 'Now I'm a whore, without shame, selling myself every night. Because of lu I did it, aduh Gusti,[1] forgiiive!' And she wept violently.

'Forgiiiiiive, Gusti, aduh Gustiiiii!' the woman repeated in long-drawn wails, screaming up to the scorching hot heaven, hurling upward her despair, begging for human help, begging for human consolation, begging for human protection, begging for human mercy, begging for human love and solace.

'Why did I get like this, aduh, Gustiii! Who turned me into this …?' she wailed, flinging her laments to humanity.

The little woman tore her own hair with both hands, beat her breast, threw herself on the ground, wailing in a high voice, 'Help me, God, why did I get like this, who turned me into this?'

The young fellow looked at her, made a step towards her, shoved her with his foot half-heartedly and said, 'You whore!'

And then he walked away.

---

1 Gusti = Lord, in Javanese.

October

'JUST LISTEN to their talk for a while,' Suryono was saying to Sugeng. 'Sometimes their discussions are quite good, though frequently they get off the track, and then they're way up in the clouds. It's really amusing when what's-his-name begins to discuss the Oedipus complex by – who was that writer, he's dead, I forget his name …? But nevertheless they're friends of mine. They're good people – only a bit mixed up. They think they're helping their country by discussing intensively all sorts of questions. At first they said that these discussions were needed to find out what sort of problems face us. When we know what the problems are it will be easier to solve them, they said. The pity of it, as I see it, is that these intensive discussions with high-flown theorising have now become an end in themselves, and are no longer a means as originally intended. But they mean well!'

Sugeng said nothing. He didn't care too much what Suryono was telling him. When Suryono had invited him to attend a meeting of the discussion club run by Suryono's friends, he was actually not too eager to go. Why should I go along? he had asked. But Suryono insisted that he join him, and, after all, Suryono's father was someone to reckon with because of his great influence in the party that had done such wonders for him since he'd joined – and so he went along.

Suddenly Suryono, blowing his horn hard and clamping down the brakes, swore.

'You pig!' he shouted.

An old woman carrying a baby ran in fright to one side of the street.

'Lucky the brakes are good, if not she'd be dead. Crossing the street without using her head,' Suryono raged and cursed. 'How will Indonesia ever get ahead? If they can't even cross a street?'

'Ah, don't be like that,' said Sugeng. He remembered the time before he had joined the party, and how difficult it was then to live as a civil servant. 'Such people have very hard lives. Maybe she didn't hear the horn because she was hungry, and was full of worries about how to get food for tonight.'

'Ah, that's not true. When people are hungry their senses are sharpened, that's what I read in an article by a doctor,' answered Suryono.

Inwardly though, he recognised the justice of Sugeng's remark, and this annoyed and angered him even more. I don't like this man, he thought, of Sugeng sitting beside him.

As Suryono stepped on the accelerator again he was suddenly seized by a feeling of depression. A feeling which for a number of times had been creeping up on him at the most unexpected moments. While he was enjoying himself with Dahlia, in the middle of a good meal at a restaurant, when he was on the point of signing a cheque or when he climbed into his fine car. What it was that disturbed him so he found it impossible to say precisely, but it made him feel uneasy, as though something were wrong, and behind it all loomed a kind of fear. Just what kind of fear he couldn't make out exactly either. So he ended up just feeling put out, and often was annoyed with the people who happened to be around him.

It was thus that he had had his first quarrel with Dahlia. Dahlia had sensed a change in him, and had asked him whether he was tired of her. Her question made him angry and he had inquired rudely, did she want money or didn't she. But on that occasion he'd soon asked her to forgive him, and amity between them had been restored. He had taken Iesye out to a restaurant once, and while they were happily sitting down to their meal this odd feeling had emerged again as he saw a little beggar-girl approaching their table. Because this strange fear was mingled with his annoyance and uneasiness at the sight of her, he'd flown into a rage and had snapped at the little beggar so harshly that the child fled in fright. Iesye had then got very angry, refused to go on with the meal and asked him to take her home right away. In the car, up to her home, he had begged her to forgive him, but Iesye had remained silent and would not speak to him. He tried hard during the following two weeks to rehabilitate himself in Iesye's eyes, but she remained unmoved. The harder he tried, the more distant Iesye became. All this convinced Suryono, however, that he really loved Iesye, and must marry her were he to attain happiness in life. He became very jealous if he saw or heard that Iesye was going out with another man, especially if he heard that she was out with Pranoto.

He kept going to the evening discussions mainly to catch a glimpse of Iesye and to watch how Pranoto behaved towards her. He also felt that it was easier to get to talk with Iesye at these meetings. All this unpleasantness came to his mind because of Sugeng's earlier remark, and he felt deeply upset and rather angry. But he restrained himself. He reminded himself how much they needed Sugeng. But even so he couldn't calm down. It's easy for him to talk, but isn't he out for what he can get like the rest? he said to himself. No sooner had this thought crossed his mind than it seemed as if a sudden shaft of light pierced him to the heart. It became clear to him at that moment what it was that he was doing, what his father was doing, what Husin Limbara was doing for his party and what they were asking Sugeng to do. He was appalled, and a terrible feeling of shame and guilt mixed with fear gripped his heart. But a moment later this feeling was gone again. Deliberately suppressed. He recalled Husin Limbara's words, 'We are doing all this to further our people's struggle for social justices to defend the Pantjasila as the foundation of our state. Ours is the only political party that firmly upholds the Pantjasila as the basis of the state. The Islamic parties want to create a Darul Islam[1] state, the communist party wants to create a communist state and so on. That's why our party has to win the general elections. In order to win, the party needs money, and plenty of it. Therefore, we are simply doing our bit in the struggle to save the Pantjasila. That's the reason we are doing all this, and we've got the full approval of the party's council.'

Suryono thus reassured himself with Husin Limbara's words, and was able to enjoy driving his Dodge sedan again. Also his annoyance with Sugeng disappeared and he turned to him.

'Have you bought a car already?'

'Ah, not yet. I'm still hesitant. If I buy a car, the people at the office will suspect there's something fishy.'

'What are you afraid of? The minister will protect you. If people start asking questions, couldn't you say that you got a present from your family? Put it down on your wife's name. How much did you get this month, a hundred thousand?'

'A little less,' Sugeng replied.

'If you apply for priority to get a car, as head of a division, you're sure to get it. On this priority you can get something like a Zephyr – costs only sixty-two thousand. You could resell this car for one hundred and twenty-five. Then you can buy yourself a second-hand car for about fifty thousand, they're decent enough, and you are left with a clear seventy-five thousand profit,' said Suryono.

'Maybe, I am not sure yet what to do with so much money got so easily,' Sugeng told Suryono. 'I never dreamed that I'd ever get so much money with so little effort. I used to feel very envious seeing other people with fine houses, cars, lots of money, going in and out of restaurants as they pleased. But now, with that much money, I'm a bit scared.

'Scared? Why?' asked Suryono. His resentment of Sugeng returned at once. Sugeng had reawakened his anxiety. Yet he wanted to hear Sugeng describe his apprehensions.

---

1 A state based on Islamic principles.

'Perhaps because I think like an official,' Sugeng responded. 'But I do feel somehow that even though all the licences we issue are legal and are approved by the minister himself, what we're doing is wrong. Why, for example, do we give preference to the Hati Sutji[1] corporation, a corporation chartered only a month ago, with a staff of only one director, who has no office, no staff, no experience and no business connections abroad? While other import firms, also run by our nationals, who have been in business for years, operating on a completely bona-fide basis, aren't supposed to get anything? Ah, and there's lots more. For instance, there's that business run by a group of veterans claiming to represent tens of thousands of other veterans; I happen to know, they aren't veterans at all, and they haven't done a thing for a single veteran. When I think of all this I get scared. I'm afraid that what we're doing is improper and that we've overstepped the limits somewhere.'

'Ah,' said Suryono. Doubts assailed him once more. But for his own peace of mind, he had to dispel Sugeng's fears. He had to convince Sugeng that they were right.

'You're too much of a bureaucrat! That's all. Don't you remember what Husin Limbara said? It's all for the sake of our people's welfare. We must look at these things in wider perspective.'

'I could feel at peace if it were really just for that one purpose,' Sugeng replied. 'But why should I be getting hundreds of thousands of rupiah? Why are so many people making fortunes out of it? They certainly don't pass on everything to the party?'

Suryono was silent, he recognised the truth of Sugeng's words. Doubt and anxiety rose in him again.

'Well, just tell me – why?' Sugeng was pressing.

Suryono did not answer. He tried to cover up his own anxiety by laughing.

---

1 Pure Heart.

'Ah, because we're just not used to having tens of thousands of rupiah in our pockets. But what does it amount to, anyway? Just think how much the Dutch and the Chinese have scraped up here over the centuries!'

Sugeng wanted to retort, but the car had reached Pranoto's house and Suryono was greeting Murhalim, who was leaning his bicycle against the wall.

As they got out of the car Murhalim said, laughing,

'Hallo millionaire, when did you exchange your car for an even larger one?'

Suryono, undisturbed by Murhalim's insinuation, laughed and introduced Sugeng.

'Here's a new friend I brought along. He wants to participate in our discussions.'

The hell I do! Sugeng thought to himself. A lot of nice phrases!

Sugeng and Murhalim shook hands.

'What's tonight's discussion about?' Suryono asked Murhalim.

'Pranoto will speak on the problems Western technology poses for our intellectuals.'

Aduh, more empty talk, Suryono commented inwardly.

They went inside. Sugeng was introduced to Pranoto, Iesye, Yasrin and six other people. The room, not too large, was already full.

'What I have to say are just a few basic ideas, what I hope to get are your reactions, brothers. As I stated last month, Western technology presents a problem to our intellectuals, because its impact upon our people who are still traditionally oriented ....'

Suryono covered up a yawn with his left hand and looked stealthily at Iesye.

Iesye, feeling that she was being looked at, turned towards Suryono and smiled. Suryono smiled back, felt very happy and was now prepared to pay attention to Pranoto's discourse.

'The special problem of our people in confronting Western

technology,' said Pranoto, 'is that we've been given no time, there is no transitional period. We either have to accept and use it or we'll just have to go on being a backward nation. We must accept and use this Western technology not just for the people's physical well-being, but also to ensure their spiritual freedom. In essence the problem can be reduced to a "to be or not to be" for our people. If we want to see our nation strong and independent we must accept Western technology. To reject it is to pass a death sentence on our own people. In facing this choice, many Indonesian intellectuals are hesitant. Their attitudes vary. Some reject it completely, because they consider the values of Western life incompatible with the spirit of the East, and see Western values as shallow and materialistic (which is true in part). Others want to adopt only what seems valuable and useful to them and reject what they don't like, but such people never specify just which Western values they prize and which they consider harmful, or how one could consciously make the distinction and put it into practice. I believe that we must accept them as a whole, the good and what we now regard as bad, and let our people make up their own minds, in the creative process of adaptation.'

Murhalim said at this point, 'If brother Pranoto has finished presenting his basic ideas, may I intervene now?'

Pranoto did not object, but added,

'There are still a few aspects of the problem I have not yet touched upon, but I'll be able to bring them up in the discussion later. It's all right by me if brother Murhalim wants to speak now.'

'First, I'd like to observe that although the problem of Western technology certainly exists for our intellectuals we stress this problem far too much. It's as though we're bewitched by the West, and every aspect of thought is inevitably drawn to the West. It's almost as if we were radios tuned in to a single wave-length, receiving broadcasts from only one station – the West. For me the question is, why the West? And, as I see it, this continued orientation to the West won't lead us anywhere. Don't you realise that eighty or ninety per cent of our people are Moslems? The majority is fanatically religious even though ninety-nine per cent of them have no real conception of the spirit of Islam. Even among Islamic leaders themselves there are very few who understand it, its dynamic power to guide not only the spiritual life of the individual but also the total reorganisation of society. I remember Ies once raising the question of whether a revitalised and creative Islam could give us an answer to the problems challenging us today. Since then I have been thinking the question over, and I've tried to find an answer in some modern books on Islam. After reading these books (I'd be the first to admit that my studies have been far from complete), I have become convinced that keeping on with the West means approaching the problem on the wrong foot. Islam does possess standards and a spiritual dynamism to organise and run a modern state. However, the present leaders of Islam are still unable to reveal its treasures. One must admit that this fault, or deficiency, is not peculiar to the Indonesian Islamic leaders alone. On the contrary, in countries which pride themselves on being Moslem, we see how, behind the façade of Islam, the people have been exploited from century to century. The condition of the fellahin in feudal Arab countries is even more pitiful than that of the working class in capitalist countries. The Islamic leaders of Indonesia must have the courage to open their minds to modern technology. It would be well to avoid using the term *Western* here, as it could easily arouse irrational prejudices. It would perhaps be advisable to refer instead to *modern* technology, to avoid the reactions usually aroused in many of us at the mention of the word West. I don't believe there is a single person in Indonesia who would want to reject modern technology – modern industrial techniques for producing the goods needed by our people, beginning with nails, wheels, screws, medicines, cars, railway equipment, ships, planes, radio, television, radar, rifles, bombs, tanks, guns and even atomic energy.'

'I agree, of course, with the substitution of modern technology for the term Western technology,' said Iesye, 'but, in spite of the change of label, the actual influence of modern technology on society and on the spirit of our people will still be the same as if we used the term Western technology. This will certainly revolutionise our people's mind and spirit and will shake the very foundations of their traditional values.'

'And what is the harm in that?' Suryono interpolated. 'Why should we be afraid if the traditional foundations of our society are shattered?'

'I didn't mean to say that I'm afraid,' Iesye replied quickly. 'On the contrary, our society is so backward and lacking in initiative that I'd be only too glad to see a drastic change. Then perhaps, because of modern technology, the Indonesians will become a people able to stand on their own feet, master nature and assume their responsibilities to the nation and to humanity at large.'

'That's a very nice statement,' said Yasrin, 'but it's not likely to lead to any definite conclusion. We reject the Japanese methods of adopting modern technology, that is using dictatorial means under the aegis of the Tenno Heika[1] as they did before the Second World War. Nor can we accept the dictatorship of the proletariat, as practised in Soviet Russia or in the People's Republic of China, to introduce modern technology to build up the country. The Indonesian nation has chosen the way of democracy. And we must have the courage to bear the consequences of this choice. Once modern technology has been introduced, let social development in our country take its own course, whether Islam possesses enough dynamism to further the penetration of modern technology, or the socialist ideology paves the way, or the Oriental soul is strong enough to support it. However, I must frankly admit to you, brothers, that I'm not a bit clear about what is really meant

1 Emperor.

by the Oriental soul. Personally, I have no objections to the drastic changes which the introduction of modern technology may bring about in the basic values of our society or the spirit of our people, provided, however, that we do not destroy the principles of democracy. These changes are actually essential if our nation is to develop rapidly.'

'Ah, I don't agree with brother Yasrin's view that modern technology can just be allowed to penetrate and that one can rely on subsequent developments to shape the future of our homeland,' Murhalim cut in. 'I am convinced that Islam, with its dynamism rediscovered, will provide a solid base for receiving modern technology!'

'May I just make a comment?' asked Suryono, and continued, 'While listening to your talk, I got the impression that the real problem for our nation is not modern technology, whether from West or East. Since Kipling wrote "East is East and West is West ..." the world has changed a good deal. Modern technology is not the exclusive monopoly of the West. An Eastern nation has been able to master it too. The problem we face is on what basic principles our country's development should be directed. On the present democratic basis, which does not satisfy us? On Islamic principles as proposed by brother Murhalim? On a dictatorial basis as the admirers of the people's democracies want? Even the Islamic basis that Murhalim wants carries the seeds of dictatorship in its exclusiveness and rejection of all alternatives. As we can see today, the attempt to develop our country and people along democratic lines has failed. Isn't it possible that this has happened not because of the failings of the democratic system, but because too many of our people are still unprepared for democracy?

'One of the basic assumptions in a democracy is that every person living in it must have enough intelligence to make conscious choices. How many of our people really understand what it is that they must choose? In our country a skilful demagogue can easily mislead the masses. In my opinion the problem is one of leadership. If the leadership of our country, which used to be so united, were to re-establish its unity, and on the strength of this unity govern the country, following the gradually developing ability of the people to build democratic institutions, that would be the best answer to the problem of our country's leadership.'

'So you agree to dictatorial methods?' interposed Iesye.

Suryono looked gratefully at Iesye for this sign of her attention, and said,

'Yes, but only for the initial phase. What are ten years, twenty years, in the history of a nation? Let people like Sukarno, Hatta, Sjahrir, Natsir and others like them, stay in power to guide the development of our state and nation.'

'You mean a sort of collective leadership?' asked Pranoto.

'Yes, and I think that a collective leadership corresponds to the instincts of our people. In the villages, where life is based on the gotong royong[1] system, one can find the predisposition for such collective leadership.'

'The question is whether personal and party antagonisms have not now become so sharp as to make it impossible for the leaders to re-establish their unity,' said Pranoto.

'That certainly is an important factor,' replied Suryono. 'And, the way I see it, it is pretty unlikely that our leaders will unite again.'

'In that case the alternative is that some group will emerge and take over the leadership of the state,' said Pranoto.

'The communists?' asked Murhalim.

'Or possibly the Moslem group,' Pranoto answered.

'It would be difficult for the Moslem group, since they're badly split, and neither do they have a militant organisation ready to act like the P.K.I.[2] has,' said Murhalim.

---

1 A system of reciprocal aid.
2 The Indonesian Communist Party.

'Another possibility is complete anarchy,' interrupted Sugeng suddenly, who had just been sitting and listening all this time.

'That also is quite a possibility,' added Pranoto, 'which implies disintegration of the state for which the lives of so many of our young people have been sacrificed.'

Pranoto then looked at his watch and said, 'It's really a pity, but our time has run out just as our discussion was getting to the most interesting and thought-provoking basic problems. I suggest that each of us make a deeper study of the problems we have touched upon. We could ask Murhalim, for instance, or another friend with enough interest and time, to formulate the conception of a state based on Islamic principles.

'It's true, of course, that too many of Islam's foremost representatives only cling to Islam's ancient glory without trying to make use of Islamic principles to solve our contemporary problems. So also, perhaps, we could ask Suryono to elaborate further the principle of collective leadership for our country. The consequences of the introduction of modern technology into Indonesian society could be examined more closely by comparisons with what happened in Japan, for example.'

After having taken Sugeng home Suryono took Iesye for a drive in his car, and on a quiet street in Kemajoran Baru he stopped the car, took Iesye's hand and drew her close to him.

'Ies ...' Suryono whispered.

He kissed her ear, his lips moved to Iesye's cheek, then with his hand he slowly turned Iesye's face until his lips met the girl's lips and then their mouths were locked in a strong, deep kiss.

Suddenly Iesye withdrew and moved away from Suryono, as his hand tried to clasp her breast.

'Don't, Yon,' said Iesye.

'Why?' asked Suryono.

'I'm not sure about you yet,' Iesye said.

'Not sure how?' Suryono retorted. Dahlia flitted through his mind. Somewhat perturbed, he thought, does Iesye know?

'As I listened to your talk just now, I believed I could trust you. And I felt as though I cared for you,' said Iesye. 'But then I began to wonder once again if you weren't just playing with words. And then, you are still young, but suddenly you're wallowing in money. It seems abominable that young people should spend their time just trying to get rich while our people are in such a desperate condition. I don't know what to think of you, Yon.'

Suryono was still, staring into the night through the wind-screen, and admitting to himself – You're right, Ies, you know me. I don't know myself who I am and what I want. I've lost hold, I'm full of anxiety and fear.

Suryono turned the ignition key, started the engine and drove off.

'Come, I'll take you home,' he said abruptly.

'You're not angry?' Iesye asked.

Suryono turned to her, again he felt their closeness and bending his head he caressed Iesye's cheek with his lips.

'How could I be angry with you?' he said.

Iesye held his hand, and the car rolled back into Djakarta.

City Report

Tony and Djok ordered the betja driver to stop at the corner when they noticed Suryono's car alone in the deserted street. They short-changed the betja driver who drove off swearing at them, and proceeded to hide themselves behind a dark tree.

'This is good pickings, Djok,' said Tony, grinning. His large, strong teeth glistened in the darkness. Tony adjusted his pistol-holster inside his shirt behind the belt, and Djok clutched the handle of his knife.

'Let them get going first,' said Tony. 'It's easier to rob them when they're in the middle of it. They'll be scared stiff and give up their wallets fast, and then scoot when we tell them to get out.'

'Nah, now, almost,' said Tony when they saw Suryono drawing Iesye close to himself and then the two kissing.

Tony and Djok cautiously moved closer to the car, Tony's hand ready to pull out his pistol.

Then Iesye withdrew, Suryono started the motor and before Tony managed to decide on a new plan of action the car had rolled away and was out of sight.

'Ah, shit! Maybe they saw us coming,' said Tony.

'Looks like they didn't make it.'

November

ADRIZZLING rain had been falling incessantly since early dawn. The morning wind was blowing in hard from the sea. The wind whirled up dry leaves, darkening the mist which billowed in the streets. The wind sneaked into the houses, making Raden Kaslan press Fatma's young and warm body closer to his own; making Suryono sink into deeper slumbers in his room while dreaming of Iesye; the wind blew into editor Halim's room, who was sleeping apart from his wife because the night before they'd had another quarrel; disturbed Sugeng's sleep, filled with nightmares; made Husin Limbara's afflicted shoulder ache more painfully in the morning chill; and caused the sago-palm leaves on the thatched roof of Pak Idjo's hut to rustle; and, having penetrated inside, hovered around Ibu Idjo and Amat who sat chilled near the balai-balai, the morning wind swept by.

Ibu Idjo sat very still near the balai-balai; Amat sat very still near the balai-balai. They had shed all their tears since Pak Idjo had drawn his last breath at ten o'clock the preceding night. The oil lamp had long since gone out.

Ibu Idjo's sorrow at the loss of her husband was mixed with relief. At last he was liberated from the torture of an illness which they had been unable to cure because they never had enough money to go to a doctor and buy the necessary medicines.

Now only she and Amat were left with the children. And Ibu Idjo was confident that she and Amat would manage to carry on. There was still the horse, and the delman cart was still there. Amat was working already, as a garbage coolie. All that remained to be done now was to bury Pak Idjo.

The atmosphere in Raden Kaslan's workroom had been tense for some time. Raden Kaslan had been silent for a long while, unwilling to participate further in the discussion. Halim sat looking at Husin Limbara with a cruel smile playing on his lips. Then, with studied slowness, he took a cigarette out from a pack on the table, put it into his mouth, replaced the cigarettes on the table, took a match from the table, lit his cigarette, then inhaled deeply and puffed the smoke upwards. Raden Kaslan watched Halim's gestures with terror in his heart. Husin Limbara said to himself that the man was dangerous but could be bought, and decided to pay Halim's price.

'Brothers,' Halim then said in a cold voice, 'the government which we are supporting at the moment is not popular in the eyes of the people. If I wanted to, I could write even more sharply and violently about this government than the opposition does. The opposition newspapers don't know even one half of what I know and have seen with my own eyes as to the doings of this government.' And Halim looked sharply at Husin Limbara and Raden Kaslan.

Raden Kaslan lowered his eyes. Husin Limbara, with great calm, looked fixedly at Halim and in the end it was Halim who averted his glance.

'My newspaper has suffered great losses as the result of supporting the government. But every time I ask for support I am put off as if I were a beggar. I am tired of begging from you, gentlemen. Why should I be begging from you? It's you, gentlemen, who're indebted to me.'

'But how about the bank loan for the printing plant, and the several hundred thousands we have given ...?' said Raden Kaslan suddenly.

Halim turned to Raden Kaslan and said, smiling,

'What does this loan of six million for the printing plant amount to? And the few hundred thousand rupiah — they're chicken-feed. Especially if we compare it to the hundreds of millions you've been making on all these deals …!'

'What you really want then, brother, is …' asked Husin Limbara coolly.

'I refuse to be merely your tool,' said Halim. 'If we're to work together I must be treated as an equal.'

'But you've already got a seat in the parliament!' said Husin Limbara.

Halim laughed sarcastically.

'How generous your gracious gift! A seat in a provisional parliament soon to be dissolved, after the general elections only a few months hence. Of what significance is that?'

'But you asked for it yourself, brother,' Husin Limbara retorted.

'Of course! But surely you realise that this isn't enough and is only temporary anyway,' Halim shot back.

'Ah, if you wish, we can include you in the list of party candidates for the elections,' said Husin Limbara. He felt somewhat relieved – so that's what's worrying Halim. 'This I can guarantee, don't worry,' Husin Limbara added.

'That's of no use to me,' said Halim. 'You know as well as I do that it's better for our plans if I'm known in public as a non-party man.'

'Brother Halim wants a greater share of the money,' said Raden Kaslan. A light smile appeared on Husin Limbara's lips. As chairman of the party he'd had considerable experience in dealing with people like Halim. Here he felt on firm ground once more. If the problem was one of money he, Husin Limbara, could settle it.

'Ah, is that all?' he said. 'But you know yourself, brother Halim, that we have to be very cautious in such matters just now. Every day the opposition's newspapers persist in tearing into the various special licences. The party itself doesn't know how much longer it can shield the minister concerned without getting embroiled in difficulties with the other government parties.'

'All right, brother, just listen to a little proposition I have for you here,' said Halim. 'Through my connections I have reliable reports that the opposition parties have worked out a plan of campaign for attacking the government in their Press. If you examine carefully the content of the opposition papers over the last few weeks, you will see that their campaign against the government is quite systematic. One of the opposition papers exposes something, it is then picked up and exaggerated in the headlines of the other newspapers, and, being centrally directed, all this does not fail to make a strong impression on the public. In contrast, the pro-government Press isn't co-ordinated at all. Each newspaper goes its own sweet way, expressing its own reactions; in short, the voice of the government Press is neither united nor strong, but disjointed and ineffective in combating the opposition's campaign.'

'This, alas, is very true, brother Halim,' said Husin Limbara. He had become interested in Halim's argument and forgot about the money problem still to be settled.

And inwardly Raden Kaslan too had to admit the merit of Halim's expert analysis of the press problem.

'I have worked out a plan of how the pro-government Press should co-operate to fight the opposition,' Halim continued, 'and I want to propose that within the shortest possible time a meeting be arranged between the editors-in-chief, the directors of the pro-government Djakarta Press, the leaders of the government parties, and the more important cabinet ministers. At this meeting the basic policies for our campaign to fight the opposition should be outlined. As the famous military saying goes, "attack is the best form of defence". Similarly the pro-government Press should take the initiative and attack, and not, as at the present, just react defensively every time the opposition takes the offensive. So far the majority of the pro-government newspapers, with the exception of mine, have merely reacted to the contents of the opposition Press. This is a mistake. We can't win over public opinion in this way. Look what's happening now. One has to admit frankly that the average circulation of the pro-government newspapers is going down, while that of the opposition Press is growing steadily. The government papers cannot survive without organised support. My idea is that we must establish a press service to collect, prepare and distribute systematically materials for our press campaign. These materials will then be published in all the newspapers which support the government, either as news reports, news comments, interviews and so forth.'

'Very good, very good,' said Husin Limbara.

'But we must launch it under the guise of an independent press organisation and not one tied to the party,' continued Halim. And that's why the organisation will need a budget, an office and a staff of its own. According to my estimates, about five hundred thousand will do for a start, including the purchase of equipment such as typewriters, desks and so on, and salaries for the employees.'

'The financial part we can discuss with our colleagues,' said Husin Limbara. 'As for the plan, it's very good. Excellent.' And he rubbed his hands.

And once again Raden Kaslan mentally had to applaud Halim's skill in making so persuasive a presentation.

'Apart from this feature service, I also want to propose the establishment of several other friendly newspapers,' Halim continued. 'So we can emerge as the leading press organisation. Our voice simply doesn't count in the one which exists now.'

'Good, good. This can easily be arranged,' said Husin Limbara.

'Nah,' said Halim, 'if you agree, I can start making the preparations right away if the money is made available immediately. But, all this aside — as I've already indicated, my

own newspaper continues to suffer losses because it supports
the government's cause. I'm fed up with begging for support. To
avoid any further quibbling about money, I'm asking for a loan of
at least eight million to finance my newly established import firm
– it's already been approved.'

Halim picked up his briefcase from the floor by his chair and
took out an issue of the *State News*.

Husin Limbara took the sheet from Halim and read the item
on the chartering of the import firm Ikan Mas.[1]

'Leave this with me, brother,' he said. 'I'll discuss the loan
with the ministers concerned.'

'I'm confident,' said Halim, 'that you'll succeed. Because,
if not, I'll no longer be in a position to continue my support for
you.'

Husin Limbara laughed, and then suddenly said,

'Wouldn't it be better not to invest the whole eight million in
this one import corporation? You must realise that the import
field is now the main target for opposition attacks. Why don't
you start up some other enterprise, some mines or a factory for
instance, and divide the loan, drawing it under two names?'

'You're quite right there, brother,' Halim replied, laughing.
'Provided I'm sure of getting the loan, there'll be no trouble
dividing it up later.'

'So where do we stand now?' asked Raden Kaslan, who had
been silent throughout this interchange. 'Does it mean that from
now on I'm no longer to be involved in the financing of Halim?'

Husin Limbara was quiet for a moment, turning things over in
his mind. Then he said,

'Yes, I'll see to it that brother Halim's request is met. As for
co-ordinating the pro-government Press, I can settle it at once;
you can go ahead with the preparations immediately. The cost isn't
too heavy.' He then stood up, saying, 'Nah, I hope we've finished

1 Goldfish.

our discussion, and our co-operation will be even firmer than it was before.'

Halim rose too, picked up his briefcase and said to Husin Limbara,

'My car may not have come yet. Could you give me a lift to my office?'

'Certainly, certainly,' Husin Limbara responded.

Halim's car had in fact not arrived, and they left Raden Kaslan behind to marvel at Halim's slickness. Just imagine, the fellow talked for just half an hour, and managed to wheedle out over eight and a half million ....

In the car Halim was saying to Husin Limbara,

'Raden Kaslan didn't seem very happy during our discussion ....'

'Ah, he's getting old. And given to changeable moods. He's put in an application to have a Dutch car-importing firm transferred to him and it hasn't been approved yet.'

'But he's got so much already, and still he isn't satisfied,' said Halim. 'Import firms by the dozen, in his own name, the name of his wife, his son and whoever else. It's really amazing how greedy people can be. Who knows how much more goes into his pockets than goes into the party treasury?'

Inwardly Husin Limbara was saying, Yes, but you, my friend, are you any less greedy than that scoundrel Kaslan? You had a bank loan for the printing works, hundreds of thousands for your newspaper, a seat in parliament and are now due to get over eight million – if that isn't greed!

But he smiled at Halim and said,

'Well, there're all sorts of people in the world. No one's satisfied. The rich ones want more power, the rich ones want more wealth. Just look at the opposition parties. What are they shouting for? They've got no responsibility whatever for the welfare of our country and the people. Continually harassing the government, without a let-up, so the really important work of building up the country gets held up because we're forced to deal with an opposition that's gone off the track. How can the government do its work if it's constantly harassed?' Husin Limbara sighed, deeply deploring the sordid ways in which these others played politics.

Ah, just keep talking to your heart's content, do you really imagine you can pull the wool over my eyes? Halim grinned to himself. Large-scale looting is what *you're* perpetrating in the name of the people. Well, you think you're using me, but it's me who's using you. And laughing softly, Halim said,

'You're right, of course, brother, the leaders of the opposition are all stooges of the capitalists and colonialists. They should all be wiped out.'

Then the car, its brakes screeching and its tyres squealing on the pavement, came to a sudden stop as the driver just managed to avoid colliding with a betja.

Husin Limbara and Halim were thrown forward, Husin Limbara's glasses fell on the floor. Halim, being younger, quickly regained his balance and said,

'Lucky we didn't hit him.'

'Hell!' swore Husin Limbara, and as the car passed the betja, whose driver stood waiting in fear, Husin Limbara stuck his head out of his newly polished Cadillac. 'Look first before you cross, lu! Follow the traffic rules!'

And then he said to Halim, 'And betja drivers should be wiped out, too. They're just causing traffic accidents.'

'Moreover, they're a blot on the dignity of man!' said Halim mockingly. Husin Limbara looked at him, caught the joke in Halim's remark and laughed. His annoyance with the betja driver disappeared, and he said,

'Ah, you talk just like a member of the opposition!'

And they both laughed.

Pranoto was writing an article in his room. The walls around him were lined with books on metal bookshelves, just like in a library. Otherwise the room was very simple. A small bed in one corner. Near his desk on a low table stood an electric record-player, and at its side a hi-fi radio set. According to Pranoto the records, especially of classical music, did not sound well without the hi-fi hook-up.

When he had first sat down to write, everything he meant to say seemed very clear in his mind. But as he went along he had to stop more and more often, dissatisfied with what he'd set down – he felt the sentences he'd formed didn't convey clearly what he'd really intended to say.

Pranoto got up, put on a record, Schubert's Quartet No. 14 in D minor. He stretched out on his bed, listening to the beginning ... Schubert's music – 'Death and the Maiden' – merging with his own artistic sensibilities produced in him a feeling of great loneliness. Pranoto began to contemplate his own self.

Here I am, he said to himself, thirty-four years old, still unmarried. Six years spent in the foreign service, then he'd given it up. And now publishing a cultural and political journal. He remembered the time when he had worked for the Indonesian delegation in New York. Two years in New York. Liz, Martha, Connie and much else. Connie stood out vividly in his mind. They were still corresponding. Pranoto smiled to himself sadly. His relationship with Connie was a kind of dream, like living in another world. Something that couldn't be realised under present circumstances without destroying its essence. He knew with certainty that though he loved Connie he could never make up his mind to marry her. Pranoto had always prided himself on his practical sense, and in his letters to Connie he had repeatedly pointed out that it was impossible for him to marry her, no matter how strongly his heart, filled with love for her, urged him to do so.

I love you too much, Connie, he often wrote, *to marry you and to bring you here into the life of my own people. You wouldn't be able to live on my earnings, as an Indonesian woman and wife could. Your standard of living is so much higher than ours. And I wouldn't want my wife to live any differently than my own people. I wouldn't want to see my family become an island to itself, far above other Indonesian families. Even though you say that you can make the sacrifice, I cannot accept it. Therefore you're free to live as you please; my love imposes no ties on you. And I say to you, I love you, love you ever so much, will always love you whatever you do, even if you marry someone else, my love for you will never change and I'll always be with you in spirit. I have a duty to fulfil towards my own people here, to vindicate the struggle of my friends who have laid down their lives in the revolution for the liberation of my people. These friends of mine have not died to free my country and then have it bled white by immoral and unscrupulous politicians. Our young people have therefore a duty to work here in our homeland, to open the eyes of the people, to raise their standard of living, until the whole of our people is capable of consciously taking the reins of their destiny in their own hands.*

Connie had written back, saying that reading his letter had made her love him all the more and had made her even more determined to be at his side during his struggle.

I love you, wrote Connie, *and you know how strong my feelings for you are. You say that if you married me you would feel obliged for my sake to create a separate island, alien to your society. How incredibly little you think of my love for you. Do you imagine that we American women are incapable of loving a man strongly enough to be happy to sacrifice everything for him? What does it matter having to bear the hardships you describe in your letter, having to live in one room, having to share a house with two or three other families and me having to give up the comforts of American life? As if you didn't know there are plenty of Americans who live in badly crowded apartment houses, and, speaking of comforts, I'm sick and tired of hearing about America's prosperity. This expression has been a curse for our people, and I now experience it myself — it has become a curse upon the love that binds us together. Do you really think that we can't live without an elevator, without a pressure-cooker, without a fruit-squeezer, without a washing machine, without lipsticks, permanent waves and various other products of our giant industries? Don't you know that there are many Americans who long for a life such as in your country, without the complexities of the machine age and all its consequences for human beings? You must realise that I love you, that I want to live by your side, to help you in your struggle to elevate your people. Am I asking too much, my dearest?*

And Pranoto had written that he felt deeply how very fortunate he was to be blessed by a love as great as Connie's, but that evidently she hadn't fully understood what he had meant. He found it very hard, in fact, to tell her this — but to understand the conditions in his country fully, she had to realise that while physical hardships could be overcome by the power of love, there were other things which could not, no matter how great their love.

Here in my country, Pranoto wrote, *there's a plague of mistrust and suspicion of all foreigners, especially the white man, and Americans, Britons, Dutchmen, Frenchmen — they're all lumped together — all are wicked imperialists and capitalists. And an Indonesian with a Dutch, English, American or French wife is automatically suspect and is distrusted by his own people, particularly if he happens to be opposed to the communists or fanatic nationalists. He is finished then; and far from being any help to him his wife only impedes his efforts to fight on. That's why, no matter how much I love you, and though I know how selfless your love for me is, we must both have the courage to renounce our love to my struggle in my people's cause. I will always be longing for you, Connie, my love!*

But Pranoto never sent this letter to Connie. After re-reading it he had felt that it was too hard, even cruel, and that it didn't really reflect what was in his heart — which was crying out for Connie. Also, he was still torn by doubts that he found impossible to resolve.

Pranoto smiled bitterly. He recalled how ardently he always insisted that the Indonesians of his generation regarded themselves as heirs of all humanity, that no national barriers stood in their way and that human values were the same all over the world. And now he could not make a decision for himself.

Instead of the unsent letter, he answered Connie with a love-letter which spoke mainly of his longing for her.

How incredibly happy I was, my darling, he wrote, *to get your wonderfully noble letter. I want to assure you of one thing, so you never doubt it — my everlasting love for you. I have almost succumbed to your reasoning. But I am not yet convinced for myself that marrying you and bringing you among my people will bring you happiness, the happiness I want you to have. So please be patient, my beloved, and wait a little longer.*

Pranoto woke up with a start from his musings as he heard the humming sound of the phonograph as the record came to the end. He sat up on his bed, rubbed the bridge of his nose, pinched his eyebrows. He felt even more desolate and lonely than usual. He stood up, went back to his desk, examined the piece of paper in the typewriter, his unfinished article. He forced himself to re-read what he had written. It was a great effort to continue the work, he felt.

'That's his story – do you think it can be done?' said Sugeng to Suryono. They were both in Sugeng's workroom. A workroom as yet empty. Suryono was thinking it over.

'Should it come off, it would mean a clear half a million for us,' he said.

Sugeng had just finished telling him how three days ago a certain Said Abdul Gafur had come to him with a proposal. According to Said Abdul Gafur, a friend of his, who was an Arab real estate owner, was eager to sell some of his property located rather strategically in the centre of the city. But unfortunately, several of the buildings on the property were occupied by government offices, so no one was willing to buy it. But if one could arrange for these government offices to be moved somewhere else, the property would become available for new housing construction and could be sold for as much as five million. And, Said Abdul Gafur had said, if Sugeng could arrange this, there was a cut of half a million waiting for those who got it done.

'But you should realise,' said Suryono, 'that the property is worth far more than five million. I'm sure Said Abdul Gafur will want a big cut for himself. I'll talk it over with my father, we'll see what the party can do. But we'll have to make sure to get a bigger share. Half a million for the party, and half a million for the two of us. Just tell your Arab that if he's prepared to pay one million we'll see it gets done.'

'If this comes off I'll resign from my post as an official,' said Sugeng, 'and go into business on my own. I want to start my own enterprise.'

'Of course, it's much better, what's the use of being a civil servant!' Suryono responded contemptuously.

Idris sat very still by the window of his bedroom. He had been sitting like this for the last quarter-hour. He'd just had a quarrel with Dahlia. He had been suppressing his feelings about his wife too long. All sorts of vile thoughts and suspicions had kept haunting him. He had seen her constantly acquiring more and more things she couldn't possibly afford on his earnings as an inspector of education. Expensive batik cloths, beautiful jackets, not to mention gold jewellery with precious stones, perfumes and so on.

That afternoon when he got back from the office he could contain himself no longer. It was not finding her home that triggered everything off. It was only after he had finished eating that Dahlia had appeared, carrying a bundle of several batik kains.

'I've kept quiet all this time, but, by Allah, you'd better tell the truth now and tell me just where you get the money to buy all this. It's impossible on my salary,' he had started, in an agitated voice.

Dahlia looked at him with great surprise, she had never expected such an outburst from her husband. For months now she had been going and coming as she pleased, bringing things home without Idris raising any questions.

But her shock didn't last long. She knew her power over Idris. Dahlia counter-attacked at once.

'Aduh, so you've gone so far as to suspect your own wife. Perhaps you think that I've stolen them all?'

Idris was groping for an answer, hesitating whether or not to utter the crucial accusation. But Dahlia, sensing his hesitation, quickly pursued her advantage. Coming a step closer she said,

'Or do you think I'm selling myself to buy all these things?'

Her voice rose to the angry pitch of an injured wife, quite unjustly suspected. It conveyed the indignation of a woman who had to bear the hardships of being a civil servant's wife and suddenly being accused of the worst by her own husband.

Idris felt that he had lost the initiative, but did not see his way to regaining it.

Dahlia pushed on with her attack.

'You should be grateful and appreciate my efforts to supplement your salary and bolster our income a bit. But you're doing just the opposite. If you really want to know how I manage to buy all these things, all right, I'll tell you – by trading in a small way, buying and selling kains and jewels among my friends. These kains I've just bought will be resold later.' And Dahlia picked up the bundle of batiks which she had brought from the shop – on credit. She still didn't know how she was going to pay for them, whether to ask Suryono to settle the debt, or the young Indian manager of a shop she patronised on Pasar Baru, who kept trying to approach her whenever she came in to do some shopping.

'Apart from trading, I run some raffles among friends. That radio over there in the dining-room, do you think I bought it out of your salary? And our new bed – from your salary, too?'

By this time Idris was completely crushed. And when, on top of this, Dahlia began to cry, sobbing bitterly and saying, 'Ah, if you don't like me any more, why don't you just divorce me?' he felt faint all over. As though he were laying his heart on the floor for Dahlia to trample on, he reproached himself in a hundred ways for having entertained such evil thoughts about the wife he loved. He sat very still by the window, not knowing how to win her back.

'I 'lready got work driving betja, 'Mun,' said Itam to Saimun in their hut. 'No joking how hard foreman can be. If you're sick one week he won't take you back. He said we get paid by the day. When I was sick he got 'nother man do my work. Lucky I got work driving betja!'

'How 'bout betja driving-licence?' asked Saimun.

'Tauké[1] don't care, have or not have driving-licence. If not

---

1 Chinese boss.

have driving-licence, must make bigger deposit. Deposit for one day and one night, usual twenty rupiah, but me, I must make deposit twenty-five rupiah.'

'Aduh, 'Tam, far too much, nuh?'

'Yah, but we, what can we expect, 'Mun? If there's no other work at all, see? Me, I've no schooling. Know nothing. Read – cannot. Write – cannot. Become skilled – cannot. Most I have – two hands and two feet. Lu, better off, see. Only thing left to do for lu, apply for licence. Then lu can be sopir.[2] Lu 'lready can write 'n read some.'

'That's it, 'Tam,' said Saimun. 'Me, from the beginning I ask you to come take P.B.H.[3] lessons, but lu just lazy.'

''T's just fate, 'Mun. Has not every man his fate? We here just submit to the Lord. If lucky enough to earn living, well, thank God. If not, just croak.'

'Don't talk this way, 'Tam, Easy!'

'Really, sometimes me, I feel like I'm going crazy, 'Mun, living like this. Feels like we just trampled on. If to stay in the village, want to work sawah[4] – cannot, 'll be killed by grombolan. If run away to city, life just suffering. How lu think, how can it be if you're sick then you lose the work? So how to be if it's this way? Then you see our high people, who always doing fine. Lu ever see them stand in line for salt, for kerosene, for rice, like us in the kampung? No, never. Most we see them line up in cars.'

'That's true, 'Tam,' Saimun replied. 'Me, I also often think and think. In our life, see, no change – under the Dutch or under our own people, no different. Me, I don't 'nderstand a thing 'bout these politics, see. But I can feel for myself, and hear friends talk. Sure, our life now has no joy at all. Nothing's fixed. Nobody cares about our lot. If hungry – 'llright, be hungry by yourself. If sick – 'llright, be sick by yourself. If dead – 'llright, be dead by yourself.'

---

2 Chauffeur.
3 Organisation to combat illiteracy.
4 Irrigated rice-fields.

'Nah, if I 'lready feel like I'm near crazy, sometimes I get to think, 'llright, just steal, that's all. If not steal, 'llright, rob. Don't care 'nymore what'll happen!'

''T's true,' said Saimun. 'Me, I also feel that way once 'n while. One time, when still learning drive the truck, motor goes dead, truck 'n middle of street; aduh, how people in big shiny cars swearing at me — telling me, lu, if you don't know how to drive, don't drive, yak! Our own people so terrible stuck-up. I'd not be bitter if he, who wants to pass, were the number of Pak President. And his name were also Pak President's. 'T's only proper to give way — lives he not in the palace and 'vrything's set. But if our own people, who're not the president, carry on like this, aduh, I can't take it, 'Tam. Are we not all human? Only they have money, and we're the people who don't.'

''Mun,' said Itam, 'friends say when driving betja luck can be fairly good. More so if we get know addresses of women. Tips then good, too. Speaking 'f women, yesterday I see Neneng on Sawah Besar market. Aduh, she wants not know me any more.'

Saimun held his breath hearing Itam mention Neneng's name. Since Neneng had left their hut last August, Saimun had tried four times to approach her and persuade her to return.

'She's 'lready fine show,' added Itam. 'All dressed up, clothes neat, lips painted red. I greet her, doesn't even answer.'

Itam stretched himself out on the balai-balai and lit a kretek cigarette.

Saimun recalled the moment when he had tried for the first time to approach Neneng. It was almost a month after she had left them to go to Kaligot. At first he had been reluctant to enter the house where she worked, because there were so many other women in it, and Saimun did not know how to behave toward all these other women who kept looking at him. But later he got up enough courage to enter because he noticed that Neneng was sitting on the front verandah with a few other women. When he entered, Neneng, seeing him, got up and ran inside. Saimun didn't dare to follow and look for her, and he quickly went out again, not daring to stand and wait for her outside either.

The second time, when he came there, he just managed to catch a glimpse of a man who was drawing Neneng with him into the inner room. He was so upset at that moment that he ran away as fast as he could.

The third time, two weeks later, he came across Neneng at the Sawah Besar market. He greeted her, but the woman kept walking on as if she'd never known him.

Neneng's behaviour had greatly depressed Saimun. But he didn't give up hope, and when a week later he accidentally met Neneng on the street he greeted her again. And again Neneng did not return the greeting. But Saimun, gathering courage, followed Neneng while saying to her,

'Neneng, why you like this? I mean no harm. Just want to see you. Want to see that you're well.'

And only then the woman answered, in a dull, sad voice,

'Bang,[1] what's the use looking for me? I'm now a dirty woman.'

At these words Saimun felt as though his heart was being cut to pieces, and without a moment's thought he said,

'Leave that house, 'Neng ayoh; let's go back to our hut.'

'And like before, with you and Itam, bang,' Neneng replied. 'It's the same as my life now. Let it be, bang, I'm 'lready a woman like this. Let it be!'

'Aduh, 'Neng, we'll get married if lu want,' suddenly sprang from Saimun's mouth without him being aware of the meaning of his own words, of the fact that he couldn't support a wife while his earnings were not even enough for himself alone and while he still suffered many ups and downs and hunger.

'You're really good, abang, but me, I'm ashamed,' said Neneng,

---

1 Short for *abang*, elder brother.

quickening her steps.

And she did not listen any more to what Saimun tried to tell her, coaxing her as he was, until he began to feel embarrassed as people started to stare at him – chasing after a woman in the middle of the street in broad daylight. He stopped and let Neneng walk on by herself in front.

'Ah, 'Tam,' said Saimun to Itam who was puffing out dense clouds of cigarette smoke, 'me, I don't know any more why we're born to be human beings! Only the Lord knows what he wants with us!'

And Saimun sat there, musing.

Yasrin was walking in the scorching heat of Djakarta towards Achmad's office. He had received a letter from Achmad, the contents of which he rather liked. Achmad had written that cultural activities in Indonesia had been left in the hands of bourgeois intellectuals like Pranoto and his friends far too long. The result had been a total lack of progress in developing a genuine cultural movement 'among the people, by the people and for the people'. In Achmad's words, these bourgeois intellectuals who profess to be supporters of Indonesian culture and claim to be heirs to universal human values are stuck in theorising, analysing, writing pseudo-intellectual essays full of pretentious words and terms borrowed from Western books. They're so absorbed in this kind of masturbation that they're quite satisfied with just publishing manifestos, producing analyses, dreaming about a fine arts academy, a popular theatre, a museum of modern art, etc., etc …. It all starts with a barrage of propaganda but soon disappears without a trace, just like in the old Malay saying – 'Very, very hot are a chicken's droppings.'

And so, Achmad had written, *my friends and I, who have long appreciated you as a poet, are convinced that you, too,*

are fed up by now with the sterile activities of these bourgeois
and compradores; we feel sure that you're eager to plunge into
the arena by contributing your great creative power to struggle
for our nation's cultural development. We therefore very much
hope, brother, that you'll be willing to come to a meeting at my
office to discuss the subject.

Yasrin was rather flattered by Achmad's letter.

Actually, he had been feeling dissatisfied with himself for quite some time. This dissatisfaction had been quite vague and general, but after receiving the letter three days ago, the reasons for his discontent had become clear to him. It was quite evident now that Pranoto and his group had been just exploiting his name as a front to show their concern for the people, because his poems always dealt with the life and sufferings of the masses. He remembered one of his poems being praised by Pranoto in the journal *Culture*. Pranoto had written that Yasrin was Indonesia's most important poet since Chairil Anwar. Yasrin ranked perhaps even higher than Chairil Anwar, Pranoto had written, since evidence that some of Anwar's poems had been plagiarised had detracted from his reputation as an original poet.

So far, all he'd got from his friends was praise. Meanwhile, several members of their club had received invitations to visit the United States or some other Western country, like England or France, but his own turn had never come. He had once asked to be given a chance, but his request had not been given the proper attention. It was even conveyed to him indirectly that it was difficult for his colleagues to get him an invitation to the United States or England since he couldn't speak the language. He had been very hurt to hear this. He had retorted by asking why the Chinese or the Russians, for instance, invited Indonesian artists, even though these artists didn't know a word of Russian or Chinese. But to this question no satisfactory reply had been given. All he'd received was just an intimation – did he want to be a propaganda tool for the communists?

Since receiving Achmad's letter, Yasrin had become convinced that his proper place was not with Pranoto's group. I've been lost all this time, Yasrin thought to himself. Why didn't I see how completely bourgeois someone like Suryono is? He goes on talking about the misery of the masses and the disintegration of the state, but money's really all he's interested in. Look how fast he's made his fortune! And for such a young man to have a car of his own and live it up the way he does! When you remember the stories of friends that Suryono's wealth comes from his father's connections with the party, it's perfectly obvious that Pranoto's group is just indulging in words, without any honest and sincere desire to serve the masses, or the proletariat – the workers and the peasants.

And now that he remembered how many times in the past he had written in defence of democracy, criticising the communists and their totalitarian system, he felt ashamed of himself. I've certainly been blind all this time, he thought.

He also reminded himself that though Pranoto, the unofficial leader of their study club, was good enough at 'analysis', he'd never had any contact with the people, had never really known the people. Wah, he just uses the autolette or the tram – never, as far as I know, goes on foot! He remembered how he had once invited Pranoto to eat with him, squatting at the roadside, and how Pranoto had refused saying,

'Aduh, Yasrin, how can you eat there? Isn't it awfully dirty? Just look how they rinse the spoons and plates in a jar where the water's never changed.'

Yasrin felt resentful as he remembered these words of Pranoto, although at the time he had answered merely by laughing. But now, since receiving Achmad's letter, he suddenly felt that he had been badly humiliated by Pranoto. I eat every day squatting by the roadside like this, Yasrin said to himself, and Pranoto says it's dirty. By Allah!

And by the time Yasrin had reached Achmad's office he was almost ninety-nine per cent determined to join Achmad and stop working for the journal he and Pranoto were publishing together. He had even formulated his reasons for leaving Pranoto — it was all so clear in his mind: he had decided to abandon their kind of cultural activity in order to devote himself to the people's culture, among the people.

In Achmad's office three other persons were already waiting. Achmad stood up quickly, overjoyed to see Yasrin arrive.

'We've been waiting for you. We were afraid you'd not be able to come at all. Let me introduce you first — this is Sjafei, people's poet; Murtoho, people's painter; and Hambali, people's short-story writer.'

They sat down, and Achmad opened the meeting by telling them that the time had now come when all artists, poets, writers or painters must get together to generate a real people's culture. He surveyed the cultural scene in Indonesia, pointing out that it was still dominated by a feudal atmosphere. It was self-evident that their now-independent country could not possibly tolerate the continuation of feudalistic influences on culture, and that these would have to be consciously replaced by a people's culture.

'That's why we've been building up a fund large enough for this struggle, and to start with, we'll have to set up a people's cultural movement. This GEKRA[1] will publish a really militant cultural magazine. In asking you four, brothers, to come here today, it was my intention to invite you to work as full-time activists for this publication. For the time being it'll come out once a month. But, the magazine aside, our task will also be to establish branches of GEKRA all over the country, organise exhibitions of books, of paintings, organise literary competitions, a popular theatre and

---

1 In Indonesian = *Gerakan Kebudajaan Rakjat*, hence the abbreviation GEKRA.

to create new people's dances and music. We've got a lot to do, and I hope we'll get through with all these preparations without losing too much time.'

Achmad's statements got Yasrin all excited. His blood was pulsing and he felt as though he couldn't wait to start.

Achmad then went on to explain that each activist would receive a monthly stipend of a thousand rupiah, and that they would be sent in turn to survey the various regions of their country. Later on arrangements would be made for them to be invited to study methods of cultural organisation in the People's Republic of China, in Russia, in Czechoslovakia and other people's democracies.

They then decided upon the division of labour, and Yasrin was given the job of heading the people's cultural magazine which was to appear at the beginning of the new year. He was to get an office in a house on Tanah Tinggi where the Proletarian Library Foundation, which was publishing Indonesian translations of books by Russian and Chinese authors, had its headquarters.

They took leave of each other with mutual assurances of co-operation in the cause of the people's cultural uplift and the destruction of the residue of feudalistic cultural influences. And as Yasrin was walking home an extraordinary joy seemed to flow through his veins, warming his whole body, making him feel as if he were bobbing along on a street of balloons, bouncing him upwards as if to propel him up into the sky.

And he felt as though he couldn't restrain the joy that flooded his being; he wanted to fill the air with cries of joy – I will now be working for the people, now I know where I am and where I'm going. Achmad's explanations came into his mind again, how they would bring justice and prosperity to all the people, how social classes would be abolished and all men would live in happiness. To attain this, Achmad had said, we must be united, uncompromising and merciless towards our enemies, the stooges of the imperialists and capitalists, the remnants of the feudal and bourgeois cliques.

He was just about to go into his house when he remembered that he still owed his landlady, Ibu Warmana, a month's rent for his room and board. But now he had no need to come home feeling uncomfortable. His total debt was only three hundred rupiah, and next month he would have a salary of one thousand. He'd have no trouble paying off his arrears for two months immediately. And he was suddenly struck with amazement at the idea of getting one thousand rupiah each month; never before had he had such a large income. His earnings had always been irregular. If he happened to publish some poems in Pranoto's journal he would receive a honorarium of fifty up to one hundred rupiah at the most. And only once had he been given two thousand rupiah by a publisher for a collection of his poems. But this money was soon gone – he had had a good many debts that had to be settled. To supplement his income he did all sorts of writing, book reviews and even stories for children. But all this never brought in more than three or four hundred rupiah a month. And now suddenly he was to get a salary of one thousand rupiah every month. And just before they had parted Achmad had even mentioned that should he need some money before the end of the month he could ask for an advance.

Yasrin entered the house, whistling, and as he opened the door to his room and stepped inside, Wiria, Ibu Warmana's son, an S.M.A.[1] student who shared his room, greeted him with,

'Aduh, you must be very pleased, abang, whistling like this.'

Yasrin laughed, and sat down on his bed.

'Dik,'[2] he said, 'next month I'll buy you the book you couldn't buy yourself for lack of money. As my first present I'll buy you the works of Shakespeare. Don't you worry.'

---

1 *Sekolah Menengah Atas* = 'Higher Middle School'.
2 Abbreviated *adik*, younger brother or sister.

Because Wiria was sharing the room with Yasrin, he cherished the idea of becoming a poet and writer himself. He loved Shakespeare; his dream was to possess Shakespeare's works in their original, English version.

'Wah,' said Wiria, sitting up and looking at Yasrin, 'where will you get the money from, abang?'

'Beginning from today your abang is chief editor of a proletarian magazine, supporter of the people's culture, with a salary of one thousand rupiah per month.'

Wiria uttered a cry of joy, and immediately begged him,

'And you will include some of my writings, too, abang, yes?'

Yasrin consented easily. There were no difficulties left in his life or in the world, as far as he could see. He was back in the true line of battle. Everything had become simple and clear: the enemy to be annihilated; the aim to be pursued; and the way to attain it — that was clear, too. There was to be no mercy for, or compromise with, the enemies of the proletariat!

Yasrin stretched out on his bed. Its mattress was worn thin and the shabby sheet, once white, was now a greyish colour. At the head of his bed, near the window, stood a shaky table covered with old newspapers. On it were piled some books he had been able to pick up second-hand, or had borrowed from friends without ever returning them. All these books must be changed, too, Yasrin thought, turning over on his belly and looking at the books — *Darkness at Noon* by Arthur Koestler which he had once liked. That'll have to go! *For Whom the Bell Tolls* by Ernest Hemingway — a bourgeois writer — blasé, as he'd said himself, though earlier Yasrin had dreamed of being able to write as lucidly as Hemingway. The books by Maxim Gorky will remain, of course, he said to himself. And Yasrin was already thinking of the moment he'd buy himself a new pair of trousers and a new shirt. It was so pleasant to imagine what one longed to have and at the same time to know that it was within one's power to get it.

Evening. A heavy rain had been dripping steadily over Djakarta since the late afternoon. The air was grey and half of the sky was overcast with black clouds which threatened much heavier rain still to come. On the street, people on bicycles who were braving the rain pushed on at top speed, but many were seeking shelter under the trees along the road. Betja drivers had lowered the awnings over their front seats, and lovers seated inside could embrace cosily while driving through the evening rain. The wheels of motor-cars swished along the wet asphalt and their yellow lamps were like the eyes of wild beasts in the darkness of the night.

People sleeping under the bridge tried to protect themselves from the sprays of rain blown in by the wind, screening themselves with worn-out mats and praying that the rain would not turn into a downpour. And the people who slept in the big water-pipe that was waiting to be laid underground moved deeper inside, away from the opening where the rain was dripping in.

From time to time the heavy rolling of thunder rumbled above them, and it looked as if the rain was gradually growing heavier. Inside a car Raden Kaslan sat with his hands folded on his belly, looking out through the windscreen. The wipers swished back and forth, sweeping away the rainwater. At his side Husin Limbara sat in silence, engrossed in his own thoughts. Husin Limbara's elegant Cadillac turned into the driveway of the Hotel des Indes, and Raden Kaslan and Husin Limbara stepped out.

'Be back by midnight,' Raden Kaslan told the driver.

They entered the restaurant.

'Let's sit and drink something until the rain eases or stops,' said Raden Kaslan.

They ordered coffee and some titbits.

'Is everything really all fixed, nothing will leak out?' asked Husin Limbara.

'Ah, you needn't worry; if it's Raden Kaslan who's arranging things, it's sure to be well done.'

'But ...'

'There's always a first time for things like this,' said Raden Kaslan, and, sipping his coffee, he added, 'For us older men who're near or over fifty, it's a very good way. You'll see for yourself. Indonesian women don't like to do it. But Indo[1] nonnas[2] like it very much. The French kiss!'

'What's the name again of the nyonya who's fixing it?' asked Husin Limbara.

'Tante Bep. You'll meet her.'

Meanwhile the rain outside had begun to let up.

Raden Kaslan summoned a hotel boy and ordered him to call a betja for them.

In the betja Raden Kaslan was saying to Husin Limbara,

'It's better to go there by betja. If we went by car, who knows who might be passing by and recognise our car? If it happened to be an unfriendly reporter it could get into the newspapers.'

And Raden Kaslan burst out laughing.

The betja soon brought them to Petodjo, and, following Raden Kaslan's directions, it entered an alley, and then stopped before Tante Bep's house.

'Shall I wait, tuan?' asked Itam, the betja driver.

Raden Kaslan looked at the sky where clumps of dark clouds were still hanging, felt the thin drizzle and said,

'All right, just wait here.'

He then hurried inside, drawing Husin Limbara in after him.

Tante Bep, who was waiting for them in the front room, rose quickly to shake hands with both Raden Kaslan and Husin Limbara.

'Aduh, tuan,' Tante Bep was saying, 'I had begun to think you wouldn't come at all because of the rain. We agreed on nine o'clock, it's already close to ten now.'

---

1 Indo-European, i.e. Eurasian.
2 Miss, damsel.

'Have the nonnas come?' asked Raden Kaslan eagerly.

'They're here, inside. They almost went home. Come on, go in, please!' said Tante Bep.

Husin Limbara, drawn along by Raden Kaslan, went inside while Raden Kaslan was saying jokingly,

'This friend of mine's still a virgin, still a bit shy!'

Tante Bep laughed.

She took them to the verandah at the back. Two Eurasian girls were sitting at the table. They just sat looking on as Husin Limbara and Raden Kaslan sat down.

'Good evening, Eve,' said Raden Kaslan to the one with black hair. She had a lovely figure and wore a gown cut so low that half of her full white breasts were showing.

'This is a friend of mine,' said Raden Kaslan introducing Husin Limbara to Eve. And Eve, remaining seated, extended her hand with a slight smile.

'I haven't met this nonna yet, isn't she lovely, too?' said Raden Kaslan.

'This is Eda,' said Tante Bep, introducing her.

Eda's hair was of a russet colour, she was slightly smaller than Eve, and indifferently she gave her hand, first to Raden Kaslan, then to Husin Limbara.

'Nah,' said Raden Kaslan, 'which one of them do you want? You're the guest of honour tonight, and you may choose. As for me I want Eda here, she's new!' and he caressed Eda from behind her chair.

Eda slapped the hand grasping her breast and said,

'Not so fast, jongen!'[3]

'It's ten o'clock already,' said Eve. 'Come on, it'll be getting late.'

Eve drew Husin Limbara into the room adjoining the verandah, and Raden Kaslan drew Eda with him into the middle room.

As soon as they were inside Eve turned the key in the door, and

---

3 Boy, in Dutch.

said to Husin Limbara,

'If it isn't locked Tante Bep is likely to peep.'

Husin Limbara sat down on the bed. From the moment they'd entered the room Eve's behaviour had changed completely. The nonchalant attitude she'd kept up on the verandah had vanished and she was a young woman greatly taken with Husin Limbara. Her eyes, her smile and the movements of her body excited the fifty-year-old man.

While on the verandah he'd still felt rather confused, and when Raden Kaslan had invited him to go inside he had been hesitant, but now, alone with Eve, he was delighted to feel the pulsing of his aroused blood. He was getting on — it had been a long time — he could hardly remember having sexual relations with a woman. He had stopped doing anything with his own wife long ago. But now he felt the surging joy of his virility once again as he saw Eve taking off her clothes one by one, and then coming to him in only her bra and panties. Eve took hold of Husin Limbara's hand. Husin Limbara trembled, his breath tightening. The experienced Eve had seen it all before. She helped Husin Limbara off with his jacket and then he lay back on the bed watching Eve slip off her bra and panties, and, swinging her hips, go towards the door and turn off the light. The room was now in semi-darkness, some light still filtering from the back verandah. Then Eve came over to the bed and whispered,

'Do you want a French kiss?' And she laughed softly.

Outside in the drizzling rain, now falling more heavily again, Itam sat huddled in his betja, clasping his shoulders with his chilled hands, waiting.

On that same rainy night, Fatma came to Suryono's room. Suryono was reading a Western. Fatma locked the door, and Suryono knew at once what his stepmother desired. During the past few weeks all the initiative had been coming from his stepmother. Fatma herself had brought up the subject several times, but Suryono had always managed to avoid it up till now. During these last weeks Suryono's feelings had become more and more mixed up. Fatma, his stepmother, Dahlia, Ies — the three of them were in his blood, each attractive to him in her own way. Yet Fatma was gradually being pushed to the background by Dahlia and Ies, and Dahlia in turn was being supplanted by Ies. None of this was clear to him yet, but some subconscious process had already thrown him into a state of great confusion and robbed him of his peace of mind. It was as though his life were threatened every moment by some great disaster and destruction. Just from what direction and in what form the danger or calamity would descend upon him he couldn't imagine.

Fatma came to Suryono as he lay on his bed, sat down at his side, drew his head into her arms and kissed his mouth in a long-drawn, deep kiss. She whispered,

'Aduh, I'm longing for you so! It's been two weeks since we've had a chance.'

For a moment Suryono decided to resist Fatma's caresses, but his intentions were dispersed like smoke blown by the wind by Fatma's passionate kiss ....

Later, when they had calmed down, Fatma got out of the bed and sat down in a chair. Suryono lit a cigarette and said to her,

'Have you ever stopped to think of the future?'

'I don't understand what you mean,' said Fatma.

'This can't go on for ever. Sooner or later Father will find out,' said Suryono, 'and what will happen then?'

'Ah, even if he does find out, what can he do to us? Don't I know he's playing around with other women himself?'

'Yes, but I'm his son and you are my stepmother!'

'So what?' said Fatma. 'Besides we've enough money, no need to worry. We could move out of this house any time we like.'

'You don't care about my father at all?' asked Suryono.

'I'm too young and he's too old for us to be together.'

'It's strange that there should be no emotional or spiritual bond between myself and my father at all now,' said Suryono, addressing himself mainly. And he remembered that when he was a child the relationship between himself and his father, as father and son, had been very close. But then later he had spent many years in his uncle's care while at school, far from home. Having no brothers or sisters, and having lost his mother in addition, the old intimacy with his father had vanished imperceptibly. Moreover, watching his father's activities during recent months had in no way enhanced his respect for him. From time to time he even felt contempt for his own behaviour as well. Emotionally he knew that what they were doing was wrong; that even though it was all quite legal, to exploit the party's power to enrich oneself was still improper, somehow. And it was the same with his relationship with Fatma. He felt that it was not proper, yet every time he succumbed again. It was the same with his acceptance of the special licences. He felt that it wasn't right for him to be getting them, but the hundreds of thousands these licences yielded excited and pleased him, reminded him of Dahlia's caresses, the bright polish of a new car, the pleasure of eating in a fine restaurant, the weight of the wallet in his pocket. Unable to resist this temptation, he even experienced a kind of pleasure in trading his special licences.

'What did you say?' Suryono asked suddenly, coming out of his musings and noticing that Fatma was speaking.

'Ah, you weren't even listening, where on earth were your thoughts?' Fatma said, showing her annoyance. 'You've been like this a lot lately; is there another woman?' she asked, the woman in her speaking.

Suryono gave a little laugh.

'I'm upset. Haven't been feeling too good the past few days. God knows why...' he said.

'You didn't answer my question. Is there another woman?'
Fatma asked again.

Suryono looked at Fatma, and decided to test her.

'And if there were, what then?'

Fatma laughed, and said,

'If there is, it's none of my business. I'm not *your* wife, but your
father's. But if another woman is giving you trouble, tell me about
it, maybe I can help you.'

'Aduh,' said Suryono, somewhat startled, 'you don't have any
morals.'

'Do you have any? Morality is just a burden, just causes people
trouble,' Fatma replied, laughing. 'People should do what gives
them pleasure while they're alive to do so, that's all. Don't rack
your brains about things you're not responsible for. I care for you,
and I'm happy when you're carefree, and that's why I want to help
you. Come on, tell me!'

Suryono laughed.

'By Allah!' he said. 'I've never met a woman like you!'

Fatma laughed, too. Took a cigarette from the table and lit it.
She puffed the smoke into Suryono's face, and said,

'I'm still young, but I've had my lessons in life. Listen to this.
I've told you once before how I came to marry your father. But you
don't know the whole story. Before I married your father I was
already a widow. My husband was killed during the revolution. He
was a lieutenant. I loved him, and with his death my love died too.
Unfortunately his rank was too low for him to be remembered by
the government, and he was not included among the "great heroes
to be remembered by the people". Naturally no one paid any
attention to me as his widow, either. I wasn't given a single penny
of support after his death. I had to live. I moved down to Djakarta
where my aunt put me up in her house. Believe me, a young and
pretty woman has no trouble making money if she's prepared to
use her body and beauty. But I was very cautious. I chose the men

with whom I would sleep very carefully. That's the only way to take good care of your body, protect your reputation and see to it that your price stays high. It's always like this with men, the more difficult it is to get a woman the more they desire to possess her. That was how I met your father, Raden Kaslan. I was not attracted to him. He was too ostentatious about what he could get with all his money. As though just having money let him do anything he pleased, even buy a person entirely. The more I withdrew from him the more he longed to dominate me. So I told him that I would submit to him, but only on one condition; that he would marry me. And so he married me. He married me not because he loved me or cared for me, or because he really desired me passionately. No, the first night after our wedding he just slept through it, snoring – he'd drunk too much. After that he didn't come to me very often because I didn't like to do what he asked. But it seems that your father gets satisfaction from having a young and good-looking wife, is pleased to hear his friends admire her beauty and to see how other men are trying to approach me. Your father is satisfied; he knows that he owns something that many others would enjoy having. That is what I mean to him. Why should I try to be moral as far as he's concerned if he's completely immoral himself? Besides, as we sit here talking, he may be playing around with another woman!

'I've learned from life that you must seize whatever you desire, and whatever makes you happy, quickly and without hesitation. And that there's no use worrying about what might happen later. Our fate is in the hands of the Lord.'

Suryono smiled at the contradiction in Fatma's statement which mentioned the Lord. Inwardly he wished he could be as free of doubt as Fatma was in facing life.

'There are three women in my life now,' Suryono told Fatma, answering her story about herself with one about himself. 'You, someone called Dahlia, also married, and Ies, an unmarried girl.

I care for all three of you, I love you all and each time I am with one of you I feel happy and at peace, satisfied and pleased with life. I'm happy to be alive right now, and feel no need to think about tomorrow or the day after. With Dahlia I experience another kind of joy, though it's somewhat like the feeling when I'm with you. With Ies my feeling of joy is different, it's full of hope and promise for the future and I feel as though, if given the opportunity, I would not hesitate to face life with Ies for ever.'

'Have you slept with both of them yet?' asked Fatma, the woman.

But Suryono did not notice the jealousy in her face.

'With Dahlia, but not with Ies.'

'What is Dahlia like?'

'Like you.'

Fatma laughed.

'To speak like a mother to her son, it would be good for you to forget Dahlia and concentrate on Ies. But apparently the girl does not fully respond to your feelings towards her?'

'Could be,' Suryono said. 'Sometimes it seems as though my own doubts are mirrored in her.'

'Don't worry,' said Fatma. 'Everything will come out all right by itself. The fire that now consumes you and Dahlia will stop burning some day, and, when the time comes, between the two of us too, maybe, but it won't matter. I'm not dreaming of living with you as husband and wife, though it's quite an attractive possibility.'

Fatma smiled, and quickly added, 'But I suppose it's impossible, isn't it? Or maybe if your father dies? I know the way a man must act to overcome a girl's hesitation,' she said, after a pause, 'but I'm not going to tell you. I'll lose you too soon. So you'll have to find out for yourself.'

Fatma stood up, pressed her cigarette-butt against the ashtray, bent over, kissed Suryono and went to the door.

'Sleep well!' she said, and closed the door behind her.

Yasrin had just finished informing Pranoto that, starting today, he was leaving the journal Pranoto was promoting to work for a people's cultural periodical which would be launched by a group of his communist friends.

Pranoto had listened in silence while Yasrin talked.

'Well, what can I say, my friend?' Pranoto said finally. 'I fully respect your new convictions. But I'm also deeply sorry that you're leaving us. Our struggle is certainly far from over – we've still a long way to go.

'I suppose I have explained everything clearly enough,' said Yasrin.

'Oh, yes. I don't want to quarrel with your decision. But there's still something I can't help telling you. You've said that our group is nothing but a salon whose members talk about the people in a purely academic way without doing anything about it. Much talk and no action. In contrast, the communists, you say, work among the people. Don't you see that once we've chosen democracy it just can't be otherwise? We're not going to force the people to swallow our ideas. We can only inform them of these ideas and hope that people will gradually understand, accept and make these ideas their own. Therein lies the strength of democracy, but its weakness as well. But once we are determined to follow the democratic way we must have the courage to accept both its strengths and its weaknesses.'

'That's where I disagree with you,' said Yasrin. 'As I see it, all this is merely a pretence to cover up your incapacity to work among the people.'

'Look!' said Pranoto. 'What do the cultural activities promoted by the communists amount to? They send our young painters and writers to all sorts of festivals in communist countries, and when they come home they write glowing reports about the cultural activities there. What good does this do our people?'

'That's because, unlike the bourgeois clique, we're not in power yet,' Yasrin answered.

Pranoto smiled.

'Well, there's no use in our arguing about it here,' Yasrin then said.

Yasrin's leaving their club created a little stir among Pranoto's friends. Some denounced him, some approved his action. One comment was, 'At least he has the courage to choose sides.' And someone else observed rather cynically, 'Ah, all he wants is the thousand-rupiah salary. It's all the same to Yasrin whether it comes from Indonesia's pocket, from Peking, from the Kremlin or from Washington. All he sees are ten hundred-rupiah notes.'

City Report

'I suggest, gentlemen, that you settle it amicably between yourselves. Why make a case of it?' said the police commissary to the two men who sat at his desk.

'But I have the proper permit for the house,' said Abdul Manap. He took a housing-bureau certificate from his briefcase. 'Brother Suparto here had already occupied the house before I had a chance to move in, though he has no housing permit at all.'

'Our problem is that you've been fighting, brothers,' said the police commissary. 'But I hope that you'll be able to make peace.'

'I am willing to make peace if brother Suparto, who has no permit, is prepared to move out,' Abdul Manap replied.

'I am willing to move out, provided that I am given another place to live,' said Suparto.

'That's not my responsibility. It must be arranged by the Housing Bureau,' said the police commissary.

'It's not my responsibility either,' said Abdul Manap. 'So what about the order-to-vacate which the Housing Bureau has issued to brother Suparto? Aren't you going to enforce it?'

'I'm not going to move out unless I have another place in exchange, even if you shoot me dead,' said Suparto.

'Ah, don't talk like this,' said the police commissary. 'I didn't ask you to come here to start fighting again, but to make peace.'

'All I know is that I've obtained a legal housing permit, and that I'm going to occupy this house legally. And, if it comes to dying, I'm not afraid of dying either.'

'Easy, easy,' the police commissary said. 'I see that both of you gentlemen are still equally excited. There's no use our continuing this discussion any further as long as you're in this state. I suggest that you go home now, and that neither of you trespass on the place now occupied by the other until a final decision has been made.'

'Does this mean you're not going to enforce the order-to-vacate issued by the Housing Bureau?' asked Abdul Manap.

'Have patience, sir. I'll take care of it myself. Everything will come out all right.'

The police commissary stood up, forcing the other two to rise as well, and ushered them out of his room, saying,

'Now let's all be friends. We've all of us got families. Let's be patient.'

When the two visitors had left, the commissary took a handkerchief from his trouser pocket, wiped his forehead and sighed to the inspector who sat at a desk in one corner of the office,

'I'm sorry, but this is the responsibility of the Housing Bureau. Why don't they just abolish it?'

December

ASNAH SAT sewing clothes for her child. According to the doctor she could expect it by the middle of February. She had asked Sugeng to choose two names for the new baby – one in case it were a girl, and the other in case a boy were born to them. They both wanted Maryam to have a baby brother.

But her joy at the coming of the new child was now often clouded when she thought about her husband and the great change which had taken place in their family life. Their luck in getting a house of their own had not brought all the happiness they had hoped for. On the contrary, doubts kept assailing her. She didn't enjoy the refrigerator, the large radio set, the electric record-player Sugeng had bought for them. They stirred up all sorts of feelings and questions in her mind. And these feelings and questions were far from comforting.

She felt more keenly than anything that a kind of estrangement seemed to have grown between her and Sugeng. It had started when Hasnah had asked Sugeng where he had obtained so much money. At first he'd evaded giving her a direct answer, but later, when pressed by Hasnah, he had said that he was now a partner in an import business run by a friend. Hasnah's uneasiness had been further aggravated in recent months, seeing Sugeng more and more often leaving the house in the evening. When he was still an ordinary official with a rather meagre salary he'd almost never acted this way. Sugeng had of course gone out sometimes in the evening by himself; but then Hasnah knew precisely where he was going – usually to a friend's house, to chat and gossip while playing chess or bridge. But now Sugeng was gone as early as seven o'clock, sometimes even before having his supper and didn't get back till midnight or even one in the morning. Considering the advanced stage of her pregnancy, Hasnah suspected that Sugeng's frequent absences were not necessitated, as he said, by urgent work or the need to attend to some business transactions, but that there was probably a woman. But she carefully concealed these suspicions from Sugeng.

Hasnah heaved a long sigh, hearing the big clock in the middle room strike one. So it was already one o'clock. In a few minutes Sugeng would be back from the office. The clock was a large upright piece which had cost six thousand rupiah. Hasnah didn't really like it. She had been quite satisfied with their old bedside alarm-clock. She felt it was just showing off how rich they were to have this useless big clock. But Sugeng had been set on buying it. He had seen one like it in Raden Kaslan's house – and it looked very beautiful there. Hasnah herself had met Raden Kaslan only once; two weeks ago she and Sugeng had been invited to a party at his house. She had seen Raden Kaslan's wife – still quite young – had met his son, Suryono, and with her sharp feminine intuition had immediately sensed that things were not right in Raden Kaslan's family.

Back home, after the party, Sugeng was just telling her gaily about Raden Kaslan and Suryono, when Hasnah suddenly dampened his animation by observing, 'I don't know why, but I didn't like Raden Kaslan or his family. That hard old man's a bit too slippery. His tone of voice and laughter don't ring true. His wife doesn't seem to pay any attention to her husband at all. And his son is woman-crazy, I think!'

Hasnah put her sewing down on the table and went into the kitchen to see to the food. In the old days she used to cook on charcoal braziers and sometimes her eyes smarted from the smoke while she fanned the flame; but now she had a modern gas-cooker, costing no less than seven thousand five hundred rupiah, complete with oven. But Hasnah didn't enjoy cooking in her modern kitchen as much as when she had to squat down to fan the fire. Now two babus were working in the kitchen, and all she had to do was to give orders. And of course to light the gas, you didn't need anyone to blow! After making sure the meal would be ready in time for Sugeng when he got in, Hasnah went back to the middle room and then into her bedroom.

All the furniture there was new. But Hasnah's sadness at parting with their old familiar furnishings had far outweighed her pleasure in getting this new elegant bedroom-set. And now Sugeng kept saying that as soon as he could afford to stop working as an official he'd buy a car immediately.

'If I should buy a car now, while still a civil servant, people would be saying all sorts of nasty things,' Sugeng had said.

Hasnah had made no reply then; she didn't want to tell Sugeng that among themselves his friends had been discussing their new prosperity for quite a while now. Even Hasnah's friend Dahlia, when she'd visited them in their new home, had said to her,

'Aduh, your husband's got very smart at making money. Not like my husband, Hasnah. He keeps telling me that a government official must be honest. And no matter how many examples I show him of honest officials living in misery nowadays, he still wants to stay honest. He says the time will come when righteousness will come to our country and those who stay honest will have their reward. Isn't he stupid, though? If I weren't smart enough to make some money on my own ...'

Hasnah had felt as though Dahlia was beating her, blow after blow, that her heart was almost breaking with mortification. She couldn't say a single word. For quite some time she had felt sure that Sugeng must be doing something wrong to get that much money. But she hadn't had a chance to broach the question to Sugeng again. The last time she had asked him how he made the money Sugeng had said,

'Why do you keep on asking, Hasnah – what's the use? Isn't it enough for you to be getting so much every month now?'

And when Hasnah had insisted further,

'Hasnah, if you think that I'm making this money in some improper way, you must realise that I'm doing it for you. You yourself begged me to do it. Don't you remember giving me a sort of ultimatum, that if you were to have the child we must have a house of our own?'

So she had been silent, unable to answer. Deep down in her heart she admitted the possibility that it was she who had been at fault pushing Sugeng into doing something that was wrong. Perhaps she had insisted too strongly on having a house to themselves. But she'd never expected that Sugeng would get in so deep. And besides, even when she begged for a house, she'd never asked to live in luxury. What she'd imagined was just a house all to themselves, not shared with anyone else, no matter how small, no matter where – even in an alley. A table and chairs bought from a roadside pedlar would have been quite good enough. And she'd have made the little house beautiful just with the radiance of her love as a wife and a mother.

Hasnah had decided then to pray to the Lord that He might protect Sugeng and save their family. Forgive me, oh, Lord, she had prayed in her heart. And then she began blaming herself. Aduh, what have I done to Sugeng to make him like this? I'm to blame, I am the guilty one.

She was startled as she heard the sound of a car horn blowing in front of the house. She stepped outside, and what she had guessed in a flash proved true. With a broad smile, Sugeng, sitting in a car, was pressing the horn and opening the door for Maryam who had come running, dropping her toys. Hasnah forced herself to smile.

'Has, you may congratulate me now. I've been given permission to resign from the service starting with the end of the month, but from tomorrow I won't have to go to work any more.

I was expecting this, and picked up this car at once. Now we're importers. I'm a director of the Mas Mulia[1] Corporation. Ayoh, step in, let's try it out!'

Hasnah got into the car and Sugeng drove out of their yard. Maryam was squealing with pleasure.

'Aduh, Lord, protect my husband,' Hasnah prayed in her heart as the car swung on to the roadway. 'I am the guilty one, it's me that made him become like this!'

Laughing, Sugeng said to Maryam,

'Isn't your papa's car beautiful?'

Murhalim was looking out of the window of a G.I.A.[2] plane flying over Sumatra on his return trip from Padang to Djakarta. He had spent a week organising meetings of the newly established Indonesian Islamic Youth Corps. He felt very satisfied with the whole trip. Especially with his meeting with Achmad, who, as a communist activist, had come from Djakarta to strengthen communist influence in Central Sumatra. They had spent a night in the same hotel. And Achmad had boasted that the meeting he was organising on the same day as Murhalim's would draw a far greater crowd. For the fun of it, they made a bet of twenty-five rupiah. And Murhalim smiled, remembering how Achmad laid down his twenty-five rupiah, admitting defeat. The communist meeting had been a complete flop. Only about fifty people at most had turned up. On the other hand, according to a newspaper estimate, the meeting Murhalim had organised had attracted no less than eight thousand. This event had caused such a stir that several newspapers had carried the news, comparing the attendance of the two meetings.

Murhalim remembered how that evening at supper-time Achmad had said, after paying his debt,

---

1 Glorious Gold.
2 Garuda Indonesian Airways.

'But all this still doesn't prove that the people understand what you're telling them.'

Murhalim laughed.

'Achmad,' he said, 'you communists always make the same mistake. You look at people as though they were cattle, or machines you can manipulate any way you want. It's not enough for men to have a full stomach every day. They also have a soul. You don't admit that the human soul has a life of its own. The communist is an incomplete human being, because he's trained and conditioned to live only in a materialistic world. Human life is rich and varied, it's like a woven fabric with multi-coloured designs: man can love God, he can love his family, he longs to create eternal values – beauty, justice, truth and so forth.'

'Ah, that's a lot of nonsense,' Achmad replied. 'These are the ideas of your decadent bourgeoisie. It seems as though you just won't admit that religion is a socio-political factor, and that the history of religion, whether Christian or Moslem, has demonstrated its essentially reactionary and anti-popular nature. All through human history, religion has always been inseparably connected with enslavement and exploitation by the feudatory and capitalist classes. Look how the Spaniards in spreading the Catholic religion plundered, burnt and ravished the Indians in Mexico, for instance; and how in our own country the Dutch came bringing priests and the cross to help them consolidate their domination.'

'If your communist theory is true, how do you explain so many adherents of Christianity and so many Islamic leaders joining the vanguard of our revolution …?'

'Ah, but what are they doing now for the people? Nothing! Don't you see?' parried Achmad. 'And as for Islamic religious leaders, don't you know that Islam is a faith invented by bourgeois Arab traders – you can see for yourself what Islam means in the Arab countries. All through the ages the masses have always been maltreated, while the feudal cliques lived in extravagant luxury, and now look how many of our own Islamic leaders are in the race to get rich.'

'Ah, there's no use our debating this now, it'll lead us nowhere,' Murhalim answered, smiling. 'You will never accept the fact that God exists, that the evils perpetrated in the name of religion do not mean that the religion itself is either evil or wrong, but that it's men who commit wrongdoings and evil, and that there's no connection between their behaviour and the religion they profess to follow. Religious people who perpetrate deeds forbidden by the Lord break the prescriptions of their own religion, and they deceive themselves if they continue to claim to be religious.'

'That's an easy way out, to dissociate religion from the corruption we see all round us nowadays,' Achmad retorted.

'Many Moslems feel the need to renew and purify the spirit of Islam, to bring it into harmony with the teaching contained in the Holy Qur'an and the Hadith of the Prophet Mohammed,' Murhalim answered.

'Ah, you're still the same,' Achmad replied. 'You don't believe in the progress of human thought.'

'The greater the progress in human thought, the stronger man's conviction that God exists,' Murhalim retorted. 'Look at the history of man's development — at first he had no belief at all; then he began to worship fire, then trees, stones, spirits, gods and finally the one and only God.'

Achmad only laughed.

Murhalim looked out of the window again. Below him spread tall and steep mountain ranges, valleys in greens and yellows, and from time to time the brilliant light of the sun flashed on the surface of streams which gleamed in their winding course below. A yellowish-white road stretched through the countryside. From above it looked like a fine, smooth road. But Murhalim knew how it was in reality: murderous for vehicles, full of pot-holes, deteriorating with every passing year, never repaired and like a thorn in the people's flesh penetrating deeper and getting more painful all the time. And Murhalim recalled the typical resentment of an inhabitant of the region just back from Java who had told him that he had seen how the excellent paved highway between Bogor and Tjipanas was being further widened and improved, while the roads in his region were not being repaired at all. Let alone reconstruction of completely ruined roads, he complained, there isn't even any maintenance to speak of on the passable ones.

He'd experienced it himself as a passenger in a car which took over twenty minutes to cover a distance of five kilometres because the whole road was full of holes. Murhalim felt strongly what terrible mistakes the government leadership of Indonesia had been making. The sources of Indonesia's strength lay with the people of the regions outside of Java. And yet they were the most neglected and maladministered of all. Hundreds of millions were divided up at the Centre among the party big-shots for buying or setting up some large enterprises, but year after year a few pitiful tens of thousands for a small clinic 'couldn't be spared'. He recalled the words of a bupati[1] who had said to him, 'We regional people are treated like beggars. All we can do is beg from the central government. If the Centre has pity on us we get something, if not, well – it can't be helped!'

Murhalim had also heard younger people voicing their dissatisfaction with the Centre with much greater vehemence. There were some who were plainly threatening rebellion, they were just going to establish their own republic. And because the Centre was located in Java, many showed anti-Javanese feelings.

'It's our people who earn the foreign exchange, but it's spent by the Javanese,' someone had said. And Murhalim had answered that it was not the Javanese, or the people in the island of Java who were the enemies of the regional people, but the leaders now in power who were mismanaging the country. And though some of

---

1 Head of a provincial sub-division: regent.

these leaders were Javanese, they also included some local leaders from their own region. The problem was not one of the outer regions versus Java, but of getting a responsible leadership for the state, one capable of furthering the country's development.

But, as he'd seen, it was difficult to convince his friends in Sumatra that this was the basic problem. Murhalim had promised to transmit their feelings and opinions to the leaders in Djakarta, even while he knew that he could not persuade them to attend seriously to these regional problems. At most, he thought, it would go in one ear and out the other.

And suddenly Murhalim felt as though he were utterly powerless, no more than an ant. Here I am, he thought, already thirty-four years old, still unmarried, with no permanent occupation. He began to think about the divisions among the Islamic groups, how backward they were, and how important it was for the Moslem community in Indonesia to be stirred by the dynamism of true Islam. There was too much to do and too few people capable of doing it. Murhalim remembered that he had often been disturbed by a dream of a solitary man in a boat, straining at the oars until his strength gave out, overcome by weakness, unable any longer to fight the rushing current and his boat beginning to drift downstream ....

And Murhalim uttered, *'Ashadu allah illa haillallah waashaduana Muhamadrasullullah!...'*[2]

Suryono leaned back on his seat in his car, closed his eyes and held Iesye's hand. At his side Iesye leaned on his shoulder, looking out over the sea, its rolling black waves breaking into whiteness on the dark-brown sand. The strong wind felt fresh on Iesye's cheek, and the sky above was studded with stars. 'Mood music', as Suryono called it, had been streaming from the car's radio for some time now. Momentarily the interior of the car was

---

2 'There is no God but Allah and Mohammed is his Prophet.'

lit up by the headlights of another car which was turning round to park nearby. The end of the road leading from the Tandjong Priok Yacht Club was crowded with cars that night. In some of them couples kept embracing and kissing, paying no attention to the cars close by and stopping only when the headlights of a passing car suddenly shone in on them. The saté[1] vendors were doing a brisk business on the beach. And the night wind was heavy with the scents of saté spices.

Iesye looked at Suryono's face. He attracted her strongly at that moment. She had an impulse to discard all her doubts and plunge into bliss with Suryono. His face was handsome. The thin moustache accentuated his full lips, though upon closer examination the lines of that well-shaped mouth also showed weakness; it was not the mouth of a strong man, but the sensuous mouth of a man enslaved by his passions.

But neither the lines of that weak mouth nor the shape of Suryono's chin, which was rather pointed, disturbed Ies at that moment. Unconsciously, her hand slipped out of Suryono's and her fingers sank into his wavy hair, slowly winding and unwinding it. Suryono growled as though he were a satisfied tiger.

'If only you'd do this with my hair every day,' he said, without opening his eyes. 'Aduh, I'm really happy tonight.'

He took Ies's neck, drew her head towards his own until their mouths met and Ies, forgetting herself for a moment, let Suryono kiss her mouth, answered his kisses. But the next moment she pulled herself up, deftly withdrawing her lips from Suryono's kiss.

'Why, Ies? More!' Suryono begged.

'There's a car coming,' Ies said, as an excuse.

Suryono, giving in, removed his hand from Ies's neck, embraced her shoulder with his left hand and then his hand slipped downwards and his fingers pressed her breast.

Ies pulled his hand away, saying,

---

1 Bits of meat on small skewers grilled over charcoal.

'Don't, Yon!'

'Ah, why are you like this tonight?' Suryono asked, opening his eyes. 'Such a romantic night, romantic music, you can hear the waves whispering on the beach, and I'm here, and you don't want to. Why?'

Suryono sat up and looked at Ies.

'I don't understand you, Ies,' he then said. 'Sometimes you want to and let me do it, but sometimes I feel you don't want it, as though you really disliked my holding or kissing you.'

Suryono looked at Ies with a peeved expression, displeased but restraining his annoyance.

In such moments his mouth seemed to droop, and his face betrayed more clearly the weakness of his character. And suddenly, as though a pitch-dark place had been lit up in a flash by a bright lamp, Ies seemed able to see deep into the recesses of Suryono's soul, see through his face, through his wavy hair, through his love-filled words and what she saw made Ies shiver as though she were gripped by a fever. And at the same time she was overcome by pity for Suryono. Now she knew why she'd been wavering all this time, back and forth, and she now knew what her answer would be were Suryono to speak. With her feminine intuition she had sensed Suryono's state of mind and knew that tonight he would propose to her. And Ies now felt relieved, strong and confident in herself. All her doubts were gone. And for some unknown reason she suddenly thought of Pranoto. But she could not keep her thoughts on Pranoto because Suryono spoke.

'Ies, I want to tell you something!'

Knowing what she would have to tell him, Ies felt sorry for Suryono, and so she said gently,

'Yes, Yon?'

The softness in her voice conveyed something different to Suryono, and sure of his victory he embraced Ies's shoulder, saying,

'Ies, I love you. Let's get married!'

Suryono tried to draw Ies to himself and kiss her, but Ies, freeing herself of his embrace and moving away a bit, said gently,

'I am sorry, Yon, but I cannot!'

Suryono, completely surprised by her refusal, did not believe what he had heard. He put his hand back on her shoulder, and again trying to draw Ies close to himself said,

'You're joking! It's not true that you don't want to. Don't you love me?' The possibility that Ies didn't love him was inconceivable. After all this time of intimacy ... after the embraces and kisses ... and now Ies saying that she didn't want to marry him, didn't love him ....

'Forgive me, Yon,' Ies said, 'but I've pondered it deeply. You and I – we don't suit each other. Be friends – yes; but marry ... I'm not convinced we'd be happy together.'

Suryono abruptly pushed a radio button and a voice resounded in the stillness of the car, a voice telling of a bewildered heart, not understanding, having lost everything it had believed till now to be true.

'I don't understand!'

And then, deep below his consciousness, his male pride, hurt by Ies's repudiation, began to smart, and as it rose to the surface Suryono felt that now more than ever he loved Ies, even infinitely more than before; that without Ies he couldn't live, and that he would gladly do anything at all if only it would get him Ies. And all these feelings led him to cunning. He felt that Ies would withdraw further were he to press her more strongly, so he changed his tactics.

'I don't know what to say, Ies,' he said. 'Forgive me if I've hurt you. I've offended you. I know that I'm nothing, a man without any status, as a merchant a mere beginner, there's nothing I can offer you but my love.'

'Ah, it's not because of status or wealth that I refuse ....'

'I love you, Ies, without you I cannot live. Give me some clue – why won't you have me?'

Ies looked at Suryono. Were she not as fully aware of Suryono's true character as she was, this was the moment when she'd have surrendered to him. His face gave the impression of absolute honesty, as though he really meant what he was saying – that without Ies he really couldn't live on, as though without Ies his life would remain empty for ever, and that never again would he relish good laughter or have any zest for life.

'Without you my life will be utter desolation for ever,' he was saying.

'Do you want me to be quite frank?' Ies asked.

Still hoping to win her, Suryono said,

'That's what I want. Out of love I can bear whatever you may say.'

'Yon, I'm full of doubts about you because you are full of doubts yourself. One moment I see one kind of Suryono, the next another Suryono appears, and later there is still another Suryono. I really don't know with which of these Suryonos I'm dealing. Also, the quick way you get rich scares me.'

Suryono was quiet. Inwardly he admitted that what Ies had said was right. For hadn't he recently been increasingly driven by doubts and premonitions, as if a disaster were to overtake him any minute? And his sleep was filled with frightful nightmares. In his dreams he would drive a car, alone or with Ies, or with Fatma, or with Dahlia, and while going at top speed he'd suddenly feel that the car was out of control. He'd try to step hard on the brakes but they wouldn't function and the car would keep rushing onwards; his heart would be gripped by terror as the car headed either for an abyss, or towards an inevitable collision with another car, or into a crowd ... and he would scream, and wake up bathed in sweat. And when he realised that it had been only a dream, that he was in his bed at home, he would be filled with relief and glad of his safety, only to be beset the next moment with doubts and questions as to the meaning of the dream.

While remembering all this, the expression of his face was like that of a child who'd lost his way, so that Ies, who was watching him, felt great pity. And if Suryono had stayed quiet just a few minutes longer Ies might easily have changed her mind, her emotion getting the better of her reason. But Suryono decided to strengthen his case by making use of what Ies had said about himself.

'What you're saying is true, Ies,' he said. 'I've been bewildered for quite some time now, full of questions and doubts as to where I belonged in the struggle our people are waging. Sometimes I hear the ringing call of 1945, but then I'm filled with disgust watching the doings of those who claim to be our fighters and I am seized by indifference. Wouldn't you help me find myself again?'

The last phrase struck Ies as empty, meaningless, and strengthened her resolve to refuse Suryono.

'Yon,' she said, 'it's no use.'

From the tone of her voice Suryono at last understood that whatever he might say or do would not reverse Ies's decision. Resentment, anger and spite rose in him and, looking at Ies, he was gripped by an irresistible desire to subject her, to avenge her repudiation of him. He looked at Ies, and her whole body excited his passion beyond control. He threw his arms around the girl, pressed his body against hers, his mouth seeking her lips.

Ies shook her head, and said,

'Don't, Yon, don't, I don't want to!'

But Suryono didn't listen. His hand reached for Ies's breast. Ies tried to resist. They wrestled silently in the car. Ies was about to scream when Suryono suddenly released her, sat up behind the wheel, started the motor, backed up a little and swung the car towards the highway.

'All right, I'll take you home,' he said abruptly.

Ies didn't know it, but while they were struggling Suryono had spotted a patrol of three policemen on bicycles who were admonishing people who were making love in the other cars.

They were both silent during the whole trip to Ies's home. In front of her house Suryono cried,

'Forgive me, Ies, I didn't know what I was doing ...!'

Ies made no reply and rapidly walked to the entrance of her house.

Suryono stepped on the accelerator, the car jerked forward with a loud squeal. He decided to go to Tante Bep's house, to see what he could do there. In front of Tante Bep's house he noticed a betja waiting. Its driver sat in it, smoking. Suryono stopped the car behind the betja, got out and asked the driver,

'Who'd you bring here? Was there a pretty one?'

'I'm waiting for gentlemen visitors,' answered Itam, the betja driver.

Suryono went to the front verandah, and as he opened the door leading inside he stopped, startled. He saw his father, Raden Kaslan, being drawn by the hand by a young woman – Eda, Suryono observed to himself – and then he saw Husin Limbara coming from the back verandah and entering a room with his arm round another young woman. Eve, Suryono again observed to himself.

Suryono retreated slowly, reached the courtyard and, half amused, half shocked, he hastened outside. Then the comical side of what he'd seen struck him, and he laughed inwardly – Father and Husin Limbara – ha-ha-ha!

As he saw the driver again standing near his betja, Suryono thought of something and approached him.

'Bang, these two gentlemen – do they come here often?'

'Often, not quite so, tuan,' Itam answered. 'Just three times with today. They arranged with me steady to bring them here, see.'

'From where do they take your betja?'

'From Hotel des Indes, tuan.'

Suryono gave Itam a Lucky Strike cigarette, laughed softly to himself, got into his car and drove home fast. What sly old fellows, he thought. I hope Fatma is home, he thought also.

He was in good spirits again, as though having seen what his father and Husin Limbara were doing had made his own wrongdoings less wrong.

'By Allah,' he said to himself, 'if the opposition papers only knew this!'

He laughed.

But he didn't enjoy the idea too long, the possible consequences occurred to him at once.

Later, at home, he was more passionate with Fatma than usual. Fatma was both surprised and pleased.

Towards the end of December the rains became much heavier, pouring down day after day, so that many places in Djakarta stood under water. The smaller streets and alleys were a morass of deep mud. The people's hardships increased with the rains.

Dissatisfaction with the government and the parties in power also grew more and more bitter as the difficulties in storing enough of the rice, salt and kerosene needed by the population mounted. The opposition papers carried criticisms of the government and of the government parties that became harsher every day. Several newspapers openly named one party especially, and singled out the names of those of its leaders engaged in the special operations for building up the party's funds. The rising tide of discontent had become so threatening that Husin Limbara decided at last to invite the editor Halim for a conference on how to counteract it.

When the telephone rang at Halim's house that afternoon he was asleep, and relishing his sleep particularly because of the heavy rain outside. When his wife woke him up, saying Husin

Limbara was asking to speak with him, Halim said, without thinking,

'To the devil with him. Tell him I'm sleeping!'

His wife left, but was back a moment later saying,

'He doesn't want to go to the devil; he says he must talk with you, it's very urgent.'

Swearing, Halim got up and went to the telephone.

'Hallo, what is it, pak?' he said in a changed voice which concealed his annoyance.

'Wah, brother Halim, could you come at seven o'clock to my house? It's rather urgent, we must confer. If we can't fix this, all of us are in for a lot of trouble.'

Halim was shocked.

'What happened?'

'Just come along at seven!'

Halim put down the receiver very slowly. His sleepiness vanished with Husin Limbara's words. His newspaper man's instinct quickly told him what was probably troubling Husin Limbara. It was surely the precarious situation of the cabinet and the 'special operations' of the party.

'What is it?' his wife asked as soon as he re-entered their bedroom.

'Husin Limbara is scared,' Halim answered. He told his wife about the possibility of a cabinet crisis, or, at the very least, of a possible big scandal involving the financial activities of Husin Limbara's party.

'But if a scandal breaks, we'll be involved too,' said his wife.

'No need to worry,' Halim replied, 'I've already figured out how we can get ourselves out of it. You see, we're actually gedekt.¹ There's no way of proving that the loan of several million we got has any connection at all with Husin Limbara's party. And luckily I haven't become a party member. The loan agreement

---

1 Lit. 'covered' in Dutch, i.e. protected.

has been drawn up in a purely zakelijk[1] manner, and is based on our newspaper's documented circulation of forty-five thousand ....'

'Which is actually only twelve thousand,' added his wife, laughing.

Halim laughed too.

'But I didn't lie. In the loan application I mentioned that this number was based on the Information Ministry's allotment of newsprint — and it actually allows us forty-five thousand sheets daily.'

But Halim wasn't at all happy to think of his newspaper's steadily declining circulation. He blamed it on the too-active support he was giving the government, and in his conversations with Husin Limbara and other party members he never failed to stress that they had a moral obligation to compensate him properly for his losses.

'Our losses are heavy because our circulation decreases by five or six thousand every month,' Halim would say. 'And only because we defend the government and the party so staunchly.'

But he never mentioned the fact that his newspaper's circulation had actually never gone beyond twenty-five thousand, and that he'd got the newsprint permit from the Ministry of Information only by some special manipulations.

The party leaders had accepted the newsprint allowance as the basis for the loan too, and later had approved another loan for a separate export enterprise he'd also established.

All in all, his decision to help the government and to support the party, far from causing him any loss, had left him pretty well off.

Having explained all this to his wife, both of them laughed gleefully.

'They're really stupid,' said Halim. 'They think they can use us as their tools. But we'll use them. Who cares who is in power, so

1 Businesslike, in Dutch.

long as we get our share?'

No sooner had Halim said this than he suddenly saw very clearly the way he could dissociate himself from the scandal which, he thought, was bound to erupt around the government and Husin Limbara's party. He slapped himself on the forehead, embraced his wife and said joyfully,

'It's all right. I've found the way to get ourselves off the hook.'

And he was so pleased that he pulled his wife off the bed and made her dance with him, turning around the room to the tune of 'The Blue Danube' waltz he was singing at the top of his voice. Thus they whirled about in their bedroom, Halim singing, and his wife laughing.

The rain had grown heavier and suddenly a thunderbolt shook the air outside. It felt very close, but Halim didn't care; he laughed, picked up his wife, flung her down on the bed and then embraced her with great gusto ....

In the evening, at Husin Limbara's house, when Halim intentionally arrived fifteen minutes late – to let them see that they needed him and not he them – he discovered that all the party's big-shots had gathered. All eyes were on him as he entered. In a voice which was far more hospitable than usual, Husin Limbara invited him to sit down.

'Ah, here's our champion,' exclaimed Mr.[2] Hardjo, member of the party's executive council, member of the party's faction in parliament and also holding the post of director-president of a bank established by the party with government funds.

Halim took the empty chair at his side, and looked around with a gay smile on his lips.

Dr. Palau was an old party member from pre-war days, very proud of his record, always bragging about his role as chief of the united command of the Sumatran military forces during the

---

2 Mr. = *Meester*, Dutch title for lawyers.

revolutionary struggle. Since then he had managed to become a millionaire, owner of a rubber factory in Kalimantan,[1] an import concern in Djakarta, a textile factory in Surabaja and was now on the point of acquiring a Dutch motor-car importing business, also in Djakarta. He sat smoking a large cigar, his completely expressionless face giving no clue to his feelings. Next to Dr. Palau sat Mr. Kustomo, also an old party member and the party's strong man behind the scenes, with great influence in Central and East Java, the regions where the party's strength was concentrated. Mr. Kustomo had no official post, wasn't director or board-member of anything, but Halim knew that he was receiving regular honoraria from all sides as legal counsellor for various business concerns established by party members. Halim guessed he was getting at least fifty thousand a month; and probably tax-free too, Halim thought.

Next to Mr. Kustomo sat Mr. Kapolo, a youth group leader who could have exercised a strong influence in the party had he wanted to. But, lacking a strong personality, he was inclined to look for the easiest way out of any difficulties confronting him, and so was very quick to make compromises. On two occasions at the party's congresses he could have been elected party chairman had he been willing to fight, but he'd always been defeated and only made vice-chairman. He had no work to do in the party, but because he was well known as a youth group leader and had a reputation for honesty he was successfully used by the party for propaganda purposes. He was on the boards of three private concerns and acted as chairman of the board to a state enterprise.

At Mr. Kapolo's side sat Sjahrusad, a former communist who had joined Husin Limbara's party. Halim didn't trust him; he was too good a talker. He was also a member of a state bank's board of directors. And next to him sat Mr. Ahmad, the minister.

Looking at the assembled members of the party council,

---

1 Formerly Borneo.

Halim was impressed by the fact that practically all of them had huge incomes from directorships either in their own concerns or in state-owned enterprises.

'Brothers,' Husin Limbara opened the meeting. 'Our conference tonight is extremely important. This isn't an official meeting of the party's executive council, and not all of its members are present – some were unable to come, prevented by other work – but still this meeting is of extreme importance. As you know very well, brothers, the opposition parties are using their sensation-mongering Press to step up their campaign to smear the reputation of the government and the parties supporting it, our party in particular. They started by raising questions about the business transactions, the enterprises, banks and so on now run by our party, in an officially approved and legal manner, of course. However, the public is easily influenced, especially since there are economic difficulties as we must frankly admit – shortages in the supplies of rice, salt and kerosene. These shortages aren't really the present cabinet's fault – it's only fourteen months old – but the fault of the preceding cabinet. But it is, of course, difficult for the people to understand the true state of affairs. You should also know that the other cabinet parties have got wind of some of the special measures taken on behalf of some of our party members, and they have raised questions in the cabinet; in fact, several of their members have already approached our minister directly' (here Husin Limbara turned towards Mr. Ahmad) 'and asked for loans and special licences for themselves, too. And three days ago a minister of another party officially informed our minister that if they didn't get their fair share they'd leave the cabinet. Finally, it's quite possible that the opposition parties have by now managed to collect enough bits of information to put up a story that'll involve the party, the government and ourselves personally in a big scandal.

'We have assembled here tonight to discuss how to prevent this, and that's why I've invited brother Halim too, as the leader of our pro-government press association. I might add for your information, brothers, that a cabinet crisis isn't likely to break if we manage to nip the scandal in the bud. For the time being, an eventual cabinet crisis has been postponed by the approval of some special licences for leaders of the other parties. But this can't go on. In the end the issuing of loans and licences in such numbers will completely destroy the government's planning.'

'Ah, why be afraid of a scandal? What kind of scandal?' responded Dr. Palau. 'Why be afraid of the opposition? We're only doing what's going on everywhere else. The party in power always helps its own members and friends first. The same thing happens in any other country. Suppose the opposition parties were in power, wouldn't we be left out completely? Just let them go on fuming. Aiih, Pak Husin, nothing's happened so far yet, and here we are already terrified! Say, once you dare to do something you have to be brave enough to take the consequences!' And Dr. Palau slapped his chest, inhaled on his cigar and let out a dense cloud of smoke.

The others laughed. They were already quite accustomed to Dr. Palau's boastful and cocky talk. He had been made member of the council just to please the people of his region and several resistance groups who still regarded him as their leader.

'Even though there's some truth in Dr. Palau's words,' said Mr. Kustomo in a calm but authoritative voice, 'we must still consider the problem carefully and thoroughly. Politics is a high art, and good politics means heading off trouble long before it can happen.'

'That's true too,' said Dr. Palau. 'But as for me, when an enemy comes, I'll get him!'

They laughed again.

'Wouldn't it be advisable to discontinue all the activities mentioned by brother Husin Limbara as soon as possible?' asked Mr. Kapolo.

'Certainly, we've already decided to stop as soon as we reach the thirty-million-rupiah party-fund we're aiming at. And we're almost there. If we could work on undisturbed for another three months we'd be through,' Husin Limbara replied.

'If that's the case, attack must be answered by attack, and scandal by scandal, and here's our champion,' said Dr. Palau, looking at Halim.

'Hmm,' said Halim. 'These easy problems of yours can be difficult. Before I give you my ideas I'd like to know from you, brothers, approximately how long it will be before this cabinet is finished.'

'Ah.' Husin Limbara coughed, looked at Mr. Kustomo and Mr. Kustomo nodded.

'The party hasn't made an official decision as yet,' said Husin Limbara and continued, 'But even so it's quite possible that we'll return the cabinet's mandate ourselves, depending on the circumstances. Because with popular dissatisfaction growing by the day, on account of the rice, salt and kerosene shortages, it's going to be hard for the party in power to face the people at election time. People usually turn to the opposition parties in hopes of improvement. So the idea of returning the mandate on a certain pretext at a certain time before the elections, is definitely being entertained. We'll just let the opposition parties take charge of the government for a few months before the general elections – with proper assurance of course that their power will be short-lived.'

The little wheels in Halim's brain were turning rapidly and smoothly evaluating the information he just received in relation to his own interests, how best to preserve them in the face of possible catastrophe.

'And what would happen if the opposition parties managed to improve the economic conditions while they're in power?' asked Halim. 'Wouldn't they win the general elections? Besides that, they could influence the outcome of the elections in a number of ways just by being in power.'

'According to our calculations, no new government could possibly improve our country's condition within a period of six or eight months – that's approximately the interval we've in mind. And we needn't worry about the opposition parties influencing the elections. Our party has a firm hold on people in very important positions; in the civil service, in the information field and so on. We can't lose this all at once. Ah, I don't have to worry about that, at least!'

'So generally we can assume that within about two months we should know for sure whether the cabinet will continue, or whether there'll be a crisis?' Halim asked.

'More or less,' said Husin Limbara. 'And so the most important problem now is to protect ourselves from the attacks of the opposition.'

'If so, that's easy,' said Halim.

Now he knew what line to follow to save himself.

'We can only fight the opposition groups who want to stir up a scandal about us by raising one about them, much bigger than these "specials" they're trying to pin on us. We'll have to step up our earlier accusations that the opposition leaders were selling out our country to foreign capitalists and imperialists and implicate some big names too. Leave it to me. But, of course, this will involve a considerable sum of money. Probably about two hundred thousand for a start,' said Halim.

He was fishing, watching the faces of Husin Limbara and Mr. Kustomo.

'Pay him then; we're ready!' exclaimed Dr. Palau.

As soon as Dr. Palau had spoken, Halim knew he'd get the sum he'd asked for.

Halim didn't stay on long after this. He excused himself on the pretext of having to finish some writing at his office for tomorrow morning's edition.

Outside the rain was still dripping, but in his car Halim was whistling 'The Blue Danube', and in his head it kept ticking – idiots, idiots, idiots.

The scandal mentioned by Husin Limbara exploded sooner than anticipated. Two days after the meeting at his house, the opposition newspapers carried in large banner headlines the news of the 'special operations' of some of the government parties, Husin Limbara's in particular. Husin Limbara's name was mentioned as 'minister' of financial and economic affairs behind the scenes; this was accompanied by a list of the business establishments involved and their presidents, directors or trustees – all members of government parties. The name of Raden Kaslan appeared in connection with five concerns, Husin Limbara's with three, Suryono's with one. Sugeng too was mentioned as involved in an import concern called Mas Mulia. According to the reports, it had been approved by the Ministry of Justice within two weeks, and had obtained its importing licence from the Ministry of Economic Affairs within five days. The names of Dr. Palau, Mr. Hardjo, Mr. Kapolo and even of Mr. Ahmad, the minister, were also mentioned as trustees of a certain bank, which, according to the opposition Press, was contrary to the existing regulations. The newspapers printed pictures of them all as well as stories about their luxurious cars and houses in the city and in the hills of the Puntjak.

Husin Limbara came to Halim's office in person. In self-defence Halim started to attack, saying that he'd often warned his friends to exercise self-restraint, not to display their wealth in public by buying two or three cars, building large houses and even taking a second wife (actually he'd never said this to anyone). But now it was too late, and the only way out was to get the counter-campaign going. 'And I still haven't received the two hundred thousand you promised me!' Halim added.

Husin Limbara immediately picked up the telephone to contact Raden Kaslan. Raden Kaslan wasn't there. Finally he got assurances from Mr. Hardjo that the two hundred thousand would be sent to Halim by noon.

'Nah, now it's up to you, brother,' said Husin Limbara as he was leaving. After closing the door of his office, Halim laughed and returned to his desk.

He sat down, put a sheet of paper into his typewriter and began writing an editorial attacking the opposition groups.

' ... Currently the opposition groups and their newspapers are demonstrating even more clearly than before that they have absolutely no sense of responsibility towards our country and our people. With a total lack of scruples, they are flinging unfounded and indiscriminate charges and abuse at the government and the parties supporting it. And this opposition clique is shameless enough not even to hesitate in disclosing the private lives of the pro-government parties' foremost leaders, discussing their private connections with enterprises which are in no way involved with government policies.

'Even though the cabinet is only fourteen months old, it is being blamed for the shortages in rice, kerosene and salt – shortages for which it's supposed to be responsible. Even the most ignorant person, if he's any common sense left, can clearly see that it's not the present cabinet that should be blamed for these shortages, but the preceding cabinet, which was led by the opposition parties themselves.

'It's quite clear from the way they're slandering the present cabinet and undermining the prestige of the pro-government party headers, that the oppositions' tactics and aims are just the same as the foreign capitalists' and imperialists' who don't want our country to advance. As our President mentioned himself, in a speech he made a little while ago, he has received reports about the existence of a Plan A and a Plan B for the subversive activities being conducted in our homeland by foreign elements and one about the leaders of certain political parties who are getting money from foreign powers to betray our country.

'This newspaper therefore proposes to publish in the near future the names of these party leaders who have received money from foreign powers and to expose their connections with the subversive activities mentioned by the President.

'The government has been patient with the opposition parties far too long, with their newspapers continually abusing the freedom of the Press and hiding behind their democratic rights to conduct activities which are endangering the state. The Attorney General should take speedy action against those who abuse their democratic rights to destroy our beloved Republic and our Proclamation of Independence.

'It is also obvious why the attacks of the opposition on the government, and personal affairs of several individual cabinet ministers, have reached a peak just at the time when these leaders are attending the debates on West Irian at the United Nations. Their actions coincide with Dutch efforts to ruin the reputation of the Indonesian Republic abroad in order to defeat Indonesia's international struggle to regain possession of West Irian. As to just how closely the moves of the opposition and its Press are geared to these Dutch activities, the reader can easily draw his own conclusions.

'It is really regrettable that there are Indonesians who, because they are set on overthrowing the present cabinet, are prepared to sell themselves to foreign powers.

'People, beware!'

Halim chuckled, re-reading his editorial, and said to himself – Two hundred thousand is cheap enough for such an editorial!

He pushed a button on his desk, and the office messenger

appeared. Halim gave him the editorial.

'Take it to the editorial office and tell then to set it up! And tell Bung Sidompol to come here right away.'

Halim leaned back in his chair, very pleased with himself, as if he'd just finished a very good piece of work. There was a knock on the door, and after Halim called, 'Come in,' the door opened and Sidompol, the news editor, walked in.

'Sit down, 'Pol!' said Halim. 'There's some work to be done, along your line!'

He told Sidompol about the editorial he'd just written, linking the opposition and its Press with foreign subversive activities and hooking up Plan A and Plan B, once mentioned by the President, with certain leaders who were selling out their country.

He continued,

'Now you compose a front-page report, as though we'd obtained it from reliable sources close to the State Investigation Service, and so on; give it a sensational headline like – Opposition Leaders Involved in Subversive Activities? Authorities Conducting Intensive Investigation. But make sure there's nothing in it the opposition could sue us for. But the report should be suggestive enough for the readers to reach the conclusions we want. Well, that's it!'

'Okay, boss!' Sidompol got up at once and left the room.

Alone in his office again, Halim opened a desk drawer, got out a bottle of whisky and poured himself a glass, adding some ice-water from a thermos bottle. Then he emptied the glass at a gulp.

He laughed inwardly again, thinking of Sidompol actually writing the news-story they'd just made up. Halim recalled that his was the only newspaper that had been willing to employ Sidompol. The other newspapers had refused because during the revolution he'd been a traitor. At first he'd been a journalist supporting the Republic; then later he went over to N.I.C.A., working first on van Mook's staff and then with N.I.C.A.'s information service. Finally he'd gone so far as to publish a paper, subsidised by N.I.C.A., which abused the Republic daily.

When Halim was reproached by his fellow journalists for being willing to employ this ex-N.l.C.A. man, he'd answer them scornfully,

'He's my loyal dog now. He knows mine's the only place where he can get work.'

And Halim smiled to himself. So long as Sidompol worked for his newspaper he could make him write anything he wanted. Then, remembering something, he picked up the inter-office phone and said,

"Pol, don't forget to send the report you're writing to the other pro-government papers, our other members!'

It was noon; Saimun walked wearily home from the police office. He'd intended to ask for a form to fill out for getting his driving licence. But after half an hour, with a horde of people crowding in front of the window and hearing stories about the difficult tests one had to pass, he suddenly lost heart. He saw people dressed twenty times better than himself – he was in shorts and a worn-out shirt, even torn at the collar, and without shoes or sandals.

Actually he'd wandered into the police station to see what it was like there. But what he saw frightened him and he felt very small, very weak, with no hold on anything, hopeless. Aduh, it's my fate, Saimun thought. Once you're a little man you remain a little man always, you can't become anything until you die. And he suddenly longed for his village; life in the village was better and happier – if only there weren't any grombolan left to interfere. Just to smell the freshly hoed earth again and be sprayed by the falling rain, to walk at dawn on the dew-cooled grass, the dew wetting the feet, to feel the rays of the morning sun warming the whole body, to bathe in the river, to fish in the river, to snare a turtle dove, to eat a roasted corn-cob just picked from its stalk, to sleep on the grass under a mango tree. Tears stood in his eyes, when all at once he was shocked into consciousness by a heavy shove on the shoulder and a man passing on a bicycle shouted,

'Eh, look where you're going, bung, didn't you hear my bell?'

Saimun was badly shaken. Lost in his thoughts he hadn't noticed that he'd strayed into the middle of the road. And startled as he was, he tried to run to the side of the street, and was almost run over by a passing convertible. The car brushed his thigh, not too hard, but hard enough to make him fall on the pavement. The car stopped, its brakes screeching, and Suryono got out. Several cars behind him stopped too.

'Wait here a moment!' Suryono said to Dahlia, who sat at his side. 'There's always something that gets in the way!'

Suryono was very annoyed – he had just been taking Dahlia to Tante Bep's. And, even if he hadn't hurt the man he'd hit badly, it would still mean explanations to the police, and who knows what else. And the day would be wasted. But as he was approaching him, the man he'd hit was already on his feet and brushing down his trousers. A passing policeman stopped and came over.

Suryono was very glad to see that the man wasn't hurt at all, and decided not to raise a rumpus.

As he came close he heard the man say to the policeman,

'It was my fault, pak!'

The policeman turned to Suryono, saluted him, and Suryono said,

'It's all right, lucky nothing happened!'

'It's my fault, pak!' Saimun repeated.

Suryono took a five-rupiah note out of his pocket, feeling suddenly that the man he'd hit should be given a present. Since no harm had been done, he could continue with Dahlia straight to Tante Bep's house.

'It's all right, nothing happened!' said Suryono.

The policeman could not refrain from giving Saimun a last

bit of advice.

'Look out, though, when you're crossing. You're lucky nothing happened!'

Back in the car Suryono said to Dahlia,

'It's lucky nothing happened to him!' And he pinched Dahlia's thigh which was pressed close to his own.

Saimun hastened away from the place where he'd almost been killed. His gloom changed to a kind of joy. Five rupiah in his pocket meant a lot of money to him. What a good heart the tuan who owns that car has, Saimun thought, and his appearance shows it too .... It was my fault but he wasn't angry at me, even gave me a present, Saimun continued thinking; not like some other tuans, they'd just finish you off with their scolding. Saimun thought, wouldn't it be wonderful to have a master like that – whatever he'd order me to do, I'd gladly do it.

In front of the telephone building, across from the President's palace, Saimun heard Itam's voice calling him. Betja drivers usually stopped and gathered there around a food-vendor's stall. Several were eating, while others sat in their betjas waiting for passengers. Some were playing paper dominoes on the ground; and others squatted, gambling for money. Itam sat on the bench before the stall, he'd just begun to eat.

''Mun, where're you coming from?'

Saimun remembered that he hadn't eaten yet, sat down near Itam and ordered a plate of nasi ramas.[1] He told Itam of his morning's experiences.

'Aduh, 'Tam,' he said, ''t looks like I can't become a driver if things like this. My reading also not smooth yet, and how to remember in your head all the road signs, all the rules of traffic? Just looking at the police who give examinations and we're 'lready full of terror.'

'But that tuan in the car, he was very good, 'Mun,' said Itam.

---

1 Mixed rice, i.e. with side-dishes mixed in.

'Not often find a man like this. Most people who drive cars, 'lmost kill you — they're so stuck-up. As if they alone own the road. We here're just like dogs. So many times 'lready I want to fight with drivers of these showy cars. If we go slow they're angry, keep blowing horns, we must be like machines of course, push the betja quick-quick? If not go off to side fast enough, they scold us. 'T's sad to be a little man!'

In the last days of December the tensions between the govern-ment and the opposition parties, the newspapers supporting the cabinet and the opposition Press, had reached a climax. Halim's editorial and the report he distributed provoked a violent reaction. One of the opposition papers exposed the 'special' game of the minister of Husin Limbara's party, gave Sugeng's name as the ministry official involved in these special manipulations who had later left the ministry to become director of an importing concern and mentioned also the speed with which the concern had obtained the approval of the Ministries of Justice and Economic Affairs. To this scandal a new scandal was added: one of the cabinet ministers allegedly was selling his signature, granting foreigners admission to Indonesia, and the opposition papers were asking: 'Who is selling Indonesia to the foreigners — the government or the opposition?'

Hasnah could do nothing but cry all day, and would hardly speak to Sugeng any more. Sugeng seemed completely distracted, saying to Hasnah every minute,

'Don't worry, we'll be protected by the party!'

'Aduh,' answered Hasnah, 'why did you join them?'

'Didn't you insist that we move to another house?' Sugeng snapped angrily in reply, regretting it the next moment seeing how Hasnah's expression changed to one of distress as she confessed her fault. But then Sugeng also felt a kind of pleasure in unloading the whole guilt on Hasnah.

'If you hadn't insisted on a house, I wouldn't have done all this!' Sugeng said.

'It's my fault, it's my fault, I am the accursed one!' lamented Hasnah, sobbing. 'Aduh, why wasn't I patient, why did I have to ask for a house, forgive me, Lord ....'

And Hasnah wept, and wept, and wept ....

Halim soon sniffed out that the cabinet couldn't last any longer. Those parties within the cabinet who had apparently not shared in the distribution of 'specials', and were disturbed by the scandal-ous disclosures of clearly proven facts, pressed Husin Limbara's party strongly to surrender the cabinet's mandate. There was a strong probability that the Prime Minister would return his mandate before Christmas or at the beginning of the new year.

And Halim decided quickly to dissociate himself from the collapse of the cabinet he'd supported so far. He wrote an editorial for the December 24th Christmas Eve edition of his newspaper which ran as follows:

'Ever since the present cabinet was formed, this newspaper has never tired of warning and urging the cabinet to make a serious effort to secure the public good and to devote special attention to the needs of the regions outside Java. Up to now we've given strong support to the cabinet, because we disliked seeing cabinets change from minute to minute as in the past, and believed that this cabinet should be given proper time to prove its abilities. This cabinet has managed to obtain satisfactory results in a number of fields. This is especially true of the international world (which continues to shrink because of technical progress in air communications) where the government has won unprecedented and brilliant successes. The name of Indonesia has become famous all over the world, and in the United Nations our voice commands the attention of all countries.

'However, there's truth in the old saying, "There's no ivory without a crack", and although we don't agree with all the accusations launched by the opposition newspapers against the cabinet and the parties supporting it, the government's shortcomings in the questions of rice, kerosene and salt supplies, for instance, have to be admitted. Apart from this, the cabinet parties have not been selective and vigilant enough about their own members. As a result they have succumbed to temptations and abused their positions in order to enrich themselves.

'If a cabinet crisis, as we hear, is indeed inevitable, it can't be helped — let the cabinet fall for the sake of our country's and people's welfare. A further heightening of tensions between the government parties and the opposition parties, if permitted to continue, can only endanger our state and close the door to wider inter-party co-operation. Wouldn't it therefore be only right if this cabinet did indeed surrender its mandate? A new cabinet could speedily be formed which would assure firm co-operation between the parties, and harmony and peace for the nation.'

Halim was very satisfied with this. That morning he re-read the editorial, which had appeared in his newspaper, several times. Husin Limbara couldn't be angry. I haven't said anything that could commit me, and we're opening up the possibility for supporting some new cabinet. Ha-ha-ha-ha, Halim laughed, extremely pleased.

Dahlia had not been feeling well for a week and in the last few days had felt nauseous. She knew that her monthly period was a week overdue. While taking a bath, Dahlia felt her belly and decided to visit a doctor to find out whether or not she was pregnant. The trouble was that she wasn't sure who might have caused her pregnancy — Suryono, Sugeng or maybe that Chinese whom she'd accidentally met on the street, who took her to town, paid her five hundred rupiah and then saw her home, but whom she'd never seen again since.

If it wasn't the Chinese it wouldn't really matter, thought Dahlia, Idris might be quite pleased thinking he had begotten a child, but if the baby were to have slit-eyes ... Dahlia laughed, amused by this possibility. She decided to go to a doctor whom she knew was prepared to perform a guaranteed abortion for a thousand rupiah flat. She'd be able to get the money from either Suryono or Sugeng, just by telling either of them that he was responsible; maybe she'd even ask both. Dahlia became cheerful again, finished her bath and attended to her body which had undergone no change as yet.

Raden Kaslan was preparing to leave for abroad at the beginning of the new year. He told Fatma that because he had been the author of the plan for the raising of funds on behalf of the party's election campaign, it was better for him to be out of the country for the time being, and said that Fatma could join him in Europe later.

During these last days of the year Suryono stayed mostly at home. He didn't go to the meetings at Pranoto's house any more since he was ashamed to meet his old friends. Practically every night he was pursued by the nightmare of the car whose brakes suddenly gave out.

Only Fatma remained calm as if she didn't care at all about what might happen.

A kind of panic broke out among the leaders of Husin Limbara's party. It was not revealed to the outside world, however. The party newspapers were ordered to continue their violent attacks on the opposition and to say that the cabinet would continue to do its duty and that no government party was planning to have the mandate returned.

Halim's treachery had badly affected Husin Limbara, the more so because he'd been bringing Halim's name before the party leadership to help him get a bank loan and other financial support.

Then, on December 30th, the Prime Minister returned the mandate to the President. Two government parties had decided on December 29th to withdraw their ministers from the cabinet as they no longer wished to be responsible for the government's policies.

The cabinet fell.

City Report

Since noon the rain had been pouring down. But it seemed to Zakaria that instead of letting up it was becoming even heavier. The sky over the city was dark and from time to time there were outbursts of deafening thunder, with flashes of lightning cutting through the heavy, billowing, murky clouds.

Zakaria sought shelter under the roof of an ice-depot. Several other people stood there with him. Zakaria's stomach felt very empty; hunger had been gnawing at his guts for some time.

He was quite exhausted. He had just got a new job as an office messenger, and had to walk from his home to work and back again. It usually took him about three-quarters of an hour to get home; he usually got back by three o'clock and could then eat and still the gnawing hunger. But now it was almost five o'clock and the rain wouldn't stop. He didn't dare walk home in the rain for fear of becoming ill, and, more importantly, if the jacket he was wearing got wet, he wouldn't have another dry one to put on tomorrow for work at the office, unless he just wore a shirt. But his shirt was already rather worn and had several holes.

One after another the people who waited together with him went off, saying,

'Ah, this rain won't stop until night. So we'll get wet!'

Finally Zakaria was left all by himself. Near magrib time, the city was already dark, and the rain was still pouring, but Zakaria felt that it was getting lighter. By six o'clock the rain began to ease off and fifteen minutes later it stopped altogether. Relieved, Zakaria stepped out to go home. Though he felt weak, the hunger didn't bother him any more. The street was flooded with stagnant water, and Zakaria decided to cross at once.

But no sooner did he start crossing the street than a car was blowing its horn at him. Zakaria saw it approaching at great speed and jumped back to the pavement. But apparently the car's driver intentionally passed close to the pavement so that the water whirled up by its wheels splashed Zakaria from head to foot. Zakaria had jumped away hoping to avoid the spray, but was too late. The front of his jacket and trousers were soaking wet, his face and his hair were dripping.

Dumbfounded, Zakaria just stood. Then, realising that the calamity he had tried to prevent by waiting out the rain had overtaken him after all, he burst into tears which streamed down his cheeks and mingled with the rainwater splashed there already. Then a wave of violent and bitter hatred swept through his whole being. Zakaria looked at all passing cars with glaring, hate-filled eyes. And he cursed all people who had cars.

January

$\mathcal{I}$N THE first days of the new year Hasnah's baby began stirring restlessly in her womb, and she feared it would be born prematurely. Sugeng was seldom home now, day or night. Sometimes he stayed away all night. Hasnah felt the distance between them growing all the time. And all she could do was to cry and cry, always accusing herself – it was she who'd ruined Sugeng, she who'd caused the calamity that had befallen them. All the luxurious objects in the house served only to remind her of her trouble and make her even sadder. And tears she could not restrain filled her eyes every moment.

The doctor had warned her to control her emotions or she might endanger herself and especially the child she was carrying. When Sugeng was home, she hardly dared to speak to him. She'd seen how it consoled him, even cheered him, to have her admit that she was the one to blame for his wrongdoings.

Meanwhile Sugeng was busy transferring the titles of their possessions to other members of his family. He sold his car and invested the money in a business officially headed by a relative. A new house he'd just built in Kemajoran Baru was likewise registered under the name of another relative after a legal sales agreement had been drawn up, though of course no actual transaction had taken place. 'If anything happens,' Sugeng said, 'we'll at least save what little we have now.'

One day he asked Hasnah whether she'd mind if he also sold the refrigerator and changed the big radio in the living-room for a smaller set instead.

'We'll do without a refrigerator for the time being,' Sugeng said. 'We'll just buy ice.' Then he added, 'We'll get at least forty or fifty thousand for it and we'll put the money away somewhere else.'

Hasnah left everything to Sugeng. The refrigerator and the big radio set were sold. And Hasnah was even somewhat relieved not to see them in the house any longer.

But even so Hasnah could not stop crying.

'Aduh, it's my fault. Why did I keep asking for a house? I only asked for it so we'd be happier and love each other better. I didn't ask for a house to make Sugeng do wrong. I wasn't asking for luxury and riches.'

It was beyond Hasnah's understanding why their life had become what it now was. The days ahead seemed dark to her as the new year was coming. Something shadowy and frightening seemed to hang over their home, poised to drop down and crush them all at any moment; ready to destroy even the last sparks of their happiness, like Maryam's hearty laughter as she played. And it was only occasionally that Hasnah managed to forget it all and cling to her memories of the warm and intimate life she'd had with Sugeng in the past. But then it had all been long ago, in a very different world, she felt. And she'd become even more dejected, bursting into tears again and again, until her eyes were red and swollen. And when Maryam stopped laughing and, coming to her, asked, 'Why are you crying, Mother?' it seemed as if Maryam's world too had become very dark.

On January 5th Raden Kaslan left the country after a farewell party given by Husin Limbara and several members of the party council. Suryono and Fatma took him to Kemajoran Airport. Returning from the airport, Suryono said to Fatma in the car,

'Now Father's gone. We're left here. What are we going to do? I can't stand Djakarta any longer. Especially for the next few weeks.'

'Where do you want to go?' asked Fatma.

'Anywhere, who cares? But I don't want to go alone!' said Suryono. Then a thought struck him, and he said,

'Why don't the two of us go off together?'

'Ah, and what will people say?'

Fatma smiled, challenging him. Suryono understood.

'Who cares what people say?' he answered. 'Why stop half-way? What do we care, whatever happens?'

Fatma smiled. She realised that if she were to go with Suryono, a new bond would grow between them. The showdown with Raden Kaslan they'd managed to avoid so far was sure to come and would have to be faced. To go off together was different from being secretly in bed together at home. If she went off with Suryono she couldn't possibly remain Raden Kaslan's wife. Nor could Suryono very well continue to be his father's son. If I marry Suryono, Fatma thought, I certainly won't lose anything. He's young, handsome, has money. I'm rich enough myself, too. Even if we have to separate somewhere along the line I won't have lost anything.

'Why aren't you saying anything?' asked Suryono.

Had Suryono ever thought of marrying her? Fatma wondered. She decided that it hadn't entered his mind. She suspected that for him all this was still playing around. By Allah, even stealing his father's wife was still 'just fooling around' for Suryono!

'Don't you want to come with me?' Suryono pressed.

In his unnerving state of constant doubt and anxiety, Suryono now felt that the only way for him to regain peace of mind and soul was to go off some place with Fatma, hide there from the world and find release from all the fears and premonitions of disaster which pursued him, by drowning them in an orgy of passion and lust; it was as if he could in this way freely express his real disregard and indifference to society, politics, the parties whom he considered responsible for the disasters he felt were threatening him, threatening his welfare, threatening his very life. By defying what people thought, by asserting himself, he'd be free from the standards and judgements of others.

'Fatma, let's go,' said Suryono.

Fatma smiled again. She knew she could now do anything she wanted with Suryono.

'Well, anyway,' she said, 'we still have to consider what people will say.'

'Why worry about people?' retorted Suryono. 'If we want to, we'll do it.'

'Haven't you thought what it may lead to?'

'Who cares what it leads to?'

'Don't you think of your father?'

'What about Father?'

'This is sure to mean our divorce.'

'Ah, Father, why care about Father? When trouble came, as it did now, he just left. He's left us in the lurch now. But earlier it was he who persuaded us to join him.'

'You're his son.'

'What kind of father abandons his son when there's trouble?'

Inwardly Suryono now felt greatly relieved, even satisfied. Of course all this was his father's fault. It was because of his father that he'd got involved. He himself had never dreamed of piling up money when he first returned from abroad. It was his father's fault. Compared with what his father had done, his own affair with Fatma was nothing.

'If your father divorces me, will you marry me?' Fatma then said.

'I'm ready to marry you this very moment,' Suryono answered quickly.

Fatma suddenly felt herself very powerful, as though a man's fate were in her hands and she could twist it any way she wanted. The life of Raden Kaslan, her husband, and the life of Suryono, his son, were now completely in her power. It was gratifying to feel this power.

'How about it, Fatma?' Suryono urged again.

'Let's talk it over a bit more at home,' said Fatma. 'Why the hurry? We've lots of time.'

Ever since the Prime Minister had returned his mandate, political activity in Djakarta had reached a new pitch of intensity. Though inter-party conflicts continued to rage, behind the scenes several of the parties which had supported the retiring cabinet were establishing contact with the opposition parties. It looked more than likely that a new cabinet could be formed quickly, most probably without the participation of Husin Limbara's party.

In Husin Limbara's party the executive council had split in two. Some of the younger leaders at last dared to challenge the policies of the top leadership, and Husin Limbara was singled out for particularly violent attacks. In return, he even went so far as to threaten to resign if the party wouldn't give his policies complete and unconditional support. But then, towards the end of a council meeting, Husin Limbara was suddenly seized by a heart ailment. His physician advised him to take a vacation and not to work too hard. Husin Limbara accepted his advice and, greatly relieved, left Djakarta for a rest in his native village in the mountains of East Java.

Editor Halim changed the line of his paper completely and ordered his news editor Sidompol to interview the leaders of the opposition parties whose names were being mentioned as candidates for posts in the new cabinet. His editorials now contained criticisms of some of the old cabinet's policies and placed the whole blame for the rice, salt and kerosene shortages at its doorstep. When a number of readers sent in angry letters reminding the editor that he'd previously defended the old cabinet to the hilt and had asserted that it bore none of the responsibility for these shortages, Halim gave orders that none of these letters were to be printed.

The new cabinet was formed on January 12th. Husin Limbara's party was not in it. Halim immediately wrote an editorial welcoming the new cabinet and promising to support it as long as it was going to work for the welfare of the people and the state.

January 16th. All morning Hasnah had felt her time was very near. Sugeng had left the house early in the morning and Hasnah was waiting for him to come back and take her either to the doctor or to the hospital. If this was really the beginning of her labour, the baby would be a month early – the doctor had said it was due in February. But Hasnah had already foreseen the possibility of the baby's premature birth because of her own poor state of health during the last few months. Towards noon Hasnah could no longer bear the pains that now came at regular intervals and decided to go directly to the hospital. She asked a neighbour to telephone her doctor, quickly packed into a small suitcase the things needed for the baby, told the babu to tell Sugeng that she'd left for the hospital and, after kissing Maryam while tears streamed down her cheeks, went off to the hospital in a betja, accompanied by her friend.

She was taken at once to the delivery-room. The hospital doctor made a preliminary examination. And then he telephoned Hasnah's doctor. Half an hour later he arrived. He told Hasnah that it did look as though the baby wanted to be born. His face was a bit gloomy.

She was taken to the operating-room of the maternity ward. The neighbour who'd brought her to the hospital pressed her hand and went home.

Sugeng only returned home at five in the afternoon. Hasnah had left about noon. When he learned about it from the babu he jumped into a betja and hurried to the hospital. As he reached the maternity ward he saw the doctor who'd been attending Hasnah, ready to leave.

'How is it, Doctor?' Sugeng asked with a heavy heart.

'The mother is well, but we couldn't save the baby,' said the doctor, pressing his hand.

Sugeng was overcome by a feeling of weakness.

'May I see her?' he asked the doctor.

The doctor took him to a 'second class' room; a four-bed room with only two beds occupied. On one of them a woman who'd just had her child lay reading. Opposite her lay Hasnah.

'Just look at her, don't try to talk!' said the doctor. 'She's too weak.'

The doctor left Sugeng. Sugeng stood near the bed, looking at Hasnah as though he was nailed to the spot. He was very pale, all blood seemed to have been drained from his veins. His lips were as white as a sheet, and low, choking moans escaped from them. Tears welled up in his eyes, streamed down his cheeks. Then Sugeng stooped to grasp Hasnah's hand. He sat down on the edge of the bed, and remained there silently, until Hasnah opened her eyes and looked at him. She tried to smile at him with her eyes, didn't quite succeed and closed them again while Sugeng whispered to her softly,

'Has, Has, it was all my fault, not yours; I should have known when to stop!'

Crushing remorse overwhelmed Sugeng till his heart felt like bursting. He remembered all his wrongdoings, starting with his yielding to the temptation to make a lot of money, and then still more money, and later playing around with women because he had too much money and didn't really know what to do with himself. And he now saw clearly how cruelly he had treated Hasnah, piling the whole responsibility and guilt upon her shoulders because she'd been urging him to get a house for themselves. He saw now that Hasnah's plea was but the desire of a devoted wife who longed for a good family life, undisturbed by other people; and that it was he, Sugeng, who was guilty of going far beyond what Hasnah had wished for. He remembered how happy they'd been when they were newly married, and later when Maryam came, and though they'd led a simple life they'd been at peace with no dark clouds threatening them.

I beg you to forgive me, Has, Sugeng was murmuring in his heart. I want to start all over again; I want to start clean again; if you'll forgive me I can face everything – whatever may happen. I won't run away, I'll be strong if only you'll go on loving me.

As though she'd heard the murmur in Sugeng's heart, Hasnah opened her eyes and looked at him. Their eyes met, and Sugeng bent down and kissed her forehead. Then Hasnah closed her eyes again. Sugeng sat very still holding her hand, oblivious to everything that was going on around him and the bed where Hasnah lay until a nurse came, tapped him on the shoulder and said that it was time for him to leave.

January 20th was Pranoto's birthday, and he'd invited his friends over to celebrate. That evening, in his room, he re-read the letter he'd got from Connie the day before, although he'd read it over several times already. Connie never forgot his birthday. After congratulating him, she'd gone on to write that since he'd now reached the age of thirty-four she hoped he'd be able to look at things more sensibly and propose to her at last.

I'm not getting any younger, Connie wrote, *I'll be twenty-eight in July of this year – an unpopular old maid, longing for a lover who doesn't return her love. How I long to be with you to celebrate your birthday, just the two of us together – only you and I.*

Pranoto stopped reading when he heard a knock on the door. The babu announced that the guests had begun to arrive. He went quickly to the front room and saw that the first to arrive was Ies.

'Congratulations on reaching old age!' Ies joked, and Pranoto answered,

'I feel greatly honoured tonight, because you're my first guest. This promises me happiness.'

He seized Iesye's hand, and as they looked at each other Pranoto saw something in the radiance of her eyes which completely flustered him. He let her hand go and said,

'What'll you have to drink? I'll go get it.'

'Anything, so long as it isn't alcoholic,' Ies replied.

Pranoto went inside, still disturbed by what he'd seen shining in Ies's eyes. And while he was pouring Coca-Cola into a glass, he suddenly remembered, he'd seen the same radiance before … in Connie's eyes!

'My God!' The English expression escaped involuntarily from his lips.

Ies, for me — it's impossible. Isn't she with Suryono? he said to himself.

To calm himself down he lit a cigarette before he went out with the drink for Ies.

Later, after they'd eaten, several of the guests suggested that the chairs and tables be moved aside to make room for dancing. The big lamp was turned off so that the room was lit only by a small wall-lamp which cast a dim greenish light. Pranoto got the first dance with Ies. Later on, with only a few couples still dancing, Pranoto realised that he'd danced with Ies uninterruptedly through three records, the last in a slow, swinging mood. It brought back the peculiar radiance in Ies's eyes which had so surprised him at the beginning of the evening. The night was now far gone and Pranoto, who'd had quite a few whiskies, felt as though an impulse was communicating to him from Ies's body. It made him lower his head, brush his nose along her cheek. Ies pressed her cheek against his, Pranoto tightened his grip on her body and it came close to his own. And so they danced in close embrace, cheek to cheek and body to body.

Pranoto was startled when the music stopped and the remaining guests said it was time for them to go home, it was already three in the morning.

Ies drew a long breath, looked searchingly at Pranoto for a moment as though hunting for something she'd not yet been able to discover and then, together with his other friends, she wished him a good night; and they all left, Ies escorted by the friends who left with her.

Pranoto could not fall asleep until dawn, disturbed by what he'd seen in Ies's eyes.

If only it wasn't for Connie, he thought.

He sighed. He'd never suspected that love and marriage could pose such difficult problems, so complicated that it was impossible to know where one was drifting with each new turn ....

On January 23rd the doctor told Hasnah that she could go home the next day. Sugeng and Maryam had been visiting her daily while she was in the hospital. She was beginning to reconcile herself to the loss of her baby, particularly since it was evident that Sugeng had changed completely. Every time he saw her he assured her of his love, repeatedly asked her to forgive him – Hasnah was not to blame at all, it was his fault; everything that had happened to them was his own doing. Hasnah felt that they'd be able to start afresh.

Towards noon of the 23rd, while Hasnah lay reading, a stretcher was wheeled into her room and the nurses lifted a woman into the bed next to hers. With a shock Hasnah recognised Dahlia. Dahlia had not yet regained consciousness.

'Aduh, this lady is a friend of mine!' Hasnah said to one of the nurses.

'She'll wake up soon,' the nurse answered, 'and then you'll be able to talk with her.'

'What's the matter with her?' Hasnah asked.

'Abortion. Just a small operation,' the nurse replied. 'She was only a few weeks pregnant.'

A few hours later, when Dahlia had come to, Hasnah said to her,

'What a pity, this child of yours, only a few weeks! I've lost my child, too!'

'Yes,' said Dahlia.

Dahlia was inwardly cursing her own carelessness. A few days earlier she had gone to the doctor, and the doctor had confirmed that she was indeed pregnant. But her plan to ask Suryono for money had miscarried completely. He'd stopped coming to her since the beginning of the new year, and every time she telephoned him at the office she was always told that he was out. Similarly her efforts to reach Sugeng had been fruitless. Like Suryono, he too could never be reached at his office.

Finally Dahlia was forced to use her own savings. She had had to pay seven hundred and fifty rupiah plus the costs of hospitalisation.

'Lucky I'm only here for a short time, the doctor says I'll be able to go home in three days!' said Dahlia.

'I'll be able to go home tomorrow,' Hasnah told her, and asked, 'Where is your husband? I didn't see him.'

'He's out of town again,' answered Dahlia.

But she didn't tell Hasnah that she'd intentionally gone to the hospital only after her husband had left, having ascertained beforehand that she'd be back home before he returned.

On January 24th Hasnah went home. Under the circumstances – with her just getting out of the hospital, still in a weak state of health and the loss of her baby still weighing on her mind – Sugeng was very loving and solicitous. He looked after her, kept her in bed and didn't let her get up, he fetched water for her to drink and served her her meals in bed.

Before going to sleep that first night at home Hasnah felt sure that they could make a new start together and regain their lost happiness.

Sugeng put Maryam to sleep by telling her a little story. When he came and lay down by Hasnah's side she stretched out her hand, drew him to herself and kissed him slowly.

And then she fell asleep with a smile hovering on her lips.

At nine o'clock the next morning three police agents headed by an inspector came to the house to arrest Sugeng. They searched the whole house and ransacked his desk and bookcase for letters and papers. The police inspector handed Sugeng the warrant for his arrest on the charge of taking bribes while employed in the Ministry of Economic Affairs.

Sugeng told Hasnah that he'd expected this to happen, and said that he was determined to start afresh as he had said. He begged her to be patient.

In the face of the disaster that had befallen her husband and family, Hasnah, who was still sick, showed a fortitude which Sugeng had never suspected in her. Strengthened by the old hope and faith which had now returned to her (though aware that primarily Sugeng's acts had brought catastrophe upon them), Hasnah was determined to fight with all her strength to cultivate the seeds of love now sown anew between herself and Sugeng.

'Don't worry, Sugeng!' Hasnah said, as Sugeng was ready to leave with the police. 'I will be with you, always.'

Sugeng kissed Maryam who was crying, frightened by the police.

He now felt strong enough to bear anything that could happen to him. Whatever might happen, he was sure Hasnah's love would always sustain him. It would always be a cool, green island where one could take refuge from the bitter and painful ordeal that he now had to face.

Djakarta's morning papers of January 25th carried a report of the arrest of several officials from the Ministry of Economic Affairs, among them a man named S. no longer employed there now, but heading a business of his own. They also reported that the authorities concerned had wired abroad to the Indonesian Embassies to make Raden Kaslan return to the country. Furthermore, the police had uncovered a series of manipulations in the economic affairs ministry dealing with import licences and their certification, and that as a result Raden Kaslan, a well-known figure and prominent member of the party, was being recalled from abroad for questioning.

In the afternoon of January 25th Suryono and Fatma read the various reports in the newspapers, including the news that Raden Kaslan was being ordered to come home. One of the papers also mentioned the possibility of further disclosures of the operations of certain parties who had collected funds running into the tens of millions for election purposes.

Their departure had not materialised because Suryono had begun to waver as the result of Fatma's cautious attitude. But after reading that his father was being recalled Suryono again started urging Fatma to leave.

'The day after tomorrow we'll be called as witnesses,' Suryono said to her. 'Come on, let's get out of town! Anywhere!'

Fatma decided that since Raden Kaslan was now involved in such a big scandal his social position was ruined, and there was no advantage in remaining his wife any longer.

They decided to drive off to Malang in East Java the next day.

For more than a week the queues for rice, kerosene and salt had been growing with each day. During the first days they were not so long – fifteen to twenty buyers would come to a warung[1] and

---

1 Combination of small retail grocery and coffee-shop.

that would be the end of it. But two or three days later, when it became increasingly clear that the new cabinet was set on fighting corruption, the opposition – to discredit the new cabinet – launched an intensive campaign, blaming it for these shortages. A whispering campaign was spread in the kampungs that the supplies of these goods would be exhausted in a few days, and the people were urged to stock up before it was too late.

Itam told Saimun that some strangers had come to him and other betja drivers, saying they should tell all the people in their kampungs to get out in crowds and quickly buy up as much rice, kerosene and salt as possible.

On the morning of January 26ᵗʰ, when Suryono and Fatma were leaving Djakarta to go to Malang, they could see huge lines in front of the warungs along the road. They also saw many betjas with women and children in them, carrying empty bottles and baskets. And when they reached Djatinegara they even saw several trucks filled with women and children in rags, all of them carrying bottles and baskets too.

'What's all this?' Fatma asked Suryono.

'Who knows?' Suryono replied. 'All sorts of things happen in Djakarta nowadays. But whatever happens we won't be in Djakarta any more anyway. Who cares!'

By ten o'clock the police stations all over Djakarta were flooded with telephone calls from shopkeepers and district offices asking for police protection, since the crowds waiting to buy rice and kerosene were getting out of hand.

It was reported that two shops in Djatinegara had been invaded by a mob because the owners had announced that their supply of kerosene was exhausted.

Murhalim was in a betja going to Pasar Senen,[2] when his betja was held up near the railway-crossing by several dozen other passenger-carrying betjas.

2   A large market area in Djakarta.

'Come on, bung, that warung over there doesn't want to sell us kerosene and rice. Ayoh, help the people!' these passengers incited Murhalim's betja driver.

The betja driver told Murhalim either to get out or to join in and help the people. Murhalim decided to join, as he was curious to see what would happen. He'd already heard during the last few days that the crowding of the rice, kerosene and salt lines was really being instigated by a political party that wanted to mess up the situation for the new cabinet. There were many stories about trucks rounding up crowds to be transported from one place to another to fill the lines, and that betja drivers were also being given money to fill up the lines. But this was the first time he could get a first-hand impression of this organised movement.

Murhalim asked the driver whether anyone was giving them orders.

'No one's giving orders, pak,' said the betja driver. 'But we little people, if we can't defend ourselves, who's going to defend us? Just try not to line up for rice – then, when the rice is finished, must we go hungry? Those bapaks high up, they're always well off, though. They don't have to stand in lines!'

They turned into an alley and all the betjas stopped. Murhalim got out. In a crowded line, about a hundred yards long, people were shouting,

'Ayoh, hurry up, where's the rice? Where's the salt? Where's the kerosene? Don't lie! Back up the living of the little man!'

Several young men could be seen wandering up and down the line, as if giving orders. The betja drivers who'd arrived in great numbers were gathered into one group and moved up to the front, close to the warung. Among them was Itam, cheering and yelling clearest and loudest. He was very happy this morning. He'd fight for the little man. He'd fight for his own fate. They'd beat up the oppressors of the people and the exploiters of the little man. All those foreign enemies of the people would be destroyed. The little people would come to power, and everybody would be happy ever thereafter, living in a fine house, owning land, with no difference any longer between the high tuans and the common people. All this had been conveyed to them the night before by several young men who had also given them some money because 'tomorrow they'd not be driving their betjas, but fighting for the interests of the little man'.

The crowd in the line was becoming more excited. The people's shouts grew increasingly threatening. From time to time one could hear, 'Just break in! Burn! Kill!'

Murhalim stood under a tree by the roadside, looking on. He felt very worried that the warung would be invaded and its owner beaten to death by a half-crazed crowd. And there were no police in sight.

As he stood there he suddenly heard a voice near him saying,

'A beautiful sight, isn't it?'

Startled, Murhalim turned around. It was Achmad.

'Achmad!' exclaimed Murhalim, annoyed that Achmad should be joking, calling something that was so very sad a 'beautiful sight'.

'Don't talk like that. These people are degrading themselves, acting almost like maddened animals, and you say – "beautiful"!'

'Ah, as usual, you don't understand what I mean,' said Achmad, smiling. 'Look at that.' He pointed at the crowd that kept moving forwards relentlessly, like a stream of lava blazing with heat, like some wild howling animal pawing the ground and filling the air with frightening noises. 'Isn't that,' said Achmad, 'a beautiful sight? The little people who've never known their rights till now are finally daring to close their ranks and shout out their right to rice, salt and kerosene. That's just a beginning, friend. Last week they wouldn't have dreamed of doing this. Listen to what they're shouting – "The Little People Must Eat! The Little People Must Win! Down with the Capitalists!" If they dare to do this now, they'll dare to do much bigger things later. And this is not the dynamism of Islam, my friend!' Achmad added, mockingly.

Murhalim looked at Achmad with great astonishment, but then as he slowly grasped the full meaning of his words he got red with anger.

'This has all been organised. So it's true what I've heard. There's no use my arguing with you here, Achmad. It's clear that for you and your friends these people are merely objects to be manipulated, so you can achieve your political ends. You don't really care whether they get rice, whether the lamp in their hut will be lit or whether there'll be salt in their cooking-pot or not. Human beings have no value for you, you don't respect them at all! May the Lord forgive you!'

Achmad laughed loudly.

'If I were to yell out now, and point to you, and tell them that it was you who caused the shortages of rice and salt and the lack of kerosene, do you know what would happen to you? What they'd do to you?'

Murhalim looked at Achmad. He was seeing a man whom, it seemed, he'd not known at all, as though Achmad had never been a friend of his in the old days. Achmad's eyes glittered, his face shone with joy and his body seemed coiled as though ready to spring – his whole being reflected absolute faith, readiness to do anything at all to win his battle.

By Allah, Murhalim thought, if he felt it necessary he wouldn't hesitate a moment to tell the crowd to tear me to pieces!

It was to Murhalim as though he were seeing something black – something very dark, very evil – as though a fiendish spirit were passing before him. And his conviction grew all the stronger that what Achmad represented was evil, contrary to the dignity of man, contrary to the injunctions of the Lord and the precepts of Islam. Murhalim was calm again.

All at once the group of betja drivers shouted together, 'Break in! Break in!' And they started forward. But at the entrance to the warung they collided with women and children who filled the door. Seeing the betja drivers come on for an assault, the owner of the warung locked the door from the inside, and with his wife and children fled through the back, abandoning his warung.

A scuffle then started at the door, everyone wanting to get in first. The sight of the abandoned warung whetted the people's eagerness to break in and grab anything they could carry off with them. By now they had become possessed.

Something stirred within Murhalim.

No, he said to himself. No! Not here. This isn't the time.

But this something was urging him again.

'No,' Murhalim repeated. 'It's not the time, not the place.'

Achmad was looking at Murhalim with a smile.

Their eyes met.

Achmad's eyes were full of mockery — you wouldn't dare! People like you, petty bourgeois, how would you dare to act, how would you have the courage to risk your life for something? You're just a bunch of 'analysts' and talkers. Only we, the communists, have the courage, the power to act ....

Something in Murhalim's body was crying out, ascending shrilly to the tip of his tongue.

'No,' Murhalim protested again. 'It's not the place, not the time.'

Achmad's eyes were saying to him, you're just looking for an alibi, something to hide behind, something to cover up your fear! You don't dare, you're weak, you've no conviction, no fighting spirit; this is the bourgeois way of thinking, of avoiding responsibility.

Murhalim broke out into a sweat. His face was pale. His lips trembled. The voice inside him cried ever louder, its din filling his ears, deafening, commanding him, forcing him and finally ... Murhalim felt as if he were moved by some irresistible power, something that was rising from his unconscious being. It forced him to run towards the crowd pushing at the warung door. He felt that the people, misled by Achmad and his friends, must be brought back to the true way, the rightful way, the way of Allah.

A strange force seemed to fill his body. Murhalim managed to break through the crowd before the door, and he turned quickly to face the now half-maddened mob. Momentarily the hot smell from the bodies and mouths of the people he faced overpowered him, their eyes seemed to shimmer, their faces seemed to dissolve in a haze, but then he pulled himself together and could see clearly again.

Murhalim held up his hands and shouted,

'Stop! Brothers, be calm! Be patient!'

The crowd seemed to hesitate, not knowing how to react to the man who'd just come to stand before them. Hope rose in Murhalim's heart – he'd be able to calm the crowd.

'Calm down! Calm down! Brothers, I'm just a little man too. I too need rice … remember …' he shouted again, but suddenly he heard Achmad's voice yelling from behind the crowd.

'Hayooh! Attack! Burn! He just wants to confuse you!'

And at the sound of these shouted words the tide of passion welled up again in the half-dazed and frenzied crowd that had hesitated only for a moment when Murhalim had appeared. Those in front raised their arms and Itam jumped forward, swinging a log ….

'Stop! I'm your friend! I want to help you!' Murhalim cried to Itam.

He turned away, covered his face with his hands to shield it from Itam's blow, but Itam swiftly changed its direction and the log in his hands landed heavily on Murhalim's head. Murhalim collapsed. The crowd closed in. They beat him and trampled on him. Blood streamed from his head, his nose, his ears and mouth ....

At that moment a police truck arrived. Policemen jumped off and ran to the warung. The seething crowd ignored the police's order to disperse. Only the tail end of the line, which was not involved in the brawl at the door, retreated. A few policemen reached the warung entrance, and when their order to disband was not obeyed they fired a few shots into the air.

At the sound of the shots most of the crowd scattered quickly, running, but what seemed like a hard core of impassioned people didn't budge. Itam leaped towards a policeman and like one possessed, yelled,

'Hayoh! Attack! Attack!'

He landed very close to the policeman, and when the latter raised his pistol to shoot into the air Itam jumped at him. While they grappled together the barrel of the pistol was lowered accidentally; the finger, ready for the shot into the air, pulled the trigger and the bullet pierced Itam's temple. Itam crumpled to the ground. His body jerked for a moment and then his head sank down, bathed in a pool of blood that spread on the ground.

The next moment the warung was deserted. All the people had fled and only some neighbours looked on from a distance.

It had all happened very quickly. Achmad was long gone.

Murhalim and Itam lay on the ground close to each other. They both lay there in the scorching heat of the sun, a ball of red fire in the sky. Murhalim's hand was stretched out on the ground, almost reaching Itam's hair. Its fingers were slightly curved as though wanting to touch Itam. Thus the two who had wanted to fight for the little man now lay together. They had met and had been united in death. The one who'd been trampled on had fought, and the one who had fought had been trampled on. Murhalim's hand stretched out towards Itam as though inviting him to join in a common struggle.

On the same day, January 26th, Yasrin left on a G.I.A. plane for Singapore, to go on from there to Peking. He had received an invitation to attend the Festival of Asian Artists in Peking and from there he was to go on to Moscow, Prague and Warsaw. As the plane reached its ceiling and turned towards the sea, Yasrin looked down, remembered his old friends for a moment and thought – Lucky I broke so soon with Pranoto and my other friends!

He was very pleased and mentally began to compose a poem depicting the heroic struggle of the Chinese people. Later he'd send it as a souvenir of his trip to the magazine he was editing.

It was past one o'clock when Suryono and Fatma crossed the Puntjak Pass on their way to Bandung. They'd had a rest in the Puntjak restaurant, with food and drinks. But when their car reached the beginning of the descent, with a sign showing a skull and the warning: 'Low Gear!' Suryono suddenly became panic-stricken. He remembered the dream he'd had of driving in a car whose brakes suddenly gave way; he remembered his father – what he was doing to him now, stealing his wife – and all at once he couldn't face the future, imagining what would happen when his father found out, everybody found out, all his friends found out …. Abruptly he stepped hard on the brakes, pulled up the handbrake and clutched his head with both hands.

Fatma was jerked forwards, her face almost hitting the windscreen. Turning to Suryono, she said angrily,

'Aduh, my face almost hit the glass. Why did you stop so suddenly?'

Seeing Suryono putting his head down on the wheel and holding it between his hands Fatma asked,

'Are you ill?'

Suryono didn't answer but only moaned, and then he suddenly burst out crying like a little child. He didn't want to be held by

Fatma, and slapped her hand when she tried to massage his head. Fatma let him be for about ten minutes. When Suryono had calmed down somewhat, she asked softly,

'Are you ill, Yon?'

Suryono merely shook his head, looking straight ahead of him. His head, neck and back then stiffened into a rigid upright line, and he said,

'We're going back to Djakarta.'

'To Djakarta? But we want to go to Malang,' said Fatma. 'What's the matter with you?'

'We're going back to Djakarta,' said Suryono, 'and I can't drive any more, I'm dizzy; you'll have to drive.'

Something in Suryono's behaviour convinced Fatma that there was no use arguing, so she got out of the car. Suryono moved over, Fatma took his place at the wheel and at the foot of the descent she turned the car round in the direction of Djakarta. Fatma drove fast, faster than usual.

Who does he think he is? she thought. As though he were the only one with any feelings.

Suryono sagged backwards, dropped his head and closed his eyes. Accusing voices beset him:

You can't go on. You don't know what to do. You're a failure, a confused young man. You've lost your grip. You've been wrong, you're guilty, dead-ends wherever you turn. And through his mind frightening visions kept flashing of his father returning and discovering his affair with Fatma; his friends finding out about his affair with Fatma; the police coming to arrest him; Dahlia denouncing him to the police; Dahlia's husband coming in a rage .... Suryono groaned. Fatma turned to look at him. She saw him now with new eyes, saw now the whole weakness of his character showing in the lines of his mouth, the weakness of his chin .... But Fatma didn't feel pity. She simply thought that she'd been stupid to give herself to such a weak and worthless man.

Fatma stepped on the accelerator to give vent to her frustrated feelings, swerved too far to the right on a curve and so failed to avoid an oncoming lorry. It hit the front of Suryono's car towards the right. Turning over once, the car was hurled into a ditch by the roadside, hitting a large rock. Fatma was only shaken. She'd bruised her shoulder. She was dazed and felt stiff and ill. But apart from the shock she was unharmed. But Suryono, who had been hurled with his head against the door, had fainted and lay white-faced.

In a few minutes a small crowd had gathered. Fatma and Suryono were helped out of the car. Suryono was laid on the ground and Fatma sat near him.

Then the police arrived. Suryono was put into an ambulance. Fatma accompanied him. In the hospital at Bogor Suryono was examined by a doctor who said he'd suffered a brain concussion. The doctor advised against transporting Suryono to Djakarta, and suggested leaving him in the Bogor hospital. Fatma left all the arrangements to the young and very friendly police inspector who'd come to take care of the accident – he telephoned to Djakarta for a breakdown truck to haul away their car and she herself drove off to Djakarta in a taxi, after agreeing with the doctor that she'd come back the next day to see Suryono.

In the evening the Bogor hospital telephoned Fatma in Djakarta to tell her that Suryono had passed away. While shocked by the news, Fatma felt that for Suryono himself it was perhaps the best way out.

In the evening of January 26th the discussion club met at Pranoto's house for the first time in the new year. Before the meeting started they excitedly discussed Murhalim's death. Many said they couldn't understand why Murhalim had helped lead the crowd. But Pranoto told them that he'd heard from a police commissary he knew that Murhalim had not been shot by the police but was killed by a mob which ran amok and beat him to death. The first police reports stating that there had been two victims of the shooting when the police tried to control a looting gang had been given out hurriedly, and now the police were unravelling the true course of events. Several persons had been arrested. According to their confessions it appeared that Murhalim had been trying to restrain the mob when the disaster occurred.

Pranoto also told them of Murhalim's experiences during his trip to Sumatra and his conclusion that the central government should be giving them more support since the strength of the Indonesian nation actually depended on the fortunes of the regions outside Java. Murhalim said that these regions were now constantly neglected and perhaps even worse – it was almost as though the Centre was sucking out the wealth created by the labour of the regions and spending it on luxuries in the capital.

What is the actual problem now? Speaking plainly, it's to give the masses something to hold on to. Something that would make them work joyfully, make them work hard, make them strain their minds and muscles to build up the country. Nationalistic slogans used to have a magical effect in creating unity in the nation and giving fire to the revolutionary struggle. Too many of our leaders keep on throwing these nationalistic slogans around, while in fact nationalism by itself doesn't provide any content to the goals of independence to which we used to aspire. Moreover, this nationalism still worshipped by many of our leaders is mixed up with all sorts of irrational, emotional attitudes and ideas – mixed up with myths and hero-worship. The tasks of leadership are further impeded by such ambitions as the building of a grandiose national monument, the search for still more myths of all varieties, the ever-growing distrust of foreign nations, the drummed-up fears of subversive activities allegedly conducted here by foreigners as agents of the capitalists and imperialists, who are kept in the limelight to make the people feel they are constantly threatened from all sides. All this is symptomatic of the emptiness of the nationalistic slogans and their lack of creative power.

'The result is the people have become listless and don't care any more. Many become cynical and the rate of disintegration worsens. It is therefore essential to find a new rallying-point for the people. The only new rallying-point which could inspire them with the old spirit is if we could prove that work has really started and efforts are really under way to provide them with a decent standard of living. The steady decline in the value of money could be speedily reversed. All activities must be aimed at raising the level of the people's welfare, and not merely at enriching a few small cliques of leaders.

'The ways of thinking we've used so far must be discarded.'

Pranoto added, 'Relating the conditions in the regions as seen by Murhalim, the situation of the new cabinet and the riots that have occurred ... and if we'd analyse the present situation—' Suddenly Pranoto stopped because Iesye, her voice trembling, interrupted him vehemently.

'Pranoto, I'm ashamed to hear you speak. Murhalim has been killed because he wanted to defend the little man, our country's in a mess, our leaders are like drunkards without any sense of responsibility, stealing and plundering a people unable to defend itself — and here we gather from evening to evening to analyse what's wrong with our country. Isn't there anyone here who realises that the sickness of our country has already been analysed and discussed more than enough? Hasn't the moment come for all those who've any sense of responsibility for their people's well-being to act?'

'Aduh, this is precisely what Murhalim had said to me as soon as he got back from Sumatra,' said Pranoto. 'Murhalim said that we must have the courage to pledge our whole beings, our physical and spiritual selves, to the fight for the common people.

If we don't, we're sure to be defeated. According to Murhalim, the communists promise the people everything under the sun, but they also dedicate themselves completely to their cause. They live and work among the people. Although they pass off lies to the people, they also work themselves to death to build up their influence. Even though the people will realise how badly they've been deceived when the communists have won and how they're being oppressed under a totalitarian communist regime, this awareness will come too late and will be utterly futile.

'Then Murhalim said that we who have chosen democracy as the way to attain the welfare of the masses and have chosen a society which guarantees justice, the rule of law, the rights and dignity of man, must work ten times as hard as the communists, because we cannot fight with lies, deceit and empty promises as weapons. The communists promise: join us, and if we win you'll get land, a house and good wages; the property of the rich will be confiscated, and so on. We, however, must spur the people to work harder and to sacrifice more. But the masses are easily taken in by the promises of the communists, because that is human nature.

'That's why Murhalim had decided to dedicate himself completely, dedicate his whole being, to the struggle he thus outlined.'

'And now he is dead!' said Ies. 'And we're still talking and analysing here ....' Her voice broke. 'None of you are men ... just gossiping women ....' Ies got up, sobbing, and ran out of the room .... They all sat staring at one another.

Pranoto rose. He looked at his friends. He said,

'There is truth in what Ies said. Up to now we've been pretty pleased with ourselves, thinking we were serving our country and our people by analysing conditions in the peace of this room. Now the time has come for us to get out of the room!'

Pranoto walked out to join Ies.

Ies sat on the wall of the front verandah, crying to herself. Pranoto came up to her and put his hand on her shoulder. Ies took his hand.

'I was thinking of Murhalim who died, and us still talking ... I felt as though we were betraying him,' said Ies.

'I understand,' said Pranoto. 'Our mistakes are clear to me now. We thought our good intentions would just communicate with the people all by themselves, and they'd follow us automatically. But it seems that actually it isn't so. The good must also have the courage to fight the evil.'

'Isn't it too late?' said Ies.

'No,' said Pranoto. 'It is never too late to fight in defence of the good against the evil.'

Ies tightened her grip on Pranoto's hand. And suddenly in the air before him Pranoto saw Connie's face.

On the night of January 26th security measures were strengthened in Djakarta. Police patrols made the rounds more often. And on the same night, the vice squads took special action and rounded up street prostitutes soliciting customers at the roadside or riding round town in betjas. About fifty women were arrested that night. Neneng was detained while standing with a few companions in front of the Catholic church in Banteng Square.

At sundown Saimun learned from Itam's friends that Itam was dead, shot in an incident at the rice and kerosene line. He wanted to see Itam's body but was afraid, and all that night he kept standing in front of the police headquarters' office, hoping to hear something about Itam. Later, as he sat for hours at the roadside near a vendor of fried bananas, some police trucks came by and turned into the yard. They were full of women picked up in the raids. That night the police station was very busy. Not long afterwards a number of men appeared, as though on orders, claiming that their wives were among the women arrested by the police and that their wives had not been soliciting but turning down offers when picked up by the police.

Saimun joined the men claiming to be the husbands of the arrested women when they went inside, into the room where the police were conducting their investigations. Suddenly Saimun saw Neneng. He plucked up his courage and approached the group of women. As no one interfered, Saimun went up close to Neneng and said,

'Neneng, why you!'

It was the first time that Neneng had been arrested by the police and she was frightened, though her companions, who were quite used to it, had said to her,

'There's nothing to be afraid of; you'll be released tomorrow.'

But that night Neneng was badly frightened and she was happy to see Saimun.

'Aduh, kak,' she said. 'Help me. If someone says he's my husband I can go home now, they say.'

'Neng, I want to,' said Saimun. 'We'll just get married, we'll go back to the village. What's the good living like this in the city with no sense to it? Do you want?' Saimun was speaking without thinking.

Then Neneng remembered the village, its peaceful life, free of the kind of work she was doing now – a life never free of fear ... all sorts of fears ... rough men who wanted you to do indecent things ... fear of the police ... fear of the day and fear of the night ... a fear never ending – and Neneng nodded to Saimun.

A great surge of pride welled up in Saimun, and when a policeman shouted at him, telling him to get out,

'Hai, lu there, why're you getting so close, is she really your wife?'

Saimun answered bravely,

'Right, pak, this is my wife,' and he took Neneng by the hand.

And his fear of the police vanished. He was now ready to fight for a life with Neneng.

City Report

The night held the city in tight embrace. The streets were deserted. Later a torrential downpour blown in from the sea by a great storm descended on Djakarta. But all through the night dark shapes crept stealthily about, feeling their way, slipping into the houses of people who were fast asleep, thieves of the night doing their work ....